W9-CNA-645

# FRACTURED FUTURES

## Also by Monica Tesler

# BOUNDERS
## BOOK 5

# FRACTURED FUTURES

## MONICA TESLER

## ALADDIN
New York   London   Toronto   Sydney   New Delhi

*For Cameron, Nicholas, Gavin,*
*Lucas, and Connor*

## ALADDIN

An imprint of Simon & Schuster Children's Publishing Division
1230 Avenue of the Americas, New York, New York 10020
First Aladdin hardcover edition December 2019
Text copyright © 2019 by Monica Tesler
Jacket illustration copyright © 2019 by Owen Richardson
All rights reserved, including the right of reproduction in whole or in part in any form.
ALADDIN and related logo are registered trademarks of Simon & Schuster, Inc.
For information about special discounts for bulk purchases, please contact
Simon & Schuster Special Sales at 1-866-506-1949 or business@simonandschuster.com.
The Simon & Schuster Speakers Bureau can bring authors to your live event.
For more information or to book an event, contact the Simon & Schuster Speakers Bureau
at 1-866-248-3049 or visit our website at www.simonspeakers.com.
Jacket designed by Karin Paprocki
Interior designed by Mike Rosamilia
The text of this book was set in Adobe Garamond Pro.
Manufactured in the United States of America 1119 FFG
2 4 6 8 10 9 7 5 3 1
Library of Congress Cataloging-in-Publication Data
Names: Tesler, Monica, author.
Title: Fractured futures / by Monica Tesler.
Description: First Aladdin hardcover edition. | New York : Aladdin, 2019. | Series: Bounders ; book 5 |
Summary: Jasper and his friends must find a way to make peace between Earth and the Youli aliens
before the Youli destroy the human race. |
Identifiers: LCCN 2019019144 (print) | LCCN 2019021850 (eBook) |
ISBN 9781534402522 (eBook) | ISBN 9781534402508 (hardcover)
Subjects: | CYAC: Adventure and adventurers—Fiction. | Human-alien encounters—Fiction. |
Ambassadors—Fiction. | Science fiction.
Classification: LCC PZ7.1.T447 (eBook) | LCC PZ7.1.T447 Fr 2019 (print) | DDC [Fic]—dc23
LC record available at https://lccn.loc.gov/2019019144

**1**

**WE SHIFT INTO FASTER-THAN-LIGHT SPEED,**
leaving the cold and rocky surface of Gulaga behind. I
grip the hand rests and focus my gaze out the front window. Everything's a haze, but I still know the other ships
are there, the five Earth Force fighter crafts sent to escort
Denver Reddy and me back to Earth and the Last Heroes
Homecoming Tour.

Our craft is nearly empty—only the captain, a few crew
members, and two passengers. Or maybe I should say three
passengers. We're bringing Regis back to Earth. His casket is
in the cargo hold.

"It's weird," I say to Denver, who's stretched out on the

row in front of me. His arms are slung over his face, probably to block the light. "Regis traveled here in a box, and now he travels home in one." On our way to Gulaga, Denver, Regis, and I were packed like sardines into a shipping crate and then attacked by Alkalinians before we could rendezvous with Neeka, our Tunneler junior ambassador–turned–Resistance fighter, for the ride to the planet's surface. We were lucky Regis and I had our gloves. I rub my hands against the secret glove pocket Addy helped me sew into my jacket. I'll never go anywhere without my gloves again.

"At least we're not in a box with him this time," comes Denver's muffled reply. I definitely don't disagree with that. After what went down on Gulaga, I'm lucky not to be in a casket myself.

The last time I saw Regis alive was out on the Gulagan tundra during the battle with Earth Force. Minutes earlier, we'd raced to join the fight. Together. I never thought I'd willingly do anything with Regis, and now I never will again.

"I feel guilty." I'm talking to Denver, but I really just need to say the words out loud.

He sits up and stretches as he turns to face me. "Why?"

I shrug and look down at the worn carpet beneath my feet. "I've secretly wished for this moment. I mean, not this *exact* moment, but something close."

Denver waves his hand. "The demise of your nemesis?

MONICA TESLER

Who hasn't fantasized about that? It doesn't mean you caused it, kid. You're not a god, despite what your million screaming fans on Earth think." He turns back around and closes his eyes. "There's work to be done. That's where your head needs to be. And where my head needs to be is in dreamland. Wake me up when the Lost Heroes Homecoming Tour is over, will ya?"

A few minutes later, his breath is loud and steady—not quite a snore, but he's definitely asleep. How can he sleep when there's so much at stake? I could barely string together a few hours of shut-eye the last few days on Gulaga. Rejoining the homecoming tour doesn't stress me out—not that I'm looking forward to it or anything—but what comes after does. Formal talks between Earth Force and the Resistance. A visiting delegation to the Youli home world. Another reunion with Mira.

As Regis and I raced through the Gulagan tunnels to join the battle, he turned to me and said, "Bounders will be the ones who end this." His words inspired my strategy that led to a cease-fire between Earth Force and the Resistance. Now that truce is so fragile, it could unravel with a simple tug on the strings that hold it together.

Before we reached that strained peace, we were nearly annihilated. If I hadn't convinced Waters to get on board with my plan—and Denver hadn't persuaded Admiral Eames—Addy would be dead. I'd probably be dead, too. Instead, my pod mates, my sister, and I met off-site at a bounding base to hammer out the beginnings of a peace deal. It's strange that we're the ones starting to bridge the gap between Earth Force and the Resistance, but somehow both Waters and Eames agreed, thanks to Denver's urging. Since the alternative was total destruction (the Resistance) or a worldwide televised outing of your generations of lies (Earth Force), I guess you could say we had a lot of leverage.

Even though the off-site meet at the bounding base was my idea, I never could have predicted that Mira would show up on behalf of the Youli. Almost a week has passed since the meet, but I can still feel Mira's hand on my heart. I wish that moment could have lasted forever. Oddly, it almost felt like it did, like it defied time and space.

In the minutes we were alone together at the bounding base, the past and future didn't matter. I temporarily forgot how Mira left with the Youli when we were stranded in the rift. I lost the urge to beg her to stay. We were just there, together in space, sharing the most intense connection in the galaxy.

But of course it didn't last. Mira was there for a reason. She issued an ultimatum from the Youli. We would need to travel to the Youli home world as representatives of Earth. Our planet was required to appear before the Intragalactic

Council and answer for its actions. The Youli weren't messing around. As soon as Mira stated their demands, three Youli ships showed up, armed and ready for battle.

When the ships spun into spheres and bounded away, Mira left, too. It felt like she ripped my heart out and took it with her. I can still feel a hole in my chest, a bottomless cavern that can't be filled, no matter what.

The good news (sort of) is that I've had zero time to obsess about Mira. As soon as we returned from the bounding base, we went into prep mode. Earth Force and the Resistance had to hammer out the details of their cease-fire. Waters reached out to his Youli contacts to clarify and flesh out their demands. Although the primary focus is the Intragalactic Summit that is scheduled to take place in less than a month at an as-yet-undisclosed location, the Youli have insisted that Earth first send ambassadors to their planet. They've been very clear who those ambassadors should be: everyone present at the bounding base meet and absolutely no one else. That means Addy, my pod mates, and I are heading to the Youli home world on our own. I'm kind of surprised Waters and Eames agreed, but since both of them want us to get the inside scoop on the Youli prior to the Summit and neither of them are willing to waste their negotiating power on the issue of adult chaperones, we're going.

For now, though, we're broken into camps. Earth Force on

one side, the Resistance on the other, and Denver and I caught in the middle. So we're headed back to Earth. Part of the truce between Earth Force and the Resistance is that Denver and I have to finish out the Lost Heroes Homecoming Tour. It helps the Force save face with the public. I hated leaving Addy, Marco, and the rest of my friends behind on Gulaga, especially when I'm diving headfirst into the awkwardness and animosity that comes with going AWOL during your own homecoming tour.

Maybe it won't be so bad. The Force's culture of secrecy might work in my favor this time. Admiral Eames might have kept the truth about Denver's and my involvement with the Resistance to a small circle of confidantes, leaving most of the Force in the dark as to why we've been missing for a week and the tour visits had to be rescheduled. For all I know, everyone without a level-one security clearance has been fed the public narrative (the Force's feel-good word for *lie*) that Denver and I were injured in the attack at the rally in Americana East.

Two people who definitely know the truth? Cole and Lucy. By the time we said good-bye at the bounding base, some of the tension in the pod had faded. Still, there's no way they've forgiven me for bailing on the tour, going to Gulaga, and fighting with the Resistance.

Since we're traveling at FTL, it won't be long until we're back on Earth and back on the tour. Soon, Denver and I will know who buys into the Earth Force narrative, and we'll be the ones onstage repeating the lies to thousands of screaming fans.

The smoke clears, and the Eurasia West skyline comes into view out the front window. The Eiffel Tower rises high above the other buildings. When we were little, Mom read Addy and me a book about Paris. It described the city from hundreds of years ago, when you could buy bread and pastries from a corner baker and visit museums with tons of real paintings hanging on the walls. All that's gone now, but the Eiffel Tower still points to the sky, just like it did in the book.

Mira is from Eurasia West, although not from Paris specifically. She grew up in a northern district. Still, she must have left from here to travel to the Americanas. I wonder what she thought of the Eiffel Tower. Maybe she had a copy of the Paris book, too. Maybe her family will be at the rally later, hoping to hear firsthand how she died during our infamous rescue of the lost aeronauts. That's a lie I particularly hate.

We make our way to the exit ramp. A motorcade is waiting to escort us back to the tour. A group of Earth Force officers stands at attention. Off to the side is a familiar woman wearing a formal black suit and enormous sunglasses.

Why is Florine Statton here? The last thing I knew, she'd been banished to hotel voice-over work.

"Who's the suit?" Denver asks me. When I tell him, he shrugs. "Never heard of her."

He really has been missing for a long time. "Don't tell *her* that."

We make our way across the tarmac. I smell Florine long before I reach her. She's still going overboard with the rose perfume. Lucy isn't a fan of Florine, but she follows her taste in fragrance and nail polish.

Florine extends a limp hand to Denver and then to me. Her nails shine, pink and glossy. She goes through the introductions in her typical bored voice, but then she leans forward and whispers in a conspiratorial tone, "I have a business proposal to discuss later. I think you could make a fortune in celebrity appearances."

"No thanks," Denver says.

Florine laughs like she thinks he's joking.

The officers wave us toward the waiting hovers, but something catches my eye on the other side of the craft. A man and a woman in civilian clothes are waiting by a large commercial hover that isn't nearly as new and shiny as the Earth Force vehicles. The woman is crying. Her shoulders bob up and down. Her hands are wrapped tightly around her middle. The man stands stiffly with his hand placed on the woman's back.

Something about the man is . . . familiar.

The crew is unloading the craft. The cargo plank rises on

the accordion lift and lowers with baggage and goods. The next time it rises, crew from the craft push a familiar box onto the lift: Regis's casket. As soon as it comes into view, the woman bursts into sobs.

The realization hits me as his casket is lowered to the ground. That's why the man looks familiar. He looks like Regis. Those must be his parents.

Two men in suits exit the civilian hover and cross to the casket. As they wheel it back, the woman races over. She drapes herself across the box that contains her son's remains. Her sobs are loud now. Her body shudders. Her shoulders heave. Regis's father is trying to coax her away so the casket can be loaded onto the waiting hover.

An officer's hand is on my arm, steering me to the motorcade. "Let's go, Adams."

I shake him off and dart across the tarmac.

It won't do me any favors in the Earth Force popularity department, but I can't turn my back.

"Excuse me," I say, nearly slamming into the casket as I skid to a stop in front of Regis's parents.

"Yes?" the man says. He must recognize me from the webs. My face has been plastered everywhere since I returned from the rift with the lost aeronauts. I can see the confusion on his face. Why is an Earth Force hero talking to the parents of the only student ever expelled from the EarthBound Academy?

Now that I'm here, I'm not sure what to say. "I . . . uh . . . I'm . . . sorry about your son."

The woman steps away from the casket and turns to face me. Tears still stream down her face, but her crying is quiet now. "Did you know Regis?" she chokes out.

I'm not sure what to say. That yes, I knew her son, and I hated him. He tried to kill me multiple times, and that's why he was booted from the Academy. I don't think those sentiments would add anything to this horrible moment. Plus, in the end, did I really hate the person Regis had become?

"Regis and I were . . . well, we . . . he and I . . . we fought together." I take a deep breath and search for the right words. "And no matter what anyone else tells you, I want you to know that he died admirably." I stick out my hand to Regis's father. He stares at it for a second, then quickly clasps and releases my palm.

His mother grips my shoulders and then pulls me in for a hug. It's a gesture that's so motherly it makes me miss my own mom. Before she steps back, she whispers in my ear, "Thank you."

I nod at them both, then turn and jog back to the waiting motorcade, wiping away a few stray tears that I don't want anyone in Earth Force to see. I ignore the glares from the officers and slide into my seat next to Denver.

He gives my knee a slap. "Good on you, kid. You're one of the best kind."

**FLORINE SLIDES INTO THE HOVER BETWEEN**
Denver and me. I try not to roll my eyes and make a silent
wish that the ride doesn't take too long. Being trapped in a
hover with Florine isn't much better than being packed into
a crate with Regis.

As soon as the motorcade rolls out, she starts talking in her
bored monotone. She's been asked to brief us on the status of
the Lost Heroes Homecoming Tour. Apparently, she's taken
over for Jayne.

Right now, Jayne's probably back at the space station
awaiting transfer to Nos Redna Space Port to continue on to
Gulaga. Waters negotiated her release when he and the admiral

hammered out the logistics of the cease-fire. The entire time Jayne was coordinating the Lost Heroes Homecoming Tour, she was secretly working as a Resistance spy. One of her missions was to help bring me over to the Resistance. I thought we were friends—in fact, I thought she had a crush on me—but she was duping me all along. She swears that the friendship part was real, but who really knows? I doubt I'll ever be able to trust her, but now that I'm back on the tour, I miss her. She sure beats Florine.

So if Florine took over for Jayne, that must mean she's Lucy's assistant. I wonder how Florine feels about that. It must be pretty humbling for the former face of Earth Force. Then again, it beats doing hotel voice-overs. Maybe Florine sees this as a stop on her slow crawl back to celebrity.

Denver asks Florine a few questions about her career, and she instantly transforms from bored to incredibly engaged. She launches into a pitch for her show *In the Flo with Florine Statton,* which apparently still runs in syndication, and which she's hoping to shoot for a reboot, and would Denver consider coming on for an interview? She smiles, flashing her enormous teeth that are no less white than the day I met her when I departed for the EarthBound Academy on my first tour of duty with Earth Force.

Florine is rarely as enthusiastic as she is right now. She's fangirl flirting with Denver the way she used to flirt with

Maximilian Sheek. She never showed that level of animation with the Bounders. Although, of course, she was plenty animated that time we filled the suction chute trough with noodles. She came sailing in and was drowning in tofu. We nearly died of laughter.

That was all Regis's idea.

Regis, whose parents just took him home in a box.

"Mr. Adams, puh-leeeze."

Denver kicks my foot. "You with us, kid?"

I must have zoned out. "Huh?"

He winks. "Florine was just reviewing the narrative."

"Thank you so much, Denver," Florine says. "I can't stress enough how important the narrative is to the success of our media campaign. The admiral herself asked that I brief you." She flashes her ugly smile at Denver before continuing. "It is of paramount importance that you know every detail of the events at the Americana East rally. Here's what happened, the—"

"We know what happened," I say, even though it's pointless. "We were there, remember?"

Florine continues as if I hadn't interrupted. "The protestors had a large, vocal presence at the rally. Now, Earth Force is very tolerant of the right to protest. . . ."

Right. All I can see in my mind are the Earth Force officers body-slamming the peaceful protestors who watched our motorcade when we first arrived in Americana East. The last word I'd used to describe that is *tolerant*. I don't interrupt Florine again, though. The narrative is the narrative; there's no way to change it. We learned that back at the space station when we first prepped for the tour and Lucy informed me that Mira was dead (in the narrative, that is).

But I do shoot a look at Denver. He rolls his eyes.

"The protestors turned to violence," she continues. "The Force had no choice but to shut them down immediately, avoiding a calamity of tremendous proportions. Sadly, in the first moments of aggression, some spectators in the front of the crowd were injured."

I clench my fists and bite my lip to stop from screaming at her. Of course I know some spectators were injured. I found my mother covered in blood!

Florine's voice chokes up as she keeps talking. "The two of you heroically came to their aid, and you were wounded while saving them. It's a beautiful story of sacrifice. Thank God no one died." Actual tears roll down her cheeks. Geez, I never knew she had the acting chops.

"Not to be a pain," Denver says, "but don't you ever worry that these stories go too far? There were witnesses. They saw what happened."

"I have no idea what you're talking about," Florine says, brushing away a stray tear.

"Sure," he says. "All I'm saying is that this is bound to back-fire someday. One of those protestors is going to get so sick of your lies that they really will turn violent. What happens then?"

Denver knows Florine is just an Earth Force pawn. He doesn't press her for an answer. We ride in silence for a few minutes. Out the window, the Eiffel Tower is getting taller by the second as we close in on the city center.

"So Jasper and I have made a full recovery, I suppose?" Denver asks, going back to the narrative.

"I believe so," Florine says with her standard monotone. I guess Denver crushed her enthusiasm. Or maybe she's still depressed about the terrible imaginary injuries we suffered at the rally. "There was discussion of having one of you walk onstage with crutches, but I think we've moved past that idea."

I laugh. "Definitely don't ask me to use crutches. I'm not coordinated enough for that."

"*I'm* not using crutches," Denver says. "Those definitely weren't part of the terms of our return."

"What terms are those?" Florine asks.

Denver shakes his head. "Forget it."

We're quiet again. Denver's words brought us back to why we're here. The only reason Denver and I rejoined the tour is that it was part of the cease-fire terms. Florine clearly doesn't know that. She probably doesn't know there was a battle. She may not even know the Resistance is real. And I'd be willing to wager a large sum of money that she has no clue I'll be traveling to the Youli home world in a few days. The web of lies woven by Earth Force is so vast, it would be impossible to guess what Florine knows. There could be an entire secondary cover narrative that Denver and I know nothing about.

I point out the window. Denver leans over me and cranes his neck to see the Eiffel Tower in the distance. "She's a beauty! Hopefully there's time to see it up close. I'd also love to get over to the Louvre. Rumor is they've brought out one of the few remaining Monets for annual viewing."

An image of Monet's famous water lily paintings pops into my head. We studied them in school. "I didn't know you were into art."

"Art appreciation is for everyone," Denver says. "Plus, painting was a personal hobby before . . . well, before."

Before he was stranded in the rift for fifteen years, he means. I think of the Paris book that Mom used to read and picture Denver in a funny hat and black-and-white striped shirt. "Can you imagine living here back then? When Paris was Paris, not Eurasia West, and artists roamed the streets of Montmartre? Things were so much simpler then. Peaceful."

"You can think that, kid," Denver says, "but there's always been conflict. It's part of the human existence. The French

Revolution, the Korean War, World War II, the Catalan War for Independence . . ."

"So you're an artist *and* a historian?" Florine says with a thick layer of sarcasm.

"You sound more like an *Evolution of Combat* expert to me," I say.

"I'm neither," Denver says. "I just like history. You would, too, if you missed a good chunk of your own."

We cruise down a large promenade headed to a large circle with a giant arch in the middle. I recognize it from the book as the famous Arc de Triomphe. Once we veer off the main promenade, the motorcade slows down. Up ahead, a large crowd partially blocks the road. As we close in, the sound of cheering swells, and I spot signs with my name: WE'RE BOUND FOR LOVE, JASPER, WILL YOU MARRY ME?, SAVE ME, JASPER! I haven't seen that last one before. Maybe it's referring to my "heroic acts" at the Americana East rally. Long live the narrative!

"They still love you, kid," Denver says.

I shake my head. Barely a month ago, I almost lost myself to the pull of worldwide popularity. Now I just want someone to turn down the noise. "Get ready to greet your ten thousand closest friends."

"Don't joke!" Florine says sternly. "They're here for you. So put on your best smiles and stop taking your celebrity for granted. For shame!"

I press my hands to my mouth to stop from laughing. I can't even look at Denver or I know I'll bust a gut. Take my celebrity for granted? Geez. At this point I wish I'd never had it in the first place.

Florine takes out a small silver mirror and reapplies bright pink lipstick. Then she puckers her lips and runs her pointer finger across her huge, white teeth.

Denver takes a deep breath but still has to swallow a laugh before eking out a question. "How did they know we were coming?"

"It's all part of the narrative," Florine says. "You've flown here straight from Americana East following your discharge from the medical center." A cameraman for the Earth Force Affairs Network follows the hover with his lens. Florine rolls down the window, turns her smiling face to the EFAN camera, and waves.

My laughter is replaced by waves of anger. Forget the narrative. Denver and I may not have been in the Americana East medical center, but others were. There were *real* people injured in the rally, treated in *real* medical centers, including my mom.

"Showtime!" Florine says, reaching for the hover handle.

"Wait!" I block the door with my hand. "When will I be able to visit my parents?" I insisted that Waters include the visit on the long list of terms in the final cease-fire agreement.

Since the Resistance was responsible for my mother's injury, Waters didn't give me any pushback. Before I leave the planet, I get to return to Americana East and see my family.

"I don't know anything about that," Florine says. She brushes me out of the way and steps out of the hover.

That must be another nugget outside of Florine's clearance. I'll have to find someone else to ask.

We're hurried through the crowds and down a ramp leading to an underground entrance to a historic Parisian hotel that's been converted into the Earth Force Eurasia West headquarters where we'll be staying. We cross through the security gates and continue to the lower level.

The admiral and her honor guard are waiting to greet us. Cole is standing by her side. My stomach does a weird flip. I'm excited to see Cole, but I don't know what to expect. When we said good-bye at the bounding base, it seemed like things were headed in the right direction. Even Lucy and Addy were getting along. But I know he doesn't trust me. I turned my back on the Force and fought with the Resistance on Gulaga. Even though I'm neutral now, I can't escape those facts, not that I'd want to.

We used to be best friends. Now are we friends at all?

Admiral Eames greets us then steers Denver to a quiet corner. I head over to Cole.

He nods but doesn't make eye contact. "How was your flight?"

I hate how formal things are between us. "Good. Fine. I didn't expect you to be here."

Cole's eyes dart around the garage, landing on me for a second, then quickly looking away. "Admiral Eames wanted to be here when you arrived, so Captain Ridders and I joined her. We held a prep meeting for the negotiation sessions and our appearance before the Intragalactic Council."

It feels like there's a mile between us, not just a meter. I wish I knew how to bridge the distance. "How did it go?"

"Fine."

I don't ask for details about the prep meeting. I doubt he'd tell me if I did. But if I don't think of something else to say fast, this conversation will be over before it really begins.

A joke could be common ground. Cole doesn't always get my humor, but I think this one is pretty obvious. "Was it Lucy's idea to give Jayne's old job to Florine Statton?"

Cole's eyebrows pinch together as he thinks through my question. I smile. Then he smiles—only for a second, but it's an unmistakable smile. "No, it was Sheek's idea, actually."

"Really?" That was not the answer I was expecting.

"I don't know the specifics, but I've heard he owed her a favor."

Could it be? I lean forward and whisper, "Is she still black-mailing him about hiding during the Paleo Planet attack? I thought she cashed that in for her *In the Flo* flop."

Cole shrugs, but his smile's back. "Like I said, I don't know the specifics."

"Did you hear she's hoping for a show reboot?"

Before Cole can respond, another officer interrupts and tells Cole he's needed in a meeting. Cole nods and heads toward the door. Midway there, he turns. "It's good to see you, Jasper."

"Yeah, you, too," I say with a smile. Maybe there's a chance I can get my friend back after all.

With Cole gone, I scan the room. There are tons of Earth Force officers standing around and they all look . . . awkward? It only takes a second for me to realize why. Admiral Eames is still in the corner with Denver, and she's clearly upset.

"Do you have any idea how I felt?" she shouts at him. "Did you even think of me for a second? It was like reliving the Incident all over again!"

"I had no idea they were going to grab me, Cora!" Denver replies.

"How do you expect me to believe that? Everything that comes out of your mouth is pro-Resistance!"

"It's not." He shakes his head. "You're not listening. I'm not pro-Resistance. I'm pro-compromise."

She throws her arms in the air. "I suppose the next thing you're going to tell me is that you support the Youli!"

Denver sighs. "Cora, times are changing. We need to think about what's best for Earth."

"The Youli kidnapped you, Denver! They kept you prisoner in the rift for fifteen years!"

"That's not what happened—"

She holds up her palm. "I've heard enough. There is nothing you could say that will ever change my mind about the Youli after what they did to you, after what they did to *us*." With that, she marches out of the room. The officers exchange questioning glances, then rush to follow her. Soon, Denver and I are the only ones left.

I'm not sure what to do. I've never seen the admiral out of control like that. I take a couple of steps toward Denver. When he looks up, his eyes glisten with unshed tears.

He shakes his head. "I'm fine, kid. I just need some space."

**I MAKE IT TO MY ROOM WITH A FEW**
hours to relax before the rally. Given her comeback to Earth
Force PR, I figured Florine's voice-over days were over. Nope.
The hotel command system features the unnaturally friendly
voice of the former face of Earth Force, Florine Statton.

I tell her to shut up (a huge benefit of virtual Florine over
IRL Florine). Then I fling myself onto the bed, hoping for a
quick snooze before the rally. I crawl under the covers and lay
my head against the soft, cool pillow. With my eyes closed, I
let my thoughts drift. A picture of Mira fills my mind. We're
at the bounding base. Her hand is pressed against my chest.

Just as I start to doze, there's a loud knock at my door.

"Hey, Florine! Make them go away!"

Florine doesn't answer, and whoever's at the door keeps right on knocking. What's the benefit of having a hotel voice system if Florine won't even do what I tell her to?

I stumble out of bed and grumble my way to the door. "I'm coming!"

As soon as I pull back the handle, Nev and Dev pour in like a rainbow slushie, sweet and colorful. One of them grabs my cheeks while the other circles me, looking me up and down from every angle.

Please not now. Why can't I just lie down for thirty minutes?

"Oh, my poor, sweet golden boy!" one of them coos.

"Are you okay, dear Jasper?" the other says while stroking my hair. "We were so worried!"

They must have been fed the line about me being injured at the rally. The narrative is alive, well, and well spread.

"I'm okay." I gently push them out of my personal space and retreat farther into my room. "What are you doing here?"

"Dev and I were worried we wouldn't have time before the rally to transform you into your true, golden self," Nev says.

"For all we knew, you had visible wounds and horrible scars. We couldn't let you be seen like that on the webs, now, could we?"

"Really, I'm fine." Although I'd be a lot finer with a nap.

"We can see right through you, Jasper Adams," Dev says. "And what I'm seeing right now is someone quite peakish."

Peakish?

The twins look at one another and then say in perfect unison, "Time to work our magic!"

Ugh. Way too perky! Although maybe there's a bright side to this. "Fine, but hook me up with some of those lavender eye pads so I can sleep."

By the time they wake me up, it's nearly time for the rally. Once I change my clothes, I'm in full golden-boy mode, or at least I look the part. It feels weird to be wearing the Earth Force uniform again. Denver and I traded our uniforms for civilian clothes on Gulaga—not the colorful tunics that the Tunnelers and even Addy and Marco now wear, but old pants and sweatshirts that some of the officers donated to the cause of making sure we didn't look like the enemy.

Dev and Nev hurry me down to the motorcade. Most of the hovers are already loaded, so the crew waves us into Sheek's hover. When Nev, Dev, and I climb in, Sheek glares at us. A team of four stylists work on getting his hair teased up into his signature bouffant while we cruise the streets lined with screaming fans. Sandwiched between Dev and Nev, I nearly pass out from the fumes of their competing colognes.

Fortunately, the ride is quick, just over the Seine to the Champs de Mars, right in the shadow of the Eiffel Tower.

I barely catch a glimpse of the tower through the window before we're shuttled into an underground garage and ushered to the prep area.

"Hey, Jasper," a voice sounds behind me as I walk into the green room. I spin around to find Bai Liu looking down at me. "You've had quite a time of it, huh?"

I'm not sure what to say. Is this toe-the-party-line time?

She winks and whispers, "Don't worry. Denver filled me in. There are no secrets between us."

I smile. "Okay. It's hard to keep track of all the narratives."

She laughs and slaps me between the shoulder blades, almost knocking me to the ground. "Good one! Who can? Don't worry, I've got your back. I'm so ready to be done with all this homecoming crap. I don't know what's next for me, but a Bai reinvention is about fourteen years overdue, and I don't think it's going to include the Earth Force insignia. You with me?"

Before I can answer, Denver joins us. He has a plate with pizza stacked four slices high. "I'd offer to share, but I've been subsisting off fungi for the last week."

I ask him where I can find the food, and he points me to a side room. I immediately head in that direction. Denver may have been eating only fungi, but I've basically been on a hunger strike since leaving for Gulaga. I pile my plate with pizza and brownies.

As I'm about to head back to the greenroom, a familiar shriek makes me jump.

Lucy flies in, closing the door behind her. "There you are!" She races over and wraps me up in an enormous hug.

That must mean she doesn't hate me. "Hey, Lucy." The hug goes on for so long, my arms start to hurt. "How are you?" I ask when she finally steps back.

Lucy flashes her new signature style smile and flutters her unnaturally long lashes. "Excellent." Then she leans close. "But don't think for a second you're off my bad-guy list."

She waltzes over to a deep purple couch against the wall and flings herself down. "Can you believe we're in Paris? I've dreamed of this day my whole life."

I'm pretty sure that's what she said before the rally in Americana West. Apparently, Lucy's had many days she's dreamed of her whole life. "Yeah, it's pretty cool. The rally is right in front of the Eiffel Tower."

"*Le Tour d'Eiffel? C'est magnifique, non?*"

"Ummm . . . ?"

"Just say *oui* and imagine you're strolling through the streets of Paris long ago—the clothes, the culture, the elegance. And soon you'll appear on a Parisian stage as one of the planet's biggest stars."

"Speaking of that, shouldn't you be getting ready? I figured you were coming in here to hurry me up."

"I have a few minutes." She crosses her legs and examines her nails, painted the same pink color as Florine's. "So, how is everybody?"

That's an odd question. It's not like Lucy to be vague. Usually her problem is talking too much. I shrug. "Who exactly?"

Now *she* shrugs. It's not really a shrug, more like a slight tip of the head and raising of her shoulders. It's probably Lucy's signature shrug. "You know, Marco, Addy—"

"Wow. I never thought I'd hear you ask about my sister."

"Okay, fine. Don't tell me."

"It's not that, Lucy. It's—"

She leaps off the couch and throws her arms in the air. "Oh, Jasper! At least tell me Neeka's okay! I forgot to ask about her when I saw you at the bounding base, and I've felt so guilty that Neeka wasn't the absolute first thing on my mind. Cole said the battle was vicious and that lots of Tunneler ships were blown to bits. I can't stop picturing sweet, furry Neeka. Dead. Gone. Wasting away to nothing on the cold, dark tundra."

Chatty Lucy is back with drama to spare. Thank goodness. "Neeka's fine."

She collapses on the couch, splaying her arm across her forehead. "Oh, thank God!"

"It's not like there weren't casualties, Lucy. Tunnelers died that day. A Bounder died."

Lucy drops her arm and raises her eyebrow. "*Former* Bounder, although you'd never know it with how you acted at the aeroport earlier."

"You heard about that?" I forgot how fast gossip travels

around here. I should have guessed she'd know about my interaction with Regis's parents.

"Please, Jasper. Everyone's heard about it."

"Regis was still a Bounder, Lucy," I say, biting into a hot slice of gooey pizza, then putting a hand in front of my mouth to keep talking. "He just wasn't an Earth Force officer. The same can be said of Marco, Addy, all the other Bounders who stand with the Resistance."

"Are you defending Regis?" Lucy laughs. "That's something I never thought I'd hear."

"I fought alongside him on Gulaga."

"I thought you were neutral in all of this."

"I am. But when my friends are threatened, I fight, no matter what side I'm fighting on."

"Here's the problem with that, Jasper. You have friends on both sides."

"Both sides?" I ask, sitting next to her on the couch. "That implies there are only two. Try *all* sides. I have friends in the Force and in the Resistance. I have friends who are Tunnelers." I cast my eyes to the floor. "I have a friend among the Youli."

"Mira," Lucy whispers. When I nod, she asks, "How was it, seeing Mira at the bounding base after all this time?"

She's the first person to ask me that. Sure, Waters wanted to know everything about Mira and the Youli, but he didn't care about my feelings. Marco and Addy had plenty to say about Mira's arrival and the Youli's demands, but they didn't ask me how I felt about Mira. It probably never occurred to them that it was a big deal, or any bigger of a deal than seeing the others. They hadn't seen anyone from my pod until the reunion at the bounding base. Since then, we've all been busy with prep for the talks and all. But still, it would have been nice if someone had checked in with me about Mira.

"Thanks for asking," I say to Lucy. "It was strange, intense. I don't have the words to explain it, really. It was like Mira and I were connected at our core."

"Your brain patches?"

"Yes, but it was more than that."

Lucy places her hand on top of mine. "We felt it, too, Jasper. Mira was able to communicate with all of us brain-to-brain."

"I know, and that was amazing, but this was something different, something heightened. For a moment when Mira and I were alone, it felt like time froze. It was just me and Mira, and we were all that mattered in the universe. Then it ended. It felt like she ripped my heart out of my chest and took it with her."

Lucy tips her head to the side. "You miss her." When I nod, she adds, "You'll see her soon."

"I know." In just a few days, we'll be headed to the Youli home world. It may be my last chance to persuade Mira to return to Earth. I need a plan, and Lucy might be just the person to help me execute it. "I need your advice, Lucy. I need to convince Mira to come home."

"Of course she'll want to come home, Jasper."

I shake my head. "I'm not so sure." How do I explain this to Lucy? I might as well tell her the truth. "When we were in the rift, Mira told me she *wanted* to go with the Youli, that it was her own choice. And when I saw her at the bounding base, she claimed she couldn't come home. Do you think you can help me change her mind?"

Lucy smiles. It's the old Lucy smile, not her new signature smile. Something inside of my chest unclenches, and I smile back. If the Lucy I know and love is still there beneath all that makeup, then maybe there's hope things can get back to how they used to be. Friendship, a future worth fighting for, a pod united. If we can rekindle even a flicker of that, then maybe there's a chance that Mira will come home.

"Of course, Jasper!" she says. "Can we talk about it after the rally? I need to hook up with my stylist for some final prep." She leaps up from the couch and waltzes across the room, morphing from Lucy, my friend, into Lucy Dugan, the new face of Earth Force, as she goes. When she gets to the door, she turns back around and blows me a kiss.

I take a huge bite of pizza and lean back on the soft sofa cushions, feeling a tiny bit optimistic about Mira for the first time in a while.

**THE RALLY GOES BY IN A BLINK. THE**
script was the same except for Lucy's melodramatic introduction of me and Denver and our heroics, injuries, and
swift recoveries. With all that's happened in the past several
days, the roar of the crowd doesn't rev me up like before.
There's too much at stake now. And the narrative sounds
even more hollow and silly than before. Plus, Denver got
me a bit freaked with his talk about the narrative being dangerous. What if some passionate player on the periphery
of the Resistance—someone without the facts about what's
really going on, like probably every single protestor holding
an anti–Earth Force sign at each rally we've had—gets sick

of all the lies and tries to finish what the Resistance started in Americana East?

The sooner the Lost Heroes Homecoming Tour is over, the better.

After the rally, I track down Lucy and ask her to go exploring, something I loved to do with Jayne (although I'm not going to tell Lucy that). At first, she's skeptical since we're really not supposed to leave the hotel, but I do a bit of begging and promise we can pretend we're living the Parisian glam life of yore. She eats it up and practically skips out of the hotel.

We exit through a side door of a connecting building and head for the main road.

Dusk settles in as Lucy links her arm in mine, and we stroll through the Parisian streets. Most people we pass recognize us instantly. Soon, we're followed by whispers and the flash of cameras.

"Can you believe we're walking down the Champs-Élysées?" she asks me. "Did you ever imagine . . . well, actually, I imagined this dozens of times . . . but still, we're in Paris, Jasper!" She's talking too loud, and I'm pretty sure it's on purpose. She's always loved to be the center of attention.

Me? I have no interest in gathering every Parisian pedestrian within a half-mile radius like I'm the Earth Force pied piper. There's definitely no way I'm going to talk to Lucy about Mira with all these people around. "Ready for some real fun?" I ask her.

She looks at me skeptically, but doesn't say no, so I grab her hand and take off running. We dash down the long promenade until we reach the gardens, shaking the crowd as we go. I weave us in and out of hedges and around benches and flower beds until we reach a large glass pyramid at the end of the greenway. I steer us off the main path and down a side street to the banks of the Seine. When we finally pause to rest and catch our breath, we're alone.

"Well, that was a thrill, although a better warning would have been nice," Lucy says, kicking off her high heels. "My feet are killing me."

"Here's an idea," I tell her. "Wear different shoes. Why do you wear those, anyway? It's like you're walking on stilts."

"I need to look the part," she says, rubbing the arch of her right foot.

"You mean your signature style?"

She laughs, even though she's still trying to catch her breath. "Exactly."

"I prefer your original style. You know, the one with the ribbons." When I think of Lucy, I still picture her braids tied in multicolors.

"And that's why I love you so much." She leans her head against my shoulder.

MONICA TESLER

I tip my head against hers and take a deep, relaxing breath. It feels good to be with someone who knows me so well. Comfortable.

That's how I used to feel with my pod mates almost all the time. Now, even if everything goes seamlessly, even if Earth Force and the Resistance reach a lasting peace, and Earth commits to comply with the requirements of the Intragalactic Council, and our planet's future looks promising, even then things might not be all good for the Bounders.

"Have you thought about what might happen to us after the negotiation?" I ask.

She sits up straight. "I thought we were going to talk about your love life."

"I never said that."

"Yes, you did. You said you wanted to talk about Mira."

"Okay, fine, but that doesn't mean my love . . . whatever. Just hear me out first about something else." I tell her how, on Gulaga, Marco and Addy sat me down for a serious talk. "They're members of the Resistance negotiation team, but they have their own agenda: Bounders rights."

I talk to Lucy about my sister's fears. If Earth is ushered into the Intragalactic Council, if we're no longer at war with the Youli, what need is there for the Bounders? We were bred specifically to fight that war.

At first, Lucy doesn't understand. How could anyone not

see the value in the Bounders, which of course means the value of Lucy, herself? I remind her that the Bounders genes had been eliminated from the population, that it took an actual alien war for them to bring us back.

"The Bounders have value, Lucy. *We* have value beyond being war machines. We need to make sure our efforts at inclusion move forward, not backward. That's what Addy and Marco are focused on."

Lucy doesn't argue. She doesn't even make any snide remarks about Marco. She listens, then lets a heavy pause hang in the air between us.

"I need some time to think about it," she finally says. She grabs my hand and leans close. "Jasper, I'm going to tell you something, too, although I really shouldn't."

"Okay."

She blinks her eyes, her enormous lashes fluttering like tiny moths in front of her face. "I'm not sure Admiral Eames is going to keep her agreement with the Resistance."

It takes me a second to process what she said. "Wait . . . what?"

Lucy exhales in a loud puff, like she's been holding her breath. Then she lets loose a flood of ramblings. "I'm not sure. I could be wrong. It's not like I'm in the inner circle. Cole probably knows more. But maybe not. I think she's been shutting him out. She knows that he gets uncomfortable breaking a promise. And she knows he has a relationship with you, Marco, and Addy. So Cole might be in the dark, too. I really don't—"

"Are you saying what I think you're saying?" I interrupt her to ask. "Admiral Eames isn't going to honor the truce?"

"I'm just not sure, Jasper. Maybe she'll act like she is, but I have this feeling that she's planning something." She bites her lip and stares at me with her wide eyes.

"A *feeling*? That's not much to go on."

"I know, but I've got to trust my gut. Plus, it doesn't take my gut to notice that the admiral's been acting strange ever since you showed up with the lost aeronauts. She's moody and mean. She wasn't exactly nice before, but she was always steady."

What if she's right? What if Admiral Eames plans to renege on the agreement? This could be disastrous. "Does Cole know she's shutting him out?"

She shakes her head. "I don't think so. He's not exactly the quickest with that kind of stuff."

"No kidding." I press my hands together. We need to do something, anything, to stop the negotiations from getting off track. "I have to talk to Cole."

Lucy's hands are trembling. "I don't know when you'll see him next. He left for the space station with the admiral immediately after the rally." Admiral Eames and Denver got in a big blowout earlier. I wonder if that's why she left Earth so quickly.

"You're kind of dropping a bomb here, Lucy. Are you sure you don't have any details?"

She shakes her head. "I'm sorry, Jasper. If I find out more, I'll let you know. I promise."

I bow my head to my knees. If Lucy's right, the admiral could be planning to derail the peace talks. From the things she was shouting at Denver earlier, it actually seems plausible. We can't let that happen.

Lucy rubs her hand across my back. "Now let's get to why we're out here in the first place. You need help with Mira."

"I'm not in the mood, Lucy, not with what you told me."

"Oh, come on, there's nothing we can do about that now. We might as well talk about your love life." She draws me up by the shoulders. "I think it's obvious what you need to do."

Hope flickers in my gut. Could Lucy actually have a solution for getting Mira to come back? Could it be something easy?

When I look at her, she smiles. "Plain and simple, Jasper. You need to confess your love for her."

I open my mouth to protest, but Lucy raises her hand.

"Don't deny it. The only person in denial about your true feelings for Mira the last few years is you. And maybe her."

MONICA TESLER

"Lucy, I'm not going to just—"

"Don't be ridiculous, of course you're going to. So we should practice."

"Practice?"

"Of course." She turns her whole body to face me on the bench. "Now pretend I'm you, and you're Mira. It should be pretty easy because you (meaning me) will do all the talking, and Mira (meaning you) won't say anything. Like normal."

I so don't want to do this.

"So first, take her hands." Lucy scoops my palms up in her own. "Then look deep into her eyes." She leans close, opening her eyes extra wide. Framed with the spidery lashes, they look scary. "Then profess your love."

"Saying what exactly?"

She drops my hands and sits back, letting a neutral expression wash her face. "Give me a second to get in character." Then she resumes her romantic pose, hands clutched, eyes staring deeply into mine, supposedly in the role of me, Jasper Adams. "I've waited far too long to say this, but I can't deny my feelings—"

Oh my God. Puke. There is no way I'm going to do this.

She leans even closer, like she might try to kiss me. "The truth is, I'm in love with you."

A bright light blinds me, and a rustle of noise makes me jump off the bench.

"Is it true?" a stranger's voice asks. "Are the two of you dating?"

What is happening? I blink back into focus. A man holding a camera is standing right behind the bench.

"What?" His question replays in my head. *Are the two of you dating?* "No!"

Lucy grabs her shoes with one hand and my shirtsleeve with the other. "What he means is 'no comment.'" She takes off at a brisk pace, dragging me behind her.

"Miss Dugan," the man calls, "is it true you've been pining for Jasper Adams ever since you first met at the EarthBound Academy?"

"You want the truth?" Lucy says over her shoulder. "The truth is we're leaving." We're already halfway up the bank, heading for the road back to the hotel.

"Mr. Adams," he yells after us, "can you describe your reunion with Miss Dugan after escaping the rift?" he yells.

Lucy tightens her grip on my hand. "Say nothing," she whispers.

"But—"

Her glare is enough to shut me up. We dash through the streets of Paris with the photographer on our tail. Our journey is punctuated by the periodic flashes of his camera, which only pushes Lucy to run faster.

We make it to the office building next to the Earth Force

headquarters. Lucy waves her key card against the door, and it buzzes. We duck inside and race through the halls to the hotel entrance. We run past the guards and into a side hall. Finally, Lucy pulls me into a dark, empty banquet room, and we collapse against the wall, catching our breath.

"Lucy, why didn't you tell them—"

"Later," she whispers, "they could be anywhere."

"But why'd you say 'no comment'?"

"Later," she hisses.

We sit in silence—the only sound is our breath, which eventually slows to a normal pace.

Lucy buries her head in her hands. "I'm so stupid."

"That wasn't your fault!"

"Of course it was." Her voice is thick, like she's holding back tears. "I should have known better. There are eyes and ears everywhere, Jasper. They followed us down the Champs-Élysées, for goodness' sake." She grabs my arm. "What if they heard what I said about the admiral?"

I hadn't considered that. "I'm sure they didn't."

"I'm sure they did! They probably tailed us all the way through the Jardin des Tuileries waiting for the perfect compromising shot."

She leans her head against the wall and closes her eyes. A tear carves a path down her cheek, leaving a dark trail of mascara. After a minute, Lucy leans forward. She lifts her foot and shines the light from her wristlet. Her foot glistens with blood.

"You're hurt."

"I think I stepped on some glass."

"Let me help." I illuminate my own wristlet while she examines her foot. She gently runs her fingers along her skin, then grabs something and pulls. The shard brings with it a gush of blood. I remove my shoes and socks. "Here," I say, handing her the socks.

She makes a face. "That's gross. I'm not going to wear your stinky socks."

"Not any grosser than your bloody foot. At least you won't leave a crime scene trail on the way back to your room."

"Fair point." She slips my socks onto her feet then tries to stand. She moans when she tries to put weight on her foot.

I grab her beneath her elbow and help her up. We quietly make our way down the hall to the elevator, Lucy limping by my side. Fortunately, no one stops us.

Once the elevator doors close, I turn to her. "Why did you say 'no comment' when they asked about us? You could have just denied that we were in a relationship."

Lucy shakes her head. "Isn't it obvious? I'm giving them what they want. If I get them excited about you being my boyfriend, maybe they'll ignore what I said about the admiral."

"I'm sure they didn't hear that," I tell her, although if they were spying on us from the bushes, they might have. "Even if they did hear what you said about the admiral, they'd have no idea what you were talking about. It's not part of the narrative."

"Maybe not, but be prepared to run with the love story as a diversion." The door dings, and we exit on the thirty-first floor.

Great. I can almost see the headlines. *Jasper Adams, No Longer Single. Lucy and Jasper, a Match Made in Space. A Great Bounder Affair.* That kind of news won't help me convince Mira to come home. Although she'd never believe I was dating Lucy. Would she?

I walk Lucy to her room. "You need to find out more about the admiral's plans," I tell her when we reach her door.

She scans the hall. "Keep your voice down!"

"I'm serious, Lucy," I whisper. "We have to find out if your hunch is right. We need more information!"

"Then find some! You have connections, too, you know!" She opens her door and steps inside. "Go to bed, Jasper. We've got a busy day tomorrow. And I need to put this night behind me. It's been a total crapfest."

"Gee, thanks, Lucy!"

"It's not about you, Jasper. Not everything is about you. I thought you'd finally figured that out." She shuts the door in my face.

Ouch. I shuffle the rest of the way down the hall in my sockless shoes.

Once I'm in my room, I double-check that my bounding gloves are still safely sewn into my jacket. If Admiral Eames is seriously considering steering us back into war, I need to be ready. Lucy's right: tonight was a crapfest. I crawl into bed and tell Florine to wake me in the morning.

## THE NEXT FEW DAYS WE TRAVEL TO

Australia and Amazonas. Lucy keeps it business-only with me even though everyone on the planet thinks she's my girlfriend. The few times I get her alone, she lectures me. "Haven't you seen the webs?" she asks when I try to talk with her before the rally in Amazonas. "There are pictures of us plastered all over! I'm sure the paparazzi are everywhere now, hoping to catch another picture of us alone. Is that what you want? Someone to capture us this very instant and tell the whole world we're having a lovers' quarrel?"

"I really wouldn't care, Lucy, because it's not true." Although the truth is I *do* care. I hate the idea of people all over the planet talking about my love life, especially since I don't even have one.

"If there's one thing you should know by now, Jasper, it's that the truth doesn't matter. What's true? The narrative. Whoever controls the narrative controls the truth. And right now I'm in a heap of trouble for letting the media control the narrative about our poor, injured lost hero, Jasper Adams." She looks around and bends close. "Although we both know it's better than the alternative."

She means the admiral's plans to thwart the truce with the Resistance. "That's what I need to talk with you about! Did you find something out?"

Lucy glares and balls her hands into fists. "Don't. Even. Ask." She spins around on her very high heels and disappears up the hallway.

For now, I'll just have to hope that Lucy and her dramatic hunches are wrong. I shuffle back to the green room. The Lost Heroes Homecoming Tour can't end fast enough. Thank goodness this is our last stop.

Over in the corner, Denver is devouring a plate of at least a dozen chocolate chip cookies. Maybe my true soul mate is Denver, not Mira. I cross to the corner and plop down next to him on the couch.

"You okay, kid?" he asks with a mouthful of cookie.

"It's Lucy."

"Trouble in paradise?"

"We're not—"

"Kidding. We're enough alike for me to know there's only so much of her incessant talking you can take."

I grab a cookie off his plate and take a bite. It's good, but not nearly as good as Mom's. "What are you doing after the tour?"

He shrugs. "I haven't figured that out yet. I could head straight to the space station, since I'll be departing from there for the Intragalactic Summit with the Earth delegation. But the truth is, I'm not looking to spend any extra time with a bunch of officers who grew up thinking I was dead. Not to mention, things between me and Cora—Admiral Eames, I mean—are awkward. You probably guessed that."

Anyone who witnessed their fight the other day would have guessed, especially knowing their history. After the lost aeronauts returned, the rumor mill churned out a thousand stories of the famed romance between Denver Reddy and Cora Eames, two of the most promising young officers in Earth Force before the Incident at Bounding Base 51.

I steal another cookie. "You can come with me to Americana East, if you want." Fortunately, Earth Force honored its commitment to let me see my parents before heading back to space.

"I thought you were visiting your family."

"I am, but there's plenty of room at our place. My mom's a huge fan of yours. I know she wouldn't mind. Plus, we can strategize for the Earth Force–Resistance negotiations, then head to the space station together."

What I don't say is that Denver will still have plenty of time to connect with the admiral before the negotiations and the Intragalactic Summit. If it feels right, I can let him in on Lucy's hunch, and maybe he'll be able to find out the truth. He may not be on the admiral's short list now, but he has a much better chance of weaseling his way into her inner circle than I ever will.

"My mom makes great chocolate chip cookies," I tell him.

He thinks for a minute, then nods. "Sure, kid, why not?"

Wind rocks the passenger craft as it touches down at the aeroport in Americana East. The door to the boarding ramp opens to cold, pelting rain. Across the tarmac, a man holds a large black umbrella above himself and a woman wearing a long green coat.

I smile and start down the ramp in the rain. When I get closer, I realize Mom's right arm is in a sling.

I bolt the rest of the way across the tarmac as the memories of the Americana East rally rush at me. The smoke. The noise. The chaos. My father crouching over my mother, shielding her from future injury as blood soaks her shirt.

"Mom!" I stop short, not wanting to hurt her with a hug.

She waves me forward and weakly wraps her free arm around my back. "I'm fine, honey, really." When we break apart, she presses her palm against my wet cheek and smiles. "I'm so much better than fine, now that you're home."

"Your arm." I look to my dad then back to her. "I shouldn't have left you."

Dad grips my shoulder and tries to shield me with the umbrella. "Your mother told you to go, Jasper. It's what we wanted."

"Did you find her, Jasper?" Mom asks. "Did you find Addy?"

I nod. "She's okay."

Dad exhales. "Oh, thank God."

"I'll tell you everything later."

Mom lifts her left hand to her heart. "I need to know now."

"He just got here, Emma," Dad says, placing his palm on her back. "We know Addy's safe. We can talk at home."

I think Mom's going to protest, but then her eyes go wide. Her face softens into a shy smile. "Aren't you going to introduce us?"

Denver has somehow managed to secure another umbrella. He doesn't wait for my limited etiquette skills to kick in. He steps beside me and extends his hand. "Mr. and Dr. Adams, I'm Denver Reddy. It's a pleasure to meet you."

My mom's cheeks color pink and she lifts her good hand to Denver. "We're honored, Captain Reddy." Her voice is higher than normal, giddy. It must be weird to meet someone who was your celebrity crush when you were a kid, especially when the celebrity barely looks a day older.

He inclines his head. "Please, it's Denver. Thank you for your hospitality. I was delighted when your son invited me to your home."

"Call us Richard and Emma," my dad says, firmly gripping Denver's palm. "And the pleasure is ours, Denver. Now let's get out of this weather, shall we?"

When we get back to the apartment, my mom apologizes profusely for the lack of food, which is funny because there's a huge surplus of food. When she's nervous, she cooks, and she cooks a lot for me. There are cranberry scones, and banana muffins, and a fresh loaf of oatmeal bread she must have baked this morning. In the fridge is real whipped cream that I'm guessing is for the apple crumble beside it. The counter is loaded with ingredients for her famous spaghetti sauce. That must be dinner. Yum.

As promised, a plate of chocolate chip cookies waits for us in the center of the kitchen table.

"Jasper warned me about these," Denver says, eyeing the cookies.

Mom lifts the plate with her good arm. "They're his favorite."

Denver takes a cookie. He closes his eyes and slowly savors a bite. Then he grins at my mom. "Mine, too." He gladly accepts a second cookie. "You were right, kid. These are the best chocolate chip cookies in the galaxy."

Mom beams. Then yawns.

"Your mother needs to rest," Dad says.

"Richard!"

"We talked about this, Emma. The doctor's orders don't get put on hold just because we have guests. We don't want any setbacks." She rolls her eyes but allows my dad to steer her to their room. "Why don't you two take some time to relax as well?" he says when he returns to the kitchen. "I'm sure you're tired."

"Is Mom okay?" I ask. Guilt pokes at me like a dull knife. I could have protected Mom if I'd warned them about the Resistance attack at the rally.

He nods. "Yes, but she's still not one hundred percent. She doesn't want you worrying, Jasper."

I nod and wave Denver out of the kitchen. When we reach my room, Denver plops down on the beanbag my parents bought me after my first tour of duty with Earth Force. I begged them for it because it reminded me of our pod room.

"Don't blame yourself, kid," he says quietly.

He must see I'm still upset about what happened to my Mom at the rally. "What are you, a mind reader?"

"Who needs to read minds to know guilt when you see it?" He stretches his long legs out in front of him, looking eerily like Waters in our pod room. "Trust me, in our line of work someone's always getting hurt. Guilt just clouds the mind from doing what we need to do for the greater good."

I flop onto my bed. "That's what you think we're doing? Fighting for the greater good?"

He shrugs. "I don't know what I think anymore. But I'll tell you this. The peace talks and the Intragalactic Council requirements, they're important. Really important. And you just might be the key to keeping them moving in the right direction. You've got to keep your head in the game, kid."

I can't believe how much is at stake. I've barely processed the fact that I'm reuniting with my pod and traveling to the Youli planet in a few days. Why did the Youli insist we come? What if their motives aren't as friendly as we think? Maybe they want revenge for our pod placing the degradation patch on their vessel at the last Intragalactic Council. We might never make it back from their planet. And where does Mira fit in to all of this? I've been so preoccupied with my own feelings for her, I haven't spent enough time thinking about what her role will be in the upcoming negotiations . . . for the Youli and for Earth.

Denver claps to get my attention. "How many cookies can I eat and still be seen as a polite guest?"

I laugh, happy for the momentary distraction from my anxious thoughts. "There's no cookie limit. My mom probably has another batch of them in the fridge."

"Excellent." He clasps his hands behind his head. "Thanks for inviting me here, kid."

This might be the best chance I get to ask him about Lucy's hunch. Mira's homecoming, our trip to the Youli planet, the future of Earth Force–Resistance relations—all of that could be destroyed if Admiral Eames doesn't honor the cease-fire agreement. "Do you think the admiral is going to keep her word?"

"About?"

"The cease-fire."

"Of course she is."

"How can you be sure?"

"I know Cora. She's honorable, almost to a fault."

"What if she thought it was in the Force's best interest?"

Denver sits up. "Do you know something I don't, kid?"

I shrug. "Just a hunch."

"Look, Jasper, I get why you're skeptical. Earth Force has been lying to you your whole life. We've spent the last month onstage spewing the lies they forced down our throats. But this is diplomacy. The admiral would never go against her word."

Denver has faith in Admiral Eames. I guess that's something. "I hope you're right."

"Trust me, kid. Now I've got a question for you." He sits up on his beanbag and leans forward. "When are you going to teach me how to play *Evolution?*"

After I've destroyed Denver a dozen times in trench warfare at Ypres, he finally ekes out a victory. By then, the apartment is filled with the sweet and savory smell of Mom's spaghetti.

My mom seems rested and happy when we gather around the table for dinner. Denver and I practically inhale our first plates. Before going back for seconds, Denver compliments Mom on her cooking and adds, "I'm so sorry about what happened at the rally."

She looks at Denver, then at Dad, then at me. I set down my fork and nod, letting her know that it's okay, that I've told Denver the truth about what happened.

Mom turns back to Denver. "Thank you. What about you? Were you injured like they said on the webs?"

Now it's Denver's turn to cast his gaze around the table. He must assume my parents know that the narrative about *my* heroic acts and horrible injuries at the rally isn't true. Otherwise, wouldn't they have asked about that as soon as they greeted us at the aeroport?

"It's okay," I tell him. "They already know the truth about me." I turn to my parents. "Denver wasn't hurt, either."

"Then what *did* happen?" my father asks.

What should I say? Our apartment could be bugged like I thought before Addy and I left for the last tour of duty. But even if it is, so what? What is the Force going to do if I tell my parents the truth? If I refuse to stick with the narrative? They can't lock me up. They've agreed to send me to the Youli home world before the Intragalactic Summit.

I take a deep breath and launch into the story. My bound to the labs. Denver's kidnapping. Our voyage to Gulaga.

Mom clutches my hand. Her face shines with a strained hope. "Tell us about Addy."

"Addy is fine, Mom," I say, squeezing her hand. "She's doing really well, actually. She's on Gulaga with my pod mate, Marco Romero, and our Tunneler junior ambassador, Neeka." I mention names they'll recognize from stories of my tours of duty. That way they'll know Addy is with friends. As I talk, Mom's eyes fill with tears.

"Why didn't Earth Force just tell us that?" Dad asks. "Why all the secrecy? Why pretend that she's *dead*? We're her parents, for Earth's sake!"

"Addy's no longer in Earth Force."

Mom's brows knit together. "What do you mean?"

This is the part of the truth that I should probably avoid. It's safer for them if they don't know. But the thing is, I'm done with secrets. I don't have it in me to lie to my parents. Not anymore. Not when there's so much at stake. I take a deep breath and tell them about the Resistance, the battle, the Youli. Everything.

By the time I finish explaining Addy's and my roles in the preliminary negotiation and our upcoming trip to the Youli home world, my parents are beaming with pride. Yes, it's pride laced with shock and concern, but it's definitely pride.

Denver's been quiet, letting me be the one to share the truth with my parents. He stands and clears the table like a good houseguest. He's probably hoping my mom will set out some more cookies once dinner is cleaned up.

When the table's clear and my story is over, Denver steps behind me and places his hands on my shoulders. "You've raised an amazing son, Mr. and Dr. Adams. Jasper is an extraordinary young man. It's my honor and privilege to know him."

My face warms. It's kind of embarrassing for Denver to be saying this stuff about me, but I know my parents will eat it up.

"The truth is a lot to face," he continues. "It's unnerving that the future of our planet is uncertain. But personally, I'm filled with optimism. I assure you that Earth has no better representative than your son. He and his friends are the future."

**TWO DAYS LATER, I HUG MY PARENTS**
good-bye and follow Denver into the backseat of the armored
hovercraft the Force sent to take us to the departure dock for
the Americana East aeroport. Only a few ships are cleared
to land and depart from the planet, so Earth Force made
arrangements for Denver and me to catch a flight on a cruise
ship headed for the Paleo Planet. The craft stops at the space
station for refueling anyway, so they'll drop us off. The way
the officer explained it via vid chat, the whole trip should be
quick and painless.

As soon as we step off the private water shuttle onto the
deck, it's clear this trip is going to be anything but painless.

There are hundreds of passengers already on the deck. They're all waving fans about their heads. Every fan is emblazoned with a picture of either Denver's face or mine. Their high-pitched screams and squeals nearly knock me off my feet, and I'm used to screaming fans thanks to the Lost Heroes Homecoming Tour.

The crowd parts. Florine Statton waltzes forward, flanked by half a dozen cameramen.

She taps her fingers together in a flutter clap. "Our heroes have arrived!" Her voice reverberates, with each echo increasing in pitch. She must be hooked up to a high-tech amplification system.

"What on earth did you get me into, kid?" Denver asks as Florine rushes forward, arms outstretched.

"No clue," I say.

She hurls herself at Denver, bobbing her head left and right to kiss his cheeks. He's left with bright pink smooch marks. When she dives for me, I lean to the side to make sure she's only able to land a hug. Fortunately, I remember to hold my breath so I don't choke on her rose perfume.

Florine grabs our arms and steers us to face the crowd. She waves her right hand through the air in the shape of a tipped figure eight. Her elbow to my rib cage must mean she's expecting me to wave, too. I shoot a glance at Denver. He's glaring, but he obediently raises his hand and forces a smile for the crowd. The cameramen creep closer, zeroing in for close-ups before panning the crowd.

The cheers swell like a wave. Florine's handlers part the crowd. She waltzes after them, then calls over her shoulder, "Follow me, puh-leeeze!"

Heading after Florine, I whisper to Denver, "I liked her so much better when she was just a faceless voice in my hotel room."

"That sounds creepy," Denver says behind me, "but I completely agree."

We're quickly swallowed by the crowd, most of whom are women my mom's age. They reach out and touch my arms and even my hair. It's gross. One of them grabs my jacket. I jerk it back, worried that my gloves will pull loose from the lining. I glance at Denver. He's getting it twice as bad as me.

Florine directs us to the automated boarding ramp for the passenger craft. Once we've rolled to the top, she spins us around for more waving. "Welcome to the first official Paleo Planet Celebrity Fan Cruise!"

"Celebrity fan cruise?" Denver asks, careful that he has enough distance from Florine not to get picked up by her mic. "And we're the celebrities? I'd say that was a pretty important detail to disclose when you sold the whole *come spend the weekend with my family* idea."

"No one tells me anything," I say. "If I knew, there's no way I'd be here."

Soon, we get a break, thank goodness. A cruise attendant waves us aboard and leads us down the entrance hall of the craft, following a trail of faux paw prints. The walls are covered in an animated mural of the Paleo Planet. She steers us to a small private cabin with pairs of bucket seats on either side and a long table down the center. We have our own window, which for now looks out on the dark, steely waves of the ocean.

Denver drills the attendant with questions. She pulls out her tablet and reads the schedule. As soon as the craft departs, we're required to appear in the bar for photo ops. Then we have a show in the main cabin. The whole celebrity fan cruise was Florine's idea. She's bringing along her camera crew and banking on this being the big break to rekindle her career and reboot her show, *In the Flo*.

"So not only are we forced into being the celebrities for her fan cruise, but she's going to film it all for the webs?" Denver asks once the attendant leaves. "There are so many things wrong with this, I don't know where to start."

"Are you going to do anything about it?" I ask him.

He shrugs. "Doubtful. The ride to the space station only takes a few hours. I'll probably just suck it up and smile for the cameras. It's not worth the hassle to fight Florine. She scares me." Denver finds the recline lever on the side of the seat, buckles up, then tips back.

I'm about to make some jokes about how it always ends up being me and Denver on these flights, but he's already snoring. I wish I could sleep like that. I can barely sleep anywhere other than my own bed, and then only with a very heavy blanket.

We depart Earth in a cloud of exhaust smoke and shortly after shift into FTL. I keep thinking I hear a bird chirping. I brush it off since that makes zero sense, until I hear the grunt of a wildeboar. They must be playing wildlife sounds from the Paleo Planet over the speakers. They're really going all out for the authentic cruise experience. The seats in the cabin are upholstered in fake sabre cat fur. On the wall above Denver, there are photos of the mammoth herd, pomagranana grove, and towering cliffs.

I wonder if those are the cliffs near the watering hole we visited during our first tour of duty. Maximilian Sheek coaxed us off the touring hovers for a closer look. Minutes later, the Youli attacked. No one knew what was happening other than me and my pod mates. If we hadn't rushed to defend the others, who knows what would have happened? None of us might have made it off the planet alive.

It's strange to think that Earth Force is allowing all these tourists to visit the Paleo Planet just a few years after the attack. Hopefully, they've beefed up security, but would all these tourists be excited to go if they knew the truth?

I close my eyes and think of Mira holding back the herd of charging wildeboars. When the beasts passed beneath the hover sent to rescue us, Mira was gone. I thought I'd lost her that day, when in truth she'd bounded back to the Ezone. Now, though, she may be gone for good, unless I can convince her to come back with us from the Youli planet. Despite all that's happened since we left the rift, I'm still no closer to understanding why she left with the Youli in the first place.

A knock at the door shakes me back to the moment.

Denver jerks awake. "Are we there yet?"

"As if," I say.

The door swings open and two cameramen charge in, zooming for close-ups.

"Yoo-hoo!" Florine calls, squeezing in behind them. "It's time!"

I shield my face with my hands to avoid the camera. "Time for what?"

"Celebrity photos, of course!"

Denver yawns and stretches. "Might as well get this over with." He sticks his finger at the closest camera. "Do *not* use any of that footage of me sleeping, got it?"

We follow Florine and her camera entourage down a back lift

to the lower level that houses the Watering Hole, the on-craft bar and disco. The scene is totally over-the-top. Hundreds of passengers are packed onto the dance floor, shaking away to throwback tech pop overlaid with a wilder version of the animal sound effects they pumped into our cabin.

"Isn't this ahhh-mazing?" Florine says. Her entrance is starting to draw attention. Denver and I try to stay hidden behind the camera crew, but we won't be able to keep that up for long.

We wind past the bar where they're serving up purple drinks with little parasols.

"Umm . . . is that pomagranana juice?" I ask, remembering the kegs of juice they served us during our Paleo Planet picnic. We were limited to one cup a piece.

"Of course!" Florine says. "Imported straight from the Paleo Planet. We're nothing if not authentic!"

"Bring me one, will ya?" Denver asks one of the attendants.

"Emphasis on the '*one*,'" I tell him. "It makes you fart." We tricked Regis and his minions into drinking a ton of it. Of course, we all paid for it on the stinky ride back to the space station, but it was worth it.

"Seriously?" he asks. When I nod, he catches the attendant's arm. "On second thought, how about a glass of water?"

Florine leads us to a corner that's roped off with red velvet cords. There's a backdrop of the Paleo Planet watering hole (of course). Apparently, that's where Denver and I will stand for pictures with passengers.

By now, a crowd is gathering, and the crew is directing them to form a line.

"Plaster a smile on your face, kid," Denver says. He waves the first passenger over to the photo area, like he's done this a thousand times. Considering how famous the original aeronauts were before the Incident, he probably has.

I'll give Florine credit for one thing: efficiency. The pace at which she's able to send passengers through the photo area is staggering. I probably pose with over three hundred people. Each passenger is hurried in, we shake hands, Florine's staff somehow manages to arrange us for the picture while the starstruck guest rambles on about how she can hardly believe the moment is real. One guest even asks me to pinch her to make sure she's not dreaming. I don't. Half a dozen girls tell me how horribly jealous they are of Lucy. I think about telling them the truth, that Lucy's just a friend, but I doubt they'd believe me.

A few of the guests bring us gifts. A woman even more stooped than Gedney knitted Denver an orange scarf with his initials sewn on one end. A guy in his twenties made a scrapbook for me with printed clippings from the webs of all the rallies in the Lost Heroes Homecoming Tour. A woman who is so nervous she can barely speak hands me a tin box and whispers, "I heard you like chocolate chip cookies."

MONICA TESLER

When we're getting close to the end of the photo hour, the handlers hurry in the next guest in line, a woman not much older than me. There's nothing too distinctive about her. She's average height, average size, brown hair, brown eyes. The only thing that stands out is that she's sweating profusely. And rather than seeming enthused to see us like almost every other passenger who has come through the line, she almost looks disgusted. I consider suggesting she take off her coat if she's hot, but she's got such a scary look on her face that I decide against it. She glares at us and refuses to step back for the handler, so that the picture is snapped with her standing half a meter in front of us. That's fine with me. I don't know why she's sweating, but I definitely don't want to catch a virus with all I'm supposed to do in the next several days.

A few more guests come through, then Florine and her people close the line. I'm hoping we get to go back to our private cabin, but no such luck. Florine announces that it's almost time for the show to start and that everyone should find their seats in the main passenger cabin. Apparently, Denver and I are the stars of the show.

We wait in a rear hallway for the crowd to get settled in their seats. Florine announces us from the next room, and one of her handlers waves us in. We're ushered onto a small stage at the front of the main passenger cabin. The crowd goes wild, squealing and whistling and waving signs like the ones we spotted on tour. Like I noticed at the aeroport, most of the passengers are women my mom's age. It's creepy to have so many old women freaking out about me. I'd say the same for Denver, but in Earth years, he's their age. Most of these passengers probably grew up worshipping Denver.

Florine introduces us and then takes a seat in the front row like she's expecting us to entertain the crowd. No script, no guidance, nothing. Denver shrugs. Since we didn't rehearse anything, he keeps it simple and launches into our lines from the rally.

We recount the historic rescue of the lost aeronauts held captive by the Youli. All fiction, of course. Since vids of the rallies have been streaming almost 24-7, lots of the passengers know every line. They mouth the words along with us.

The passengers snap photos, nearly blinding us with their flashes. We make it through the midway mark, and I start to relax. Five more minutes, and we'll be back in our private cabin. Maybe I'll even get lucky and catch a snooze like Denver, the galaxy's best napper.

I'm describing what it was like to see the lost aeronauts for the first time, when one of the passengers jumps to her feet.

"Liar!" she screams.

I recognize her immediately. She's the sweaty guest from the photo shoot.

"Down in front!" someone behind her yells.

MONICA TESLER

"Sit your butt in the seat!" someone else shouts.

Denver shoots me a questioning look, then takes over the lines, describing their surprise to be rescued by kids.

"Lies!" The woman raises a shaky hand and points it at Denver. "All lies!"

"Shut up!" another passenger shouts at her.

Denver flashes his most endearing smile at the woman. "I think some of the other passengers would like you to take your seat."

"I stand with the Resistance!" she shouts. "And I've come to make you own up to the truth!"

Huh?

Denver shakes his head and whispers, "This is gonna suck, kid."

She reaches into her coat and pulls out a silver sphere the size of a grapefruit.

"She's got a bomb!" someone shouts.

"That's no bomb," Denver says to me. "That's a *diruo* fuse."

**"A *DIRUO* WHAT?" I SHOUT OVER THE**
erupting screams of the passengers. I quickly realize that
Denver is right. This is going to suck.

"Ever heard of a *diruo* pulse?"

"Sure." In fact, Earth Force used a *diruo* pulse at the last
Intragalactic Summit before launching our attack and planting the degradation patch on the Youli vessel. It disrupts all
shields and systems within a several-kilometer radius.

"Well, you use a *diruo* fuse to set one off, and unless you
want to be adrift in space for who knows how long with
all your friendly fans until they manage to get the systems
back online, we need to make sure that doesn't happen."

He turns to me with a grim look on his face. "Got your gloves, kid?"

As soon as I nod, Denver shoves me off the stage. I land on my hands and knees on the floor right beneath the first row of seats. "Get ready to use them and stay out of sight!" he shouts.

The cabin is in chaos. Next to me, a woman in a sabre cat bodysuit is crouching and crying. I crawl around her, heading for the end of the row. Halfway there, I sneak a peek in the break between seats.

The sweaty woman is marching up the aisle on the other side of the cabin. Her hand that holds the *diruo* fuse is shaking. What if she drops it? Will that set off the pulse?

"Quiet!" Denver shouts. "Quiet, everyone! Calm down! No one's going to get hurt."

"She'll blow us up!"

"It's not a bomb," Denver explains. "You're not in danger. That's not a bomb."

Security guards spill into the back of the cabin.

Denver flashes his palms at the guards. "Hold your position! Lower your weapons! Everybody freeze!"

The cabin quiets. Eyes dart from Denver to the woman to the guards, then back to Denver.

Denver keeps his hands extended to quiet the crowd. "I see you have a *diruo* fuse," he says to the woman. "Where'd you get that? And what's the plan here?" He shoots me a quick glance that I think means hang tight.

The woman continues down the aisle. "You admit to your lies on a live web feed, or I set off the pulse. What's your choice?"

She obviously wants to sound threatening, but she mostly sounds scared. Plus, what's the worst that could happen? She sets off the pulse, taking out the craft's systems, and we have to wait for an intergalactic tow? The stakes aren't really that high. But like Denver said, who wants to be adrift in space, especially when you're caught on a craft with hundreds of people who want a piece of you?

"You know you're going to be arrested for this, right?" Denver asks. "There's no way around that now. But if you cooperate, I can probably get the Force to go easy on you."

"I don't care about the consequences! I stand on principle! I stand with the Resistance!

"Earth Force has been feeding us lies!" she shouts at the other passengers. "They want us to believe we have no choice but to fight the Youli. The truth is the Youli want peace. The Force is risking all of our lives and using children to fight their wars, and why? So they can get richer and more powerful! This man right here—Denver Reddy—is one of their agents of evil!"

"You don't understand," Denver says to the woman. "We're on the same team. I want what you want."

She laughs. "Don't condescend to me! I'm done listening to your lies! There's a countermovement growing all around us. The Resistance. They tried to make a stand at the Americana East rally, but Earth Force stopped them. I bet none of you knew that, because Earth Force has been shoving lies down your throats. Well, I've come to finish what they started. We're going to give the people of our planet what they deserve: the truth."

As she shouts, she keeps walking toward Denver. At any second, she'll pass this row and see me. She'll probably tell me to get back onstage, and then any element of stealth I have will be lost.

I shake off another passenger who tries to use me as a human shield (so much for my celebrity) and speed crawl to the end of the row. I'm three meters from the rear hall where we entered. I double-check that the sweaty woman is occupied with Denver, rise to a crouch, and bolt.

I fling myself onto the ground in the hallway, out of view of the stage. I reach inside my jacket, split the secret seam, and pull out my gloves. I duck around the corner and eye Denver. He looks like he's pleading with the woman.

For a moment, she stops paying attention to him. She faces the cabin and waves the *diruo* pulse in the air. "Listen up!" she shouts. "Quiet or I'll set this off!"

Her words have the opposite effect. Screams build, the guests try to scatter, the guards start to advance.

"Everyone relax!" Denver shouts. "It's not a bomb. Just stay in your seats until this is over."

"It won't end until you admit to your lies." She scans the cabin. "Where's the young hero, Jasper Adams? He needs to answer for his actions, too."

Denver's eyes dart around the room. He spots me first. I wave my gloves. He gives a small nod. I slip them onto my hands and seize the connection. I reach out with my gloves and grab hold of the *diruo* fuse. I pull with all my might, and the fuse flies through the air, straight to my palm.

The woman is taken off guard and momentarily frozen. Denver leaps from the stage and tackles her. I hop to my feet and dash over. I help Denver hold her down. The guards rush to the front with cuffs, and we secure the attacker.

The guests in the cabin slowly stand. Then they erupt in cheers. Our hero points definitely got a boost with this. A guest butts her way into our circle and snaps a photo. She asks if the whole thing was staged. I laugh in her face and shoo her away.

Who on earth would stage this mess?

Denver wipes his brow. "That added a bit of excitement to the trip, kid." He points at the fuse, and I hand it to him.

"Is there a holding cell on the craft?" Denver asks one of the guards. When we find out there's not, he suggests we detain her in our private cabin. The guards protest, but

Denver insists. This should make for an interesting rest of our journey.

Denver tugs the woman up by the cuffs. She's ranting on about Earth Force lies. Denver shakes her. "Shut up. We'll hear you out in a minute." That does nothing to keep her quiet.

I lead the way to our cabin and open the door. Inside, Florine cowers in the corner. "Is it over? Are we safe?"

Leave it to Florine to hide, just like she did with Sheek on the Paleo Planet.

Denver shoves the attacker inside. "You were never in any danger, Florine. She only had a *diruo* fuse."

"We don't know that for sure, now, do we?" She looks at the woman with a mix of lingering fear and disgust. "Why did you bring her here?"

"I wanted to introduce her personally to the face of Earth Force, or, I suppose I should say, *former* face of Earth Force."

Florine smiles with her gigantic teeth as she ungracefully pushes herself up. "Touché, Denny-boy. I never claimed to be a hero like you. It seems you and Mr. Adams have things under control. I think I'll find a place to lie down and calm my nerves."

Florine exits. Denver steers our attacker by the shoulders and presses her down into one of the chairs. "We've got this," he says to the two guards standing in the doorway.

"Sir, we really don't think that's a good idea."

Denver tosses him the *diruo* fuse. "She's cuffed, and the kid has his magic gloves. You have nothing to worry about."

They still don't look like they're going to leave, but Denver closes the door on them.

Then he spins around and faces the woman. "What exactly did you intend to do? Set off the fuse and strand us in space with all these over-the-top fans? That sounds like torture for you as much as us."

She doesn't answer, just levels a glare right at Denver.

He looks at me and shakes his head.

"What's the plan here?" I ask him. I'm not sure letting the guards leave was the best idea, either. At least they could have babysat this woman while I found a seat somewhere with far less drama.

"Let's start with the truth." He folds away the center table and takes a seat across from the woman. He pats the seat next to him. Once I've sat down, he leans forward and rests his hands on his knees. "So, you stand with the Resistance, huh?"

She spits. Lucky for Denver, she's not a very good spitter. The thick drop of saliva falls short and lands on Denver's shoe.

"Lovely." He grabs a tissue and wipes it off. Then he pulls his feet clear of spitting range. "How did you find out about the Resistance's broadcast plans anyhow?"

She doesn't answer.

"Fine, but you should know you don't have your facts straight." He sits back and purses his lips, probably considering what to do with her. Then he leans forward. "I'm going to tell you a few things that are top secret, and if you repeat them to anyone outside of this cabin, they'll either tell you you're nuts or have you locked up for knowing too much. Okay?"

She hocks some snot and winds up for another spit.

Denver and I both pull our feet back as far as they can go.

He turns to me. "Why do I bother, kid?"

"Ummm . . . I'm asking the same question right now. Why tell her anything?"

"Because I think avoiding the truth causes more problems, and this whole *diruo* fuse drama pretty much confirms it."

It's hard to argue with that.

He turns back to the woman. "The thing is, you're right. Earth Force feeds the public lies. They call it the narrative."

She eyes him skeptically. "The narrative?"

"That's right. But here's the good news: things are changing. The Resistance was successful at the Americana East rally. They *did* kidnap me, and they sent me and Jasper here to Gulaga, where they're headquartered. Sure, I was mad at first, but I was also mad at Earth Force because I'm not real happy having to lie for them all the time. So now, Jasper and I are trying to change things."

"Why would I believe you?"

"Why would I lie?"

"How many reasons do you want? Everything you said out there was a lie."

"Fair point. Kid? Got any ideas here?"

Me? He was the one who decided telling his attacker the top secret, level-one-clearance truth was a good idea. Still, I can almost hear Addy in my head lecturing me about keeping secrets. I take a deep breath. Here goes nothing.

"Have you heard of my sister, Adeline Adams?" She doesn't show any sign of recognizing Addy's name, not that she should. Addy hasn't been involved in the protest movement here in Americana East for a few years. I'm sure things have changed. Grown. "Addy could have been you. She's a Bounder, like me, but before she left for the EarthBound Academy, she got involved in the protest movement. She didn't like how Earth Force wasn't being straight with the public, and she felt the way they treated the Bounders was wrong. In some ways, I felt the same, but I wasn't ready to stand against it the way Addy was. The way you are."

Maybe I'm imagining it, but I think the woman's face is starting to soften. "Why are you telling me this?" she asks.

"Addy isn't in Earth Force anymore," I continue. "She deserted. She's a Resistance fighter. When I found out where she was, I helped the Resistance transport Captain Reddy to

Gulaga. Everything he told you in here is true. The Resistance is strong and is forcing Earth Force to negotiate. We're optimistic that we'll soon reach peace with the Youli and our planet will finally enter the Intragalactic Council."

"The . . . what . . . council?"

"Intragalactic Council." I smile, remembering Waters's words from years ago, when he first gave me a glimpse of the world beyond the Earth Force narrative. "As someone once said to me, the galaxy is more vast than you ever imagined."

Soon, the captain comes on over the intercom announcing our approach to the space station. Before long, the woman across from me will be taken into custody. She'll most certainly be jailed for treason for acting against Earth Force, maybe for the rest of her life. With all the witnesses to her actions, there's nothing Denver and I can do about that. But maybe we've given her a dose of hope that the world she longs for may be dawning.

"I can't bring myself to believe you," she says, "but I want to."

"I can't blame you for doubting us," I say, "but we're telling you the truth."

She looks out the window; the space station is a flicker of lights in the distance. "I never meant to hurt anyone. I just wanted to get my point across."

Denver shakes his head. "I'm not sure that distinction is going to matter much to Earth Force. What's your name?"

"Bria."

"I can't say I like you, Bria," he continues, "but you deserved the truth. Frankly, every citizen on the planet deserves the truth." He kicks his feet up on the opposite bench.

"Why did you get your picture taken with us?" I ask, remembering her coming through the line, sweating profusely. I thought she had a virus, not a *diruo* fuse.

She shrugs. "I wanted a memento."

I look at Denver. He shrugs, too.

"Hey, kid, you got those chocolate chip cookies?"

"The ones the guest baked for me?" I ask. "You're not actually going to eat those, are you?"

"Why not?" When I hand him the cookie tin, he pops one in his mouth and gives me a thumbs-up. I guess that means they're edible.

Yeah, why not? I grab a cookie and take a bite. It's kind of stale and way too light on the chocolate chips, but I know it's ten times better than the food we'll get at the space station.

Our craft was scheduled to land in the hangar at the space station. After Earth Force was informed about the Bria incident, though, they raised the alert status to orange. All outside crafts are required to dock remotely and subjected to all precautionary inspections.

Originally, Denver and I were the only passengers who

were supposed to disembark. The rest of the passengers are continuing on to the Paleo Planet, including Florine. Her contract with Earth Force was only for the duration of the Lost Heroes Homecoming Tour. Now she's back to being a tour guide, hotel voice-over artist, and, if she has her way, web star reinvented.

Now, though, we have Bria to deal with.

We anchor a thousand meters out from the station and are soon boarded by an Earth Force fueling vessel. Florine's excited greeting just outside our cabin lets us know Admiral Eames is on board before she comes into view. That's odd. Why on earth would the admiral join a fueling and disembarkation party, especially now, with a prisoner transfer and heightened risk?

"Cora!" Denver jumps to his feet.

Okay, I take it back. I know exactly why Admiral Eames decided to board, and his name is Denver Reddy. His voice is a painful mixture of delight and desperation. I'm not the best at romance, but even I've heard enough of their exchanges (even their fights) to know that whatever used to exist between them before Denver was lost in the rift hasn't fully faded for either of them, although their romance hasn't rekindled.

She steps into the doorframe. "Captain Reddy, you're to address me as admiral." She sounds exasperated. I've heard her tell him this half a dozen times, so the count is probably at least twice that. Still, there's a softness—or maybe a sadness—in her voice that's not normally there.

I'm definitely not on a first-name basis with the admiral, so I stand and salute.

"At ease, Officer Adams." She waves two Earth Force officers into our cabin. They secure Bria and escort her away. Bria glares at the admiral as she exits. Once they're gone, Admiral Eames closes the cabin door. "Tell me what happened."

Denver describes how Bria threatened the ship with the *diruo* fuse. He mentions that I disarmed her, but he omits any reference to my gloves. He also says nothing about our conversation with Bria in our cabin.

"It's just like Jon Waters to pull a stunt like this," she says once Denver has finished.

"Waters?" I ask. "He had nothing to do with this."

She scoffs. "Don't be naive. Of course he did. He's pulling the strings in all of this."

"Jasper's right, Cora . . . or, uh . . . Admiral," Denver says. "Bria was acting on her own initiative. She knows about the Resistance and is obviously sympathetic to their cause, but as far as we can tell, she has no meaningful connection to them."

"Bria? You're calling the terrorist by her first *name*?" She shakes her head. "You were in the rift so long you forgot the basics of handling war prisoners."

A shadow falls over Denver's face. "She's not a war prisoner.

She's an angry citizen. And you want to know why she's angry? It's because you keep pushing out these ridiculous 'narratives' that have nothing to do with the truth. You're supposed to represent the *people*, Cora. You're supposed to protect the planet. From what I can tell, you're more about fueling your ambition than representation or protection."

The admiral's jaw is clenched, and her cheeks redden. I want to disappear. Yeah, they have a history, but I can't believe Denver had the nerve to talk to her that way.

They stare each other down for what feels like an eternity. Finally, she turns and exits the cabin without a word.

I look at Denver. "That was gutsy."

He drags his fingers through his hair. "Everyone's so caught up in the narrative, half the time I'm convinced they wouldn't know the truth if it knocked them on the head."

"So that's what you were doing? Knocking her on the head?"

"Figuratively, yes." He grabs his bag and tucks my cookie tin under his arm. "The truth could have avoided this."

"Maybe." I pick up my blast pack and follow Denver out of the cabin. "Although I don't give Waters as much of a pass as you. The terrorist tactics used by the Resistance—like the rally attack—will inspire copycats much more dangerous than Bria, copycats who don't care about keeping civilians safe. Waters must know that."

"You think I give Waters a pass? Definitely not. Neither of them gets a pass on this. If you ask me, our people are due for some new leaders. I'm glad you and your friends are stepping up."

I look around, making sure Admiral Eames's honor guard is nowhere close. "I doubt Eames or Waters will give up the reins. If they do, maybe you should take over?"

He laughs. "No way, kid. As soon as we get through these negotiations, I'm done." He pops one of the cookies in his mouth and takes off down the paw-print-lined hall. "Let's go. This celebrity cruise has been a nightmare, and I didn't even get in a good nap."

**FORTUNATELY, OUR BRIEF RIDE TO THE** space station from the dock is quiet and incident-free. Once we arrive, we're assigned private quarters and left on our own. I'm relieved we don't have chaperones like the last time we were here.

After a short rest, I head down to the mess hall, hoping to find some familiar faces. I'm not disappointed. Most of my remaining friends in Earth Force are crowded around one of the orange tables.

As soon as I walk in, Annette spots me. She marches right over with her hands on her hips. "I can't believe you're involved with Lucy. It's so cliché."

Again with this ridiculous rumor? I was hoping the narrative had moved on here at the space station, or that maybe the Bounders had been told the truth. Obviously, that was overly optimistic. "Hi, Annette. Nice to see you, too." She continues to stare at me with her expressionless face, so I add, "Lucy is not my girlfriend."

"Ri-i-i-ight," she says, drawing the word out like she'll play along if I want her to, but we both know it's a load of crap. "It pains me to think I used to have crush on you."

Crush? On me? That's news. "Believe what you want, Annette. At this point, I don't care."

"The indifference ploy," she says. "Don't insult me, Jasper. I know what you're about." She turns and heads back to the table.

"Ah, women," a voice says from behind.

I spin around to find Ryan standing much too close. I take a step back. He's carrying a tray filled with tofu dogs and yogurt squeezies.

I grab one of the squeezies and walk with him to the table. "Like you're some kind of expert on women?"

"Well, I wouldn't say that, exactly, but I have had my fair share—"

"Forget I asked, Ryan."

Meggi jumps up and gives me a hug. "We're so happy to see you, Jasper! Everyone was worried when we heard about what happened in Americana East!"

"How's your leg?" Orla and Aela, the twins from Addy's pod, ask in unison.

"My . . . oh, right, my leg. It's fine. Healed up fast." I can't believe they swallowed the narrative without a second thought. I figured at least they'd be asking me if it's true.

Hakim slaps me on the back. "Glad to hear it, J."

*Glad to hear it, J?* Since when am I "J" to Hakim? He was one of Regis's guys. My gaze passes between Hakim and Randall, Regis's other sidekick. Do they even know that Regis is dead? Should I tell them?

"Do you have any idea what happened to Jayne?" one of the twins asks.

Jayne, Regis . . . I can't say anything without crossing the ridiculous narrative. Maybe Bria is right. My whole life is a lie.

"No," I tell her. "I have no clue about Jayne." I've suddenly lost my appetite. "Do you guys know where Lucy is?"

"As if," Randall says. "It's not like she talks to the little people."

Ryan slaps the table. "We knew it was true!" At least, that's what I think he says. His mouth is stuffed so full with tofu dogs, his words are hard to decipher. "You're dating!"

I roll my eyes. "Just tell me where I can find Lucy."

Ryan leans forward. The smell of tofu dogs wafts over me, and I nearly gag. "Come on, Jasper, give us the scoop!"

I bug my eyes out at him and try not to breathe. "Where. Is. Lucy?"

He puts up his hands. "Don't be so touchy. No kiss and tell—I can respect that. Lucy's probably in the public relations hall."

I ignore the kiss comment and stand. "Great, thanks."

"See you later tonight?" Meggi asks.

I don't think I have the energy to do this again in a few hours. "I'm kind of tired. Maybe tomorrow?"

Hakim shakes his head. "We ship out first thing."

"All of you? Where are you headed?"

"Paleo Planet," Ryan garbles out through a full mouth.

"It's changed a ton since you were there last," Meggi says. "Lots of new construction."

"At the mines?" I ask.

Ryan nods. "Everywhere."

Really? So the admiral must want all hands on deck to make sure they get as much occludium ore out of the Paleo Planet as possible before a potential treaty with the Youli takes effect.

I'm bummed I won't be able to spend more time with them before they leave, but the idea of having to lie to my friends makes me grumpy. Maybe it's better this way.

I lift my hand. "If I don't see you later, safe travels."

I find Lucy in her pink office in the PR hall.

She clutches her hands to her heart. "My boyfriend's back!"

"Don't feed the rumors," I tell her, crossing her pink shag carpet and giving her a hug.

"Why not? We determined the story was actually helping our narrative. It's given the public something to pay attention to. There's less chance they'll get intrigued with the conspiracy theories about what really happened at the Americana East rally."

"Those aren't conspiracy theories, Lucy. They're the truth." I breathe through my mouth so the smell of roses isn't as strong. "Maybe you haven't heard, but the narrative nearly stranded us in space thanks to a would-be Resistance fighter and a *diruo* fuse."

She laughs. "Don't be dramatic."

Me? Dramatic? "As if *you* have the right to say that."

"Drama suits me, Jasper. It doesn't suit you." She sits down on her furry pink desk chair and folds her pink-painted fingers on top of her crossed legs. "As for your so-called drama on the cruise ship today, I heard it was basically over before it began. The assailant was taken into custody and will soon be returned to Earth, probably never to see the outside of a prison cell again."

I flop down on her pink velvet love seat, facing the giant screen mounted on the opposite wall. "See, that's my point, Lucy. Locking someone up and throwing away the key isn't something to be proud of, especially since the thwarted attack wouldn't have happened if Earth Force had decided to tell the truth about what happened at the rally."

"Is that why you're here? To lecture me about the truth?"

"I'm here to say hello to my *friend*. How's your foot? You're back to wearing those spikes, I noticed."

She circles her ankle. "Good as new. The doctors at the space station worked their high-tech magic."

"That's great." I kick her door closed and lower my voice. "Luce, I'm also here to see if there's any news. Do you have more information about what we discussed on Earth?"

She knows exactly what I'm asking. Is the admiral up to something? And has Lucy figured out what that something is?

"No, and I wouldn't tell you if I did. We're in my *office*, Jasper."

"I know, but we don't have much time before we leave for the Youli home world. If the admiral's up to something, we need to know now. This isn't a romance rumor, Lucy. This is our future. This is our *planet's* future."

She makes me scooch on the love seat, then slides in beside me. "I'd accuse you of being dramatic again if you weren't right. The truth is, I'm shut out. No one's telling me anything. Our imaginary romance put a roadblock into some of my regular gossip channels."

I bite my lip. We need to get past those roadblocks. "How can we find out?"

"Honestly, the best chance is still Cole. He can't be totally in the dark. The admiral relies on him too much. Still, she probably hasn't come out and told him anything specific. He'd need to put the pieces together, read between the lines."

"Not Cole's skill set, I know. I'll have to talk to him."

I'm not looking forward to that conversation with Cole. Lucy's right. He's probably clueless. And if so, he's not going to be too thrilled with me hinting that the admiral is considering reneging on our deal. That would run contrary to Cole's whole rule-abiding nature.

"Maybe tonight after our prep session," Lucy says.

Since Denver and I will be part of our planet's negotiating team at the Intragalactic Summit—and the only two neutrals—we're participating in prep sessions with both Earth Force and the Resistance. We had preliminary talks with Waters and Barrick before leaving Gulaga. We'll talk to Eames and her team here at the space station. And then we'll talk with the Resistance again via vid chat before I leave with the other Bounders for the Youli home world.

There's a lot to do, but I wish I had a few hours to catch my breath before jumping in. "The first prep session is tonight? I was hoping we'd get at least a day to transition back to space."

Lucy heads back to her desk and neatly stacks at least a week's worth of printed briefing papers. "We've been meeting daily since I got back from the Lost Heroes Homecoming Tour, and I think the Earth Force negotiating team was meeting without me before that. There's a lot to cover. Speaking of which, I still haven't caught up on everything I missed while we were on tour." She sits down and thumbs through the briefs.

That must be my cue to exit. "So I guess I'll see you tonight."

She blows me a kiss. "Bye, boyfriend!"

I roll my eyes and head for the door. As soon as it closes behind me, I take a deep breath, glad to be free of the rose-infused pink palace.

We gather around the table in Admiral Eames's conference room, the same one we reported to after escaping the rift. The last time I was here, I delivered the Youli's message to the admiral and begged her to consider peace talks. I thought it might be the only way I'd ever see Mira again. Now the Youli's message isn't so peaceful. We either show up before the Intragalactic Council and hear their demands, or they'll unleash their military might. One thing that hasn't changed: I still don't know whether Mira will come home.

So today we're preparing for the Intragalactic Summit. Earth will be attending with delegates from Earth Force and the Resistance. We're even bringing Barrick, a Tunneler, along, although his role will be as an active listener only. The Earth Force contingent consists of Eames, Ridders, and a handful of other senior officers who I've seen in the admiral's entourage but don't know well. They don't do much other than repeat the admiral's arguments and compliment her strategy. Lucy and Cole are also participating, but they're in a different category since they're part of the group the Youli has invited to visit its home world prior to the Intragalactic Summit.

Then there's Denver and me. We're supposed to be neutrals, but since we both know that the goal is to reach an agreement not only with the Youli but also within the Earth delegation, Denver's been trying to nudge Eames toward a more centrist position.

"Let me jump in here," Denver says after Eames lays out Earth Force's position—Earth reestablishes its presence on Gulaga and keeps its operations on the Paleo Planet, the Resistance disbands, the Youli backs off. "I respect that this is a negotiation, of sorts, and you don't want to come out with your last and best offer, but I also think it's important that you go into this with some modicum of realism."

"We hold the upper hand," one of the admiral's yes-men says. "We could have annihilated the Resistance on Gulaga, and Jon Waters knows it. Why would we bend to their demands?"

Denver laughs. "Well, unless something's changed, the Resistance is sitting on your occludium supply."

The admiral smiles. "Actually, they're not. The Paleo Planet has nearly as much occludium as Gulaga."

The officer on her other side pipes up. "And our survey of the surrounding galaxy determined—"

The admiral shoots him a sharp glance, and he stops talking immediately.

"What did it show?" Denver asks. "Are you considering expanding your search for occludium? Because I'm pretty sure that would violate the Intragalactic Treaty that we're now going to be expected to follow."

"That's not relevant to this discussion," the admiral says. "What is relevant is that we clearly have the upper hand."

"Even if that were true for Earth Force and the Resistance," I say, "the Youli are involved now. They've demanded our entry into the Intragalactic Council. I don't know what all the requirements for that are, but I do know we'll need to limit if not eliminate our presence from developing planets like Gulaga *and* the Paleo Planet."

"We haven't agreed to anything," Admiral Eames says. "For now, we're considering all of our options."

"Consider all you want," Denver says, "but if you don't start coming up with some concessions for the Resistance and a plan to comply with the Council's demands, the Youli will be forced to act."

"We defeated them on Alkalinia," the admiral says.

"That was a rogue attack," I say, "launched by a spin-off Youli group that wanted revenge for our planting the degradation patch. That group has claimed responsibility for most of the violent conflicts initiated by the Youli in the year I was trapped in the rift. The majority of the Youli want peace."

"You've told me that before, Adams," she says, "but your word is all we have to support that theory."

*Theory?* I grip the table so hard, my knuckles turn white. "You don't believe me?"

"Of course we believe—" Lucy says.

The admiral flashes a hand at Lucy, cutting her off. Lucy must be right. She's no longer part of the inner circle.

"Look, Cora," Denver says. I think he's deliberately using her first name to annoy her. "We've known for years that the Youli could squash us if they wanted. They think of Earth as an annoying little tot wreaking havoc on the edges of the galaxy. They may have been split the last few years, but they're not anymore. And they've had enough. If we don't fall in line, they'll make us, and no one wants that."

Admiral Eames stands. "Don't purport to know what I want, Captain Reddy. You're dismissed."

Denver rolls his eyes and pushes back from the table. "Let's go, kid," he calls when he's half out the door. "We have a video conf with the Resistance soon anyways. I'm sure they'll be far more in touch with reality than this lot. They couldn't be less."

I scramble after him, catching Lucy's wary gaze on my way out.

**WE FOLLOW THE SILVER STRIPE OF THE**
mini spider crawlers from the suction chute. I'm tempted to
take a turn and show Denver the sensory gym. Something
tells me he'd enjoyed jumping off the trampoline into the ball
pit. But there's not time. The video conf with the Resistance
is scheduled to start in ten minutes.

Gedney meets us at the door to the pod hall. I dive in for a
hug, but Denver takes a big step back. He's less than thrilled
to see Gedney. Even though Denver knows it was Waters, not
Gedney, who ordered his kidnapping at the Americana East
rally, I think he still blames Gedney. If for nothing else, he
blames him for making us ride to the Nos Redna Space Port

stuffed in a shipping crate with Regis. If you're going to hold a grudge, that's a pretty good reason.

As Gedney leads us into the pod hall, all the memories come rushing back. I can almost hear the cadets brimming with excitement and nerves the day we were first assigned to our pods. We raced through the halls, looking for our pod rooms. I was jealous of the cadets assigned to Edgar Han's pod. He was my favorite aeronaut back then. He was an accomplished photographer in his spare time, and his pod room was decorated with amazing pictures he'd taken in space. According to Cole, Han was killed in a skirmish with the Youli while I was stuck in the rift. Malaina Suarez, another original pod leader, also died in battle. The only reason more Bounders haven't died is that they've been tied up training how to pilot the bounding ships—plus the admiral is reluctant to send her precious resources into battle before she's sure how to use the bounding glove biotech for maximum combat advantage.

The Resistance has used Bounders to fight far more frequently and effectively than Earth Force, but that's not to say there haven't been casualties. Regis, for one.

Regis was in Han's pod. I remember how unfair I thought it was that a jerk like Regis got to be trained by my favorite aeronaut. Han wasn't too fond of Regis. It's easy to understand why. Regis was almost impossible to control back then, not to mention dangerous (something I experienced firsthand more than once). I wonder what Han would have thought about Regis fighting for Gulaga. Regis worked so hard to change for the better. He wasn't perfect. I still don't know if I actually liked him at the end, but I admired his effort. I think Han would have been proud of him.

We follow Gedney all the way to the last room in the pod hall. He opens the door to let me enter first. It's like wading into a frozen picture in my mind: the grass green carpet, the starry sky ceiling, the multicolored bean bags. The shelves that line the room are still filled with sensory toys: lava lamps and glitter sticks and squishy balls. Gedney and Waters knew just what we needed to feel comfortable and alert as they laid the groundwork for our training.

"Should we test the scan?" a voice calls from the back of the room.

"Remember we discussed exchanging pleasantries?" Gedney asks. "Come on out, Desmond. Say hello."

A figure rises from the far corner of the room. He's a boy, so tall and thin that his uniform drapes off of him like it's still on a hanger. Desmond . . . I remember that name . . . and he looks sort of familiar. Finally, it clicks into the place. Desmond was the rule-obsessed junior in Addy's pod. The kid must have grown half a meter!

Desmond walks over. He stares at his shoes and sticks a hand out at Denver. "Pleased to meet you. I'm Desmond."

Denver shoots me a questioning glance, then shakes Desmond's hand. "Hi, Desmond. You can call me Denver."

Desmond nods. "Should we test the scan?" he asks Gedney.

Gedney nods at me. "And this is Jasper Adams."

"I have already met Jasper Adams."

"He was in my sister's pod," I tell Gedney. "What scan?"

Desmond quickly looks up at Gedney, then back at the floor. He shifts his weight from foot to foot.

Gedney chuckles and grips my shoulder. "We just want to run a check on your brain patch, make sure everything's running smoothly before you head to the Youli home world."

"Okay." I guess that makes sense. But why is Desmond in on it? I would have thought that my brain patch was top-level clearance only. "I didn't know that my brain patch was public knowledge."

"It most definitely is not," Gedney says. "How do I put this in a way that doesn't make me sound like a comically old man? Admiral Eames is concerned with my succession. Especially since Waters is no longer under her control, she wants to make sure that I've trained an apprentice to take over on the tech front."

"And that would be Desmond?"

"It is." Gedney pats Desmond's back. Desmond winces. "I'll manage the scan, son. I'll upload the data to the drive."

"The admiral asked me to do the scan," Desmond says.

That's strange. Why would the admiral care? And why would she even be talking to Desmond?

"Do you mind, Jasper?" Gedney asks. He's already getting out a sensor and handing it to Desmond. "It will only take a second."

It doesn't appear I have much choice, I turn around and lift my hair up at the nape of my neck. Desmond runs the sensor device over my skin. It beeps.

"All done," Gedney says.

Desmond hurries from the pod room without another word.

Gedney shakes his head. "Thanks for your patience with Desmond. We're still working on small talk, but he's getting there."

I flop down on my favorite turquoise beanbag. "Another one of your Bounder projects, like Regis?"

"I'm just being a friend," he says. "Speaking of Regis, that was a very nice thing you did at the aeroport."

"Wow, word really travels fast."

"Welcome to Earth Force," Denver says.

Gedney perches on the end of a ladder-back chair like the one we practiced lifting in the Ezone during our first tour. "How does it feel to be back?"

"I wish I could say it felt like I never left," I reply, "but that definitely isn't true. At least our pod room feels the same. I'm happy some things never change."

"Change can be good, son," Gedney says, "but you also need some things you can rely on. How are your pod mates?"

I stare up at the sticky stars on the ceiling. Once Mira filled the whole room with twinkling stars, and our pod danced in the starlight. I can't imagine that happening now. Even if we were all together, we've grown too far apart. "I'm not sure how to mend things between us, but I think I need to try."

Gedney nods. "Yes, son. Tell me about your meeting at the bounding base."

I shrug. "We managed to get the job done." I think back to that day, how tense things were at first. When Mira showed up, I almost lost it. The only reason I was able to hold it together was because I knew how much was at stake. But we only knew the half of it. Mira delivered a Youli ultimatum for Earth to appear before the Intragalactic Council before bounding away again. After she left, the rest of us hung out in the mess hall for a bit, eating tater tots and trying to push through the cloud of awkwardness that clung to us. "The old bonds are there, but they're buried beneath a lot of junk."

"The more time you spend together, the easier it will be," Gedney says.

Denver stretches out on the tangerine beanbag. "Hopefully, it will be even easier when you travel together to the Youli home world. You get to ditch us grown-ups and just be teenagers together."

"I doubt that's what the Youli have in store for us."

"You might be surprised," Gedney says. "I've heard that when we clarified the demands and details of your ambassadorship, the Youli said they planned to help you improve your skills with the bounding gloves. I'd say that's something you kids can bond over." His com link buzzes. Gedney checks it and slowly pushes to his feet. "That means it's time for me to go. We can chat more later, but your vid conference with the Resistance is about to start. I promised the admiral I wouldn't take part. I'm just a neutral tech consultant."

"We're neutrals, too," I say.

"Even so." Gedney activates the tech screen on the rear wall. "You know how to operate this thing, Jasper, right?"

"Sure. See you later."

Gedney closes the door behind him.

Denver runs his fingers through the green grass carpet. "I can't believe this is where your pod meetings were. You lucked out. Why couldn't they have had these digs when I was training?"

"Maybe because they weren't expecting you to wield stolen alien biotech?"

"Okay, there's that."

"Most of the other Bounders weren't as lucky. Gedney and Waters understand how our minds work better than most. They know we'll actually relax and pay attention more easily in an environment like this than if we were required to sit at a rigid desk under bright lights."

"I'm thinking anyone would learn better under these conditions," Denver says, sprawling his arms to the side and gazing up at the ceiling.

The vid conference console lights up and emits a low beep. I stretch over and hit the accept button. A moment later, an image blinks into view. It's a stone table, and gathered around it are Waters, Barrick, Addy, Marco, and a few other humans and Tunnelers I don't know. Gulaga's online.

"Hello, Denver, Jasper," Waters says. "Are you getting this?"

"Crystal clear," Denver says. His tone says he's nowhere near forgiving Waters for the stunt he pulled on Gulaga. He tried to blackmail me and Denver into broadcasting a pro-Resistance plea across all of planet Earth. When Denver refused, Waters's Tunneler bodyguards beat him.

Addy smiles at me from across the galaxy. "Hi, J."

"Hey," I say to her and Marco. I know we're supposed to stick to business, but it still makes me ridiculously relieved and happy to see them after the Battle of the Alkalinian Seat, when I was sure they died in that poison sea.

The meeting with the Resistance goes only slightly better than the one with the Earth Force team. Waters understands that the Resistance will ultimately need to be disbanded, but he's only willing to agree to that if Earth commits to steering clear of Gulaga, pulling out of the Paleo Planet, and restructuring Earth Force to be governed by a committee that includes Resistance representatives. Plus, Admiral Eames has to resign. I look at Addy and Marco, trying to get a read on whether Waters is just posturing, but they nod along, appearing to fully support him. I have to admit, most of his demands make sense.

But it really doesn't matter how reasonable the Resistance's other positions are. Eames will never agree to step down.

"Before we sign off," Waters says, "there's something else."

"There always is," Denver says.

"You're going to have unprecedented access to the Youli during your pod's visit to their home world. Even the location of their home world is something Earth has never been able to pinpoint. Jasper, with your brain patch, you in particular are going to learn much. It will be helpful to understand the Youli players and politics before we arrive at the Intragalactic Summit, and presumably the Youli won't be as guarded with kids."

"I wouldn't be so sure about that," Denver says. "At this point, the Youli probably think these kids are the only competent ones in our lot."

Waters ignores Denver's comment and continues. "We need to know that you'll share the intelligence equally between the Resistance and Earth Force."

"I'm neutral, remember? Of course I'll share it equally."

"One more thing, Jasper." Waters leans forward, blocking the others from the camera. "You have to assume that Mira is with the Youli now. I know you have a special bond, but you need to be careful, and you need to use it to our advantage."

I squeeze my hands into fists. "I don't need advice about Mira, especially from you. We're signing off." I hit the connection button, and the image fizzles out. I instantly regret it. I didn't even say good-bye to Addy and Marco. I shouldn't let Waters get to me like that.

"Touchy subject?" Denver asks after letting me stew for a minute.

"Waters has no right to talk to me about Mira."

"Because of what you told me about your brain patches?"

"For a lot of reasons."

"Fair enough, kid, but I might have to take his side on this one. You need to be careful. Feelings get in the way."

"Like with you and Admiral Eames?"

He laughs. "More like that than I want to admit. You're pretty observant."

Denver and I sit quietly, both of us lost in thought. I close my eyes and try to imagine happier moments right here in the pod room. If only I could go back in time for a few days, I would value those moments so much more now. Back then, I wasn't worried about my visit to the Youli home world. I'd never even heard the word *Youli*. I'd just met Mira. Now she means more to me than almost anyone. But how do I tell her? And will it make a difference?

"Are you scared, kid?" Denver asks, breaking the silence.

"Sort of. I mean, we've been at war with the Youli since before I was born. It would be foolish not to be a bit worried about visiting their planet totally unarmed."

"True."

"But I'd be just as scared not going. No matter what, things are at their breaking point. You know what I mean?"

"Unfortunately, I do." He sits up on his beanbag and stares down at me. "Gedney's right, Jasper. You need to bring your pod together when you're visiting the Youli home world. I'm more convinced than ever that the future of our planet depends on you kids."

"No pressure."

"I get that it's a lot of responsibility. Trust me, I wish it weren't necessary. But I don't believe Waters or Eames sees this objectively anymore. Waters thinks he's the savior of Earth (self-appointed, obviously). Regardless of his motives, you just don't operate that way without a huge helping of grandiosity, and there's no room for that in these negotiations. As for Eames, well, I have to believe that the Incident at Bounding Base 51 changed her. It crystallized her focus: avenge Earth and defeat the Youli. I hate to think that our relationship and now my return may have contributed to the intensity of her emotions, but when a conflict is personal, you can be easily blinded.

"What I'm saying, kid, is that you've been at these prep meetings. Not only are Earth Force and the Resistance still a million kilometers apart, but they're both equally delusional in thinking the other side is going to come around to their perspective. There's only one way that changes: a small group gets together, talks through the tough issues, and bridges the gap."

"And that group is our pod."

"Exactly."

"Do you think it's odd that the Youli invited us to their home world? I mean, it's like they're setting up exactly what you described—a small group from different sides of the fight to spend an intense period of time together immediately prior to the Intragalactic Summit."

"As in, do I think it's a coincidence?" Denver asks. "No, I don't. And I don't think you do, either."

In truth, it hadn't crossed my mind until right now. Most of my thoughts about traveling to the Youli home world center around seeing Mira. Maybe that's what Waters means when he says I need to be careful and what Denver means when he says feelings get in the way. Of course the Youli's actions are intentional. Waters and Eames underestimate us. To them, we're still just kids. But that's not how the Youli see us. They know we're the key to peace with Earth.

They know we're the key because Mira told them so.

The next few days go by in a blur. There are more prep meetings that go basically nowhere. Most of the Bounders depart for the Paleo Planet. I try to snoop around and see if Lucy's hunch about the admiral adds up to anything, but every lead I try is a dead end. I attempt to talk to Cole alone, but he's almost always busy. I decide to wait to talk to him until we reach the Youli home world. He might be more willing to set aside military decorum and talk candidly when the admiral and her entourage aren't around.

There's one last thing I want to do before we leave for the Youli home world in the morning.

A guard stands post at the end of the hall leading to the prison cells. Before I can help it, a laugh escapes my throat. I'm remembering the way Lucy manipulated the guard the time we broke into the hall to pay a visit to the Youli prisoner. She had that guard practically running away to escape her hysterics. Geez. That feels so long ago. We were only twelve then. We barely knew each other.

And we barely knew anything about the Youli, the stolen biotech, the Earth Force lies, the war. . . . We had barely scratched the surface of the truth.

What *did* we know? The narrative.

I say hello to the guard, who is looking at me quizzically, probably because I'm laughing to myself. He lets me pass. I'm not sure if it's because he knows I was involved in apprehending the prisoner or if he's a bit starstruck from the whole "lost heroes" thing. I might as well milk that.

I head down the dark hall. Just like the Youli prisoner during our first tour of duty, they're holding Bria, the would-be Resistance fighter, in the last cell. This time, though, there aren't any communication barriers. There's no need for brain-talk. Plain English will work just fine.

"What do you want?" she asks when I come into her sight line. She's sitting on her cot with a book in her hands. At least they allow her to read to pass the time. "I thought you were the guard bringing my dinner."

"Sorry to disappoint you," I tell her, "although the food here sucks."

"No kidding. If I have to eat another tofu dog, I may have to go on a hunger strike." She sets the book down and lies back on her cot.

"Try plugging your nose while you eat them."

"You're here to give me food tips?"

"I wanted to see you before I left."

She crosses her hands behind her head. "Going back to Earth for some more celebrity appearances?"

"Nope. I'm heading to the Youli planet to meet up with my friends in the Resistance."

She laughs. When I don't change my expression, she sits up on the cot, planting her feet firmly on the ground. "You're serious?"

"Yeah, we told you all this on the craft."

She stands and approaches the glass barrier. "You're liars."

I shrug. "This time I'm telling the truth."

She hugs her arms around her middle. "So I did all this for nothing." She's looking at the floor, and I think she's talking to herself. At least, it doesn't seem like she's expecting a response.

"It wasn't for nothing," I say quietly. "I knew the narrative was bad, but what happened on the ship . . . Well, I've never been more certain that things need to change."

She tips her gaze, and our eyes meet. I raise my palm and press it to the glass.

"Can I ask you a question?" I ask her.

She nods.

"What do you want?"

"To get out of here, obviously."

I shake my head. "I don't think there's anything I can do about that. What I mean is, on the cruise ship . . . when you did what you did . . . what did you hope would happen? I know you said you wanted us to admit to the truth, but what were you hoping that would accomplish?"

She bites her lip and fiddles with the skin near her nails. At first, I don't think she's going to answer. Eventually, she looks up. "There's this constant stream of lies running through our lives. Even if people don't know it, they *know* it on some level. I couldn't live like that anymore. I need to live in the truth."

Isn't that what we all need? But who actually does it? Who lives in the truth? We live in the narrative or pretend to live in the narrative so that others won't know that we see through their lies. Those who call for truth end up ousted like Addy or labeled odd like Mira or locked up like Bria. That's why things need to change. Now.

"And you know what?" Bria continues. "Even if I'm locked up for the rest of my life, I will still believe in what I did."

"You should," I tell her, "because the truth is worth fighting for."

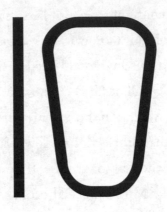

**AT 0900, COLE, LUCY, AND I MEET AT THE**
door of the Ezone so we can bound together to Bounding Base 32, the same place we met up for our cease-fire talks. Lucy is glammed up as always. Cole's face has that fresh redness you get from running. Since I learned about his intense morning schedule, which ends with a workout in the space station gym immediately before his first briefing of the day, I'd say that running is a pretty good guess for what he's been up to prior to showing up here.

As for me, I rolled out of bed about twenty minutes ago, straight into a well of anxiety. I've barely slept since leaving Gulaga, so I wasn't worried too much about oversleeping this morning. But, of course, my uncooperative body decided to stay unconscious straight through my alarm. So now I'm late and panicked. Every worry I've had about this trip to the Youli home world came rushing in like a tidal wave as soon as my feet hit the floor. Not to mention, it's probably only a matter of hours before I'm face-to-face with Mira, so I'm also full of extra jitters that have nothing to do with the future of Earth.

Gedney opens the door to the Ezone and invites us in. The dark, breezy room feels cool and familiar. That is, until Desmond steps out of the shadows.

"What's he doing here?" Lucy asks.

"We just need to run one more scan before you bound out," Gedney says.

"What kind of scan?" Cole says. "I wasn't informed."

Cole doesn't know? That's odd. "They're making sure my Youli tech is fully operational. Maybe it will help me eavesdrop on the green guys."

"You can do that?" Lucy asks me.

"I wish."

"But why are *you* here?" Cole asks Desmond. He's never liked the poor kid. Desmond's the only person in the history of the galaxy who might know more than Cole about Earth Force rules and regulations.

Desmond just stares back at Cole. I'm betting he thinks there's no reason to elaborate since Gedney already told us what they're doing.

I decide to fill in the blank. "Admiral Eames wants Gedney to teach Desmond everything he knows in case Gedney croaks, like an Einstein brain download or something."

"Really?" Cole asks. "This was a direct order from Admiral Eames?"

"Let's just get it over with," Lucy says. "It's cold in here."

Desmond runs the scanner over the base of my neck. Gedney double-checks the reading then shoos Desmond out of the Ezone.

When it's just the four of us, Gedney asks, "Okay, ready to bound? Best to hurry now."

Hurry, hurry, hurry—that's the Gedney I remember from my first tour! Like I told him before, I'm glad some things never change.

The three of us hoist our blast packs onto our backs and slip on our gloves. As we start to open our ports, clusters of light fly toward our fingertips. Cole and Lucy disappear. I nod at Gedney, take a deep breath, and bound.

I hit the tarmac at the bounding deck with both feet firmly planted. An excellent landing, if I do say so myself. I don't stay on my feet for long, though. My sister plows into me, knocking us both to the ground. I guess Addy and Marco made it here safely.

"Good to see you, too, Ads," I say as I untangle myself from my sister.

"Did you see them? Did you tell them I'm not dead?"

It takes me a minute to process what she's asking me. Oh— "Of course! Mom and Dad are so relieved."

Addy sits back on her knees. "Tell me everything."

"I took Denver home with me!"

"Oh my God! He was Mom's teen crush! She must have freaked out!"

"Pretty much."

Marco stands over Addy. "I know you've been desperate to see your brother, but can we save the *tell me everything* for the trip?" He pulls her off the ground, then reaches down to help me up. "J-Bird, always a pleasure." He quickly spins me around into a headlock.

We break apart, and then it's the five of us: Addy, Marco, Lucy, Cole, and me, the so-called neutral party. Although nothing feels neutral about any of this. For a moment, we all just stare at one another.

Cole is the first to break the awkward silence. "Has anyone checked in with the base?"

"Yes," Addy quickly answers. "The control room received confirmation that the Youli ship should be arriving in approximately five minutes."

"Just enough time to freshen up," Lucy says, turning for the station.

"I'll go with you," Addy says, taking off after her. Lucy

glances over her shoulder with a skeptical look on her face, but she doesn't tell my sister to buzz off. The fact that Lucy isn't openly hostile toward Addy is an unexpected positive.

So it's the three of us. How many times have we hung out together? A million? This used to feel as normal as brushing my teeth. Now, it's . . . not.

"What's with girls always going to the bathroom together?" Marco says.

"I think Addy was just being friendly," I say.

"I'm assuming they both need to use the facilities," Cole says.

Marco looks at me. We both burst out laughing.

"You never change, Wiki."

I think Cole may dress him down for the nickname, but he doesn't. If anything, his shoulders seem to fall a bit, like maybe he's actually relaxing. A second passes, then Cole smiles. "Have you heard the rumor?" he asks Marco. "Jasper and Lucy are dating!"

"Come on—" I start.

"Of course I've heard! It's all over the Earth webs! We can't even escape the rumors on Gulaga!"

"You know we're not—"

"I never thought Jasper could handle the drama," Cole says, "but I was wrong."

"Clearly, Wiki."

Just when I thought this agony would never end, the girls come back.

"What did I miss?" Lucy asks.

Cole and Marco choke back laughs.

"Nothing," I say. "Absolutely nothing."

If I can't get them to shut up about Lucy and me, it's going to be a very long few days.

"Check it out!" Addy is pointing off the bounding deck into open space.

In front of us, the air shimmers and bends, like a soap bubble about to pop. Then, in an instant, a silver ship spins through. It rotates faster until it's whirling so rapidly I can't track it. Next it looks like it's being squashed—it shrinks vertically and expands horizontally, all the while screeching like metal grinding against metal. After it's fully unfurled, the Youli ship rolls out a ramp of silver metal like a giant mouth sticking out its tongue. The ramp touches down on the bounding deck, leading back to the Youli ship hovering just beyond.

"The Youli have arrived," Cole says. He still wins the Captain Obvious award.

"We've got spectators," Addy says, nodding back at the bounding base station. At least a dozen faces are up against the protective glass watching us. None of them want to get too close to the Youli, apparently, but they also don't want to miss this.

"Well, friends," Marco says, "time to shuffle."

"Shouldn't we wait for someone to come out and . . . I don't know . . . greet us?" Lucy asks.

No one responds, and then I realize they're all staring at me. "I guess . . . not?"

Another moment passes. No one moves. Then Addy throws up her arms and starts for the ramp. Marco and I take off behind her.

When I'm halfway to the ramp, I check that Cole and Lucy are behind us. Some of the Earth Force officers have also ventured onto the bounding deck. One of them raises his hand in a solemn farewell. Why do I get the feeling he's sure he'll never see us again?

What I do know is that no one knows exactly where we're going. Earth Force has a general idea of where the Youli home world is, but they've never been able to confirm it. The Youli use extremely sophisticated cloaking shields. I know Gedney has been studying the technology, but Earth has nothing like it and probably won't for a long time. Also, we definitely don't have the tracking tech that the Youli have. They were able to track my pod back to Gulaga from the last Intragalactic Summit where Earth Force staged an attack and we placed the degradation patch. That sure set off a domino effect of bad events.

Addy and Marco stop at the edge of the slick silver loading

ramp. Just like the exterior of the ship, the material almost looks liquid, sort of like the occludium membrane that surrounds our own bounding ships.

Marco takes a cautious step onto the ramp. It's definitely solid. He takes another step. It can't be too slippery because he's still standing.

The rest of us crowd in behind him. We're moving in a pack now, setting aside our differences for our common mission, which I'd currently describe as "survive long enough to make it up the Youli boarding ramp."

By the time we reach the top of the ramp, we've left the security of the bounding deck. Space spreads beneath us. I didn't know this was going to feel like such a leap of faith.

Now that we're close to the walls of the ship, it's clear the material is solid, despite its liquidy appearance. It's so solid, in fact, that there doesn't appear to be a door. So while we've reached the top of the ramp, we have no clue how to enter.

I'm about to ask if anyone has a guess how to get in when the wall of the ship directly in front of us begins to move, the metal starting to ripple and unfold into the shape of a door.

I swallow my nerves. There's a decent chance that once this door is fully open, I'll see Mira standing on the other side.

But then the ship's metal stops moving, and what's left is a door-size opening for us to pass through. Mira isn't there. In fact, no one is.

"Still no welcoming party," I whisper to my pod mates.

Marco and Addy march right in. I let Cole and Lucy go next. I take a final look at the bounding base and follow my friends. As soon as I cross the threshold, the metal rushes in to form a solid wall behind me.

From the inside, the walls don't look like metal.

"We're in the middle of a cantaloupe, just like the last time we were on one of these ships," Marco says. Sure enough, the walls are orange, and the vessel has the faint smell of rotten fruit. The floor is squishy beneath our feet. I poke a finger at the wall, and it's the same squishy substance.

Addy takes a few more steps then abruptly stops. "I think there's a wall here."

Cole puts his hand out in front of him and inches forward. Sure enough, his fingers stop in what looks like the middle of the air. "Invisible wall. Fascinating."

As the rest of us explore the parameters of the wall, a chime sounds. The barriers holding us flicker and then fade.

"What was that?" Lucy asks.

"Definitely a scanner," Cole says. "I'm sure they're check-ing that we're not transporting prohibited items, especially tracking devices."

Addy extends her hand. "Do you think the wall is still—"

Before she can finish her sentence, everything changes. We're suddenly standing aboard an Earth Force passenger craft. I nearly lose my balance, catching myself on one of the tweed seats in the row behind me.

Marco turns in a circle. "What the—"

"Did they bound us somewhere?" Lucy asks.

I take a step across the space that seconds ago was an invisible wall. "I'm not sure."

"Isn't it obvious?" Cole asks. "This is VR."

"How can you tell?" Addy asks.

"Clearly they have the technology," Cole says. "The Alks didn't invent VR. I'm sure they brokered for it. I'm also sure the Youli had the tech long before Seelok and his crew. Not to mention, I'd already deduced that the interior of this ship was VR compatible."

Now that he says it, I realize the mushy orange walls are curiously similar to the walls of our common room on Alkalinia before the VR kicked in.

Marco makes a face. "If the Youli home world is anything like that snake hole, it's going to be a very long few days."

"Not to mention," Cole continues, ignoring Marco, "this craft is an old model. Aside from making absolutely zero sense, if the Youli were really going to bound us to an Earth Force passenger craft, wouldn't they choose one that was still operational?"

"So why make their own ship look like ours?" Addy asks.

Cole shrugs. "I don't know, maybe they want to make us feel comfortable?"

"Youli hospitality," Addy says. "I like it!"

As if someone heard Addy's comment, a voice comes on over an intercom. "Welcome, Earthlings. We will be departing momentarily. Please take your seats."

"That must mean us," I say. "If we're about to bound, we better buckle up."

We head over to the seats. I have my sister on one side and Cole on the other. My hands are shaking so badly that Addy has to help me fasten my straps. Now that we're about to leave, I'm incredibly anxious. I didn't spend any time thinking through the logistics. I hate bounding by ship. The Earth Force ships are bad enough. I definitely don't want to bound on a Youli vessel. What if they don't work for humans? What if something goes horribly wrong? We could end up in the rift, or worse, scattered across the galaxy.

Addy places her palm on top of mine. "Breathe, Jasper. It will be over in an instant."

I close my eyes. A chime sounds in the cabin. The next thing I know, I feel weightless, like I've been dropped into a zero gravity chamber. Then, just as quickly, the feeling's gone.

"Welcome to your destination," the intercom announces. "Please proceed to the exit."

I blink my eyes. Everything looks exactly as before.

"Is that it?" Marco asks. "We're already there?"

I exhale the breath I'd been holding since before the bound. That wasn't too bad.

"Earth Force could learn a few things about bounding in comfort from the Youli," Lucy says.

"Definitely," Cole says. "This tech is amazing. The main reason I wanted to come was to experience their technology firsthand."

"That's a surprise to no one, Wiki," Marco says.

"Enough, Marco," Lucy says as she undoes her harness. "He's Cole or Captain Thompson. Didn't you read the final term sheet of the cease-fire? No nicknames."

"Of course I didn't read it. Is that really in there?"

"No," Lucy says, "but it should have been. You better not be calling me names."

"Or what?" Addy says, rolling her eyes.

Lucy puts her hands on her hips and is clearly about to dress down my sister.

"Hey!" I say. "Let's focus on why we're here, which is presumably right on the other side of that exit. Shall we?" I stand and wave my pod mates toward the door that's suddenly appeared on the wall of the craft.

I waver between wanting to be first out or last. Will Mira be waiting on the other side this time? And if she is, what should I do? I don't want to look overeager.

What if she's not there? Does that mean she doesn't want

to see me? Did she show up at the bounding station a month ago just because the Youli told her to? What if our moment alone together meant nothing to her? Maybe our connection is all in my mind.

"You with us, Ace?" Marco asks.

I shake my head to get it in gear. "How long did you last on the no-nicknames thing? Two minutes?"

He shrugs. "Maybe. It could have been less. Let's go."

We cluster near the closed door, waiting for something to happen. Just as quickly as before, the space transforms back into the orange mush. The light in front of us intensifies, and the wall where the door was seconds ago begins to peel back. In fact, the entire vessel seems to be melting away like an ice cube under a flame.

In a matter of seconds, we're standing together on a silver platform. The ship we were on moments before has completely vanished.

"Whoa," Marco says. "We're not in Amazonas anymore."

"Kansas," Lucy whispers.

"Huh?" I ask.

"Kansas. We're not in *Kansas* anymore. It's from *The Wizard of Oz*."

"Wherever we are, it's definitely not Earth," Addy says. "In fact, it's not a planet at all."

**ADDY'S RIGHT. THIS THING DEFINITELY**
isn't a planet. There's no sign of a planet anywhere. It looks
like we're standing in the middle of open space. All I can see
is stars. There's nothing to suggest the ship we traveled aboard
was ever here. How that's possible? I have no clue.

"We must be enclosed, right?" Marco asks. "That's the
only way we're not dead."

"I think we're in a clear sphere," Cole says.

If I squint, I can just make out a metal grid surrounding
us in a sphere shape like Cole said. The grid must be holding
together a clear enclosure. I slowly turn in a circle. The exact
center is the metal platform where we're standing.

"What is this place?" I ask.

"Where are all the people, or Youli, or whatever we're supposed to call them?" Addy asks.

"There's no one here," Cole says.

"Always one to state the obvious, Wiki," Marco says.

Lucy kicks Marco's shoe.

Cole doesn't seem to have noticed. He's looking around, his eyes lit up like he's getting a sneak peek of the next edition of *Evolution*. "This is amazing," he says. "I can't believe how far they've gone to keep their planet hidden."

"What are you talking about?" Lucy asks.

"This must be a pin sphere," he continues. "Instead of bounding us directly to their planet, they brought us to a drop-off location. There are probably dozens of them in this sector, all completely cloaked. I'm sure they're linked organically to the Youli systems, just like how the Youli themselves are linked. So even though to us it seems like we're totally alone, they're watching our every move."

"Creepy," Addy says.

"So you think they'll send a shuttle to take us to the planet?" I ask.

"Doubtful," Cole says. "That would be too easy to track. I don't know what kind of tech they'll use to transport us, but I can't wait to find out."

Now that's the Cole I know. The rest of us are freaked to

find out what our so-called mortal enemies have in store for us, and he's practically bouncing on his toes with excitement to see what cool Youli tech will be rolled out next.

While Cole explains the pin sphere, Marco creeps closer to the edge of the platform.

"Careful!" Lucy shouts as Marco dangles a foot over the side.

Just as he does, the edge of the platform ripples. The silver flows out from the platform, melding into a silver path, suspended in space, angling down.

"Follow the silver road?" Marco asks.

Lucy looks at him quizzically. "What's with you and *The Wizard of Oz* references today?"

"This place looks like it was created by wizards," Addy says.

We follow Marco onto the silver walkway. As we move forward, the path unfurls before us and gently slopes toward the bottom of the sphere—or at least what feels like the bottom from the perspective of this platform.

"I'm pretty sure we're in zero gravity," Cole says. "There must be some kind of magnetlike properties that keep us anchored to the path."

"So you mean if I jumped off I'd float?" Marco asks, setting down his blast pack.

"Don't try—" But before Lucy can get the words out, Marco leaps.

I hold my breath, half expecting him to plummet to the bottom of the sphere, break the glass, and be sucked into open space, probably vacuuming the rest of us out with him.

But no. He floats, just like Cole predicted. Marco spins in midair, then somersaults. The movement pushes him away from the walkway, toward the edge of the sphere. He reclines and crosses his hands behind his head.

"Fabulous," Lucy says. "How on earth are we going to get him back?"

"I'll get him." Addy sets down her pack and jumps off the walkway.

Lucy throws her arms in the air. "Great. Now we need to rescue them both. Do either of them ever think first?"

"Not really," I say. "That's why they like each other so much."

Addy's initial momentum propels her all the way to Marco. They collide and tumble together through the sphere, laughing hysterically, then roughly colliding with the clear edge. Fortunately, it doesn't break.

"Get back here!" Lucy shouts. "If the Youli are watching like Cole said, they're going to think we're a bunch of fools!"

"Be there in a sec!" Addy replies. She says something to Marco, and then they both align their feet with the edge of the sphere and push off.

They soar across the sphere toward the walkway. At roughly

the midpoint, they start to slow down. They stop completely a few meters short of the silver walkway and then slowly begin to accelerate back to the edge of the sphere. I glance at Cole, whose face is scrunched up in thought.

"Take two!" Marco shouts once they're back at the edge. They push off hard but still can't make it all the way to the walkway.

"There must be a small amount of the magnetlike material in the sphere casing," Cole says. "It's not enough to pull us off the platform or the walkway, but it's enough to prevent them from getting back here."

"Seriously?" Lucy asks. "I can't believe this! At least they could have taken their blast packs with them. Maybe now you'll understand why I wasn't the least bit tempted to join the Resistance, Jasper. They're ridiculous."

"No worries!" Marco shouts. "We'll use our gloves."

"Don't!" Cole shouts. "We have no idea what kind of scramblers they're using here. Being stuck in this sphere is better than being stuck in the rift."

"See what I mean?" Lucy says. "They're going to get their atoms scattered across the galaxy. Can someone please go get them?"

"We can't risk using our packs, either," Cole says. "The air in here could be highly flammable, and the packs' ignitions could set the whole sphere on fire."

"Wonderful," Lucy says. "Just when I thought they—"

I ignore Lucy and sit cross-legged on the platform, searching my brain for a solution. "What if we took off our belts and linked them together? When they're close, we can swing the belts out like a rope and reel them in."

Cole shrugs. Lucy asks if I'm serious. But since neither of them comes up with a better idea, we give it a try. Once we've assembled the belt rope, Addy and Marco push off again. When they close in, I swing the rope. It narrowly misses Marco's hands.

We try a few more times but can't manage to make a connection, and Marco and Addy are starting to get tired. Each launch is shorter than the last.

While I'm trying to reel them in with the rope, Lucy is pacing the platform in a huff. Cole is sitting with his legs hanging off the path, lost in thought. He never bought into the belt rope idea. Hopefully, he comes up with another plan soon.

"This is absurd!" Lucy says. "If the Youli can monitor us organically, or whatever you said before, why don't they help us? I thought the whole point was for us to visit their home world before the Intragalactic Summit."

"I guess they want to get a look at us first," I say, "like bugs under a microscope."

"Impulsive, grossly underdeveloped bugs," Lucy says, nodding at Marco and my sister, who are currently engaged in some kind of tickle contest.

In this case, I can't disagree. "Pretty much."

Marco pushes off again. I swing the rope. It misses his hands by a solid meter.

"That's it!" Cole says like we're in the middle of a conversation. "If we're not leaving here by bounding technology, then our course has to be linear. And that means we'll need to exit from somewhere on the edge of the sphere. Let's go!"

He starts walking, and the silver path unfurls before him.

"Wait a second," I say, grabbing Marco's and Addy's packs and dashing after him. "What are you talking about? What about Marco and Addy?"

"Leave them," Lucy says under her breath.

"Simple!" Cole's smiling now. He's definitely confident in whatever conclusion he's reached. "We'll see where we end up on the silver path, and they can crawl along the edge of the sphere to meet us. It won't be a direct route, but that's the price they pay for derailing our trip."

Fair point.

I shout the plan to Marco and Addy. They give us a thumbs-up, then stretch out on their backs against the edge of the sphere. It looks like they're going to take a snooze until they know where they need to crawl.

Cole, Lucy, and I weave our way down the silver ramp

until we reach the very bottom of the sphere. As soon as we get there, a second silver platform forms. The floor is concave. Once all three of us are standing on it, the liquid silver rises around us to form a smaller, silver sphere.

"Addy!" I can't let us get separated.

A second later, the silver rolls away on one side, forming a door-size entryway.

"This must be a launch capsule," Cole says. "I bet it will take us to the Youli planet."

"Well, let's hope they make it here before it decides to launch."

"They'll make it," Cole says.

"The Youli are watching, remember?" Lucy says. "I suspect they won't leave half of us behind, even if it's the far less desirable half."

Addy and Marco slowly make their way to the capsule. By the time they arrive, they're both gasping for breath and dripping with sweat. The crawl route must have been pretty tough. They slide into the pod, and the door seals instantly.

Lucy turns her back to Marco and Addy, which isn't much of a surprise. I just laugh at them because they deserve it, and also because I doubt either one of them really regrets jumping.

With all of us piled into the capsule, it's a tight squeeze. Again I feel my nerves building. Cole said he doesn't think we're in for another bound, but that doesn't make me feel any calmer or less claustrophobic. At least I know what bounding is. Traveling by launch capsule from a pin sphere is an unfamiliar mode of transportation, and not one I signed on for. I grab Addy's sweaty hand.

The next thing I know, the pin sphere spits out our capsule. We zip through the cosmos, like we've been dropped from one of those multistoried amusement rides that lets you free-fall toward the ground, catching you mere meters before you crash.

Just like that, something snags us, but instead of bringing us to a stop, it flings us to the side. Now we're whirling through space, literally whirling, because the small capsule is tumbling. All sense of gravity is gone. I have no idea what's up or down, because really, nothing is.

"What's happening?" I whisper through gritted teeth.

"I think they're setting us into orbit," Cole says.

"Huh?" I ask.

"I think this is how they avoid us getting picked up by detection tech." Cole's voice shakes when he talks thanks to the whirling. "We look like a piece of space debris. Once we swing close enough to their system, we should get caught up in their gravity and pulled through their shield."

I take a deep breath and close my eyes. Even though I can no longer gauge our spinning, my stomach knows. I press my tongue against the roof of my mouth to ward off the pooling acid from erupting out of my throat. I knew I shouldn't have choked down so many carob-coated fruit balls during my mad dash through the mess hall this morning.

"Look!" Addy shouts.

I open my eyes. She's pointing ahead, over Lucy's shoulder. Out that side of the capsule, there's a place in space that seems to wave and bend, almost like a bounding port. We're zooming directly for it.

Before I can process whether that's good or bad, we're through. Now we're in some sort gray, gauzy haze, like a thick layer of clouds.

"I think this is a bounding shield," Cole says. "More sophisticated than our occludium shields, obviously, but the same general tech. If anyone managed to track our capsule in orbit, I'm sure they'd lose us in here."

"No kidding," Addy says. "This is thicker than Mom's spaghetti sauce, right, J?"

In response, I gag.

"Don't. You. Dare. Puke," Lucy says.

"Seriously, Ace," Marco says, "who are you, Bad Breath?"

When we bounded with Bad Breath on our way to Alkalinia, he threw up everywhere. The memory makes me gag again. I cover my mouth with both hands.

We hurtle through the haze for a long time. It seems like

nothing's changing, but if Cole's right, we're gradually edging closer to the planet, where eventually its gravity will be strong enough to yank us down.

"Something's happening," Addy says. Sure enough, the light outside the sphere is getting brighter and filled with color.

"We must be entering the atmosphere," Cole says.

Out the window, the thick gray haze shifts to an opaque ice blue, getting brighter and pinker by the second. Our trajectory adjusts. We're no longer spinning. Instead, we're bulleting in one direction and gaining speed by the second.

"And we have gravity," Cole says.

"Do we have to be upside down?" I ask, taking another deep breath to keep the nausea at bay.

Before anyone responds, our capsule breaks through the cloud layer.

Addy gasps.

"Wow," Marco says.

Beneath us, the Youli home world glistens. It looks exactly like the picture Mira showed me in my mind. Crystalline towers reach up through the rose-blue sky like lances covered in ice. They stretch through a thick layer of pink clouds that covers the ground so that it looks like the planet is built on a field of cotton candy. As we close in, I see that pale green vines climb the towers and shine their leaves at the trio of stars on the horizon.

"It's gorgeous!" Lucy exclaims.

We shoot down, gaining speed. We fly by the tips of the crystal towers with no sign of slowing. Soon, it's clear we're headed for large reflective disk built into one of the crystals.

"What is that?" Addy asks. "A solar panel? A landing pad?"

"I'm not sure," Cole replies.

As we close in, the disk appears to burp, emitting a giant bubble into the air. The bubble floats up to meet our capsule. The second they collide, the silver holding our capsule together vanishes, and we're contained inside the transparent membranc of the bubble.

As we're lowered through the silver disk into the tower, the bubble's membrane fogs. I can't see through the opaque barrier, but I can sense when the bubble stops descending. Addy and I share a glance filled with nerves and curiosity for whatever happens next.

The bubble pops.

We are standing in an enormous hall with columns reaching stories high. The space we're in is so grand there is nothing in my memory to compare it to. My closest mental references are pictures of temples built to honor the gods in ancient Greece or Egypt. We're so small compared to the size of the room that again I feel like the bug under the microscope.

Windows stretch so high, I can barely see the ceiling. On the other sides of the glass, crystal towers reach skyward and dense petals wave in a soft breeze. Inside, thick vines snake their way to the ceiling and out the windowed walls to wrap around the tower. The floor beneath us looks like marble but is so reflective that it makes me feel like I'm falling the second I look down. Everything has a greenish hue that reminds me of Youli skin, and the very air resonates with a subtle throbbing, like the unison beating of a communal heart.

Addy elbows me in the ribs. I turn. Three Youli are approaching. Inside their translucent green skin, their pink hearts beat in time to the air itself.

And Mira leads the way.

**THE MOMENT I SPOT MIRA, HER EYES**
light up, and she practically radiates with energy that showers
my brain patch with shivers.

I don't even think. I just start running . . . right into an
invisible wall. I roughly crash and fall on my butt.

Mira flicks her wrist and steps through the barrier.
Rumblings on the edge of my mind let me know the Youli
aren't too happy that she waved away the wall.

Before I can scramble to my feet, Mira's standing right in
front of me. She leans over and extends her hands.

Her fingers are cold as always, but as I fold her slender
palms into my own, a wave of warmth spreads through me.

When I'm on my feet, I sweep my arms around her and wrap her into a tight hug.

She pulls back. Her face is damp with tears. Her dark brown eyes find mine, and it's almost too intense to hold her gaze. So much emotion pours off of her—happiness and longing and relief and despair, all interwoven like a giant ball of rubber bands. I couldn't begin to separate or decipher them, so I don't even try. I just stand still and stare and try to take it all in. Take her in.

Lucy clears her throat. "Hi, Mira."

That's right. We're not the only two people in the galaxy.

I blink and step to the side. I reach down and grab Mira's hand, not wanting to let her go for even a second. She's wearing a long white gown like the one she wore when she met us at the bounding base a few weeks ago. Her blond hair hangs in a braid down her back.

Lucy, Cole, Addy, and Marco greet Mira. Unlike me, though, they're wary. They barely take their eyes off the three Youli standing behind her.

My pod mates probably haven't seen a Youli this close since the Intragalactic Summit at the end of our tour on Gulaga. And they definitely haven't seen one under supposedly peaceful conditions. As far as I know, the only Youli that Addy has ever seen were from a distance during the Battle of the Alkalinian Seat.

While my friends talk to Mira, I eye the Youli. They're green, big-headed, and tall, like aliens straight out of classic sci-fi films. I wouldn't be surprised if secret Youli visits to Earth inspired some of the original drawings of aliens and UFOs. They weren't as secret as they thought. And now, for reasons I don't totally understand but probably have to do with Mira, they aren't nearly as scary, at least to me.

Somehow I instinctively know that these three Youli are the ones who rescued us from the rift. Since they kept their word and got us out of there, I at least have some reason to trust them. And since the whole point of us traveling here is to lay a positive foundation for Earth-Youli relations before the Intragalactic Summit, with me as the neutral guy and de facto leader, I decide I should be the friendly spokesperson.

*Hi*, I say to them. *Thanks again for rescuing us from the rift.*

Addy eyes me sideways. "Are you talking to them?"

"I'm just saying hello," I tell her.

"You're actually talking to the Youli?" Lucy asks.

I smile. "Yes."

Marco nods. "Cool."

Cole's eyes light with fascination. "Jasper, you need to translate *everything*."

The Youli in the center steps forward. *Jasper Adams, we*

*meet again.* I could never forget that voice. It sounds like wind chimes. *Welcome to our world.*

The other two Youli don't send words, but positive, welcoming vibes radiate from their core.

Marco elbows me and eyes the Youli. "Well?"

"They're just welcoming us and stuff," I tell my pod mates.

Lucy steps forward. "Jasper, please translate." She flashes her signature smile before continuing. "Greetings from planet Earth. I am Captain Lucy Dugan. It is our utmost pleasure to meet you. We appreciate your hospitality, and we commit to doing everything in our power to facilitate the relations between our peoples."

I look at Mira and the Youli. *She says it's nice to meet you.*

*They don't need you to translate,* Mira says. *They understand.*

"Oh," I say.

"Did you tell them what I said?" Lucy asks.

"Sort of," I say.

"Well, *tell them,* Jasper. It's very important that you translate what I say word for word."

"They heard you, Lucy. I don't need to translate."

*Can you please ask the others if we can form a brain connection?* Mira asks.

*You mean you can talk directly to them?* I ask her. *Like at the bounding base?*

When she nods, I relay the request to my pod mates.

Marco takes a step back, like physical distance might prevent the Youli from invading his mental space. "I suppose *no* isn't an option, huh, Ace?"

"Just say yes," Lucy says. "We're here to form positive bonds before the Summit, remember?"

"I certainly assent," Cole says. "This method of communication is fascinating."

Addy looks to Marco, then to me. "I didn't know 'bonds' meant *brain bonds*, but we're in. It's not like we have a real choice anyway."

I feel the Youli expanding our communication circle to include my pod mates. By this point, it feels pretty normal for me to be communicating brain to brain, but the same can definitely not be said for them. The small taste of it they got at the bounding base from Mira did not prepare them for the utterly foreign presence of the Youli in their minds.

Marco clamps his hands against his head. "Whoa! Not loving this!"

Lucy presses her lips together. Cole's whole body is rigid with stress. Addy crouches and shields her face so we can't see her reaction.

*Welcome, young ones,* Wind Chimes says. *We have been anticipating your visit with joy and intention of purpose. We want your stay to be comfortable and productive. Please let us know at once if any of your needs have not been met. We will let* your comrade show you to your quarters. We have secured your mental network, so you will be able to communicate telepathically even when we are not with you.

Mira smiles. *I'm your comrade.*

As the Youli step back, preparing to leave, I sense a presence in our mental circle. I look to Mira, then to the Youli to see if they are going to say more.

*Thank you,* the voice says. I know at once that it's Addy. She pushes herself to standing and smiles. "That was hard."

"Nice, Ads," I whisper. "It gets easier."

The Youli stop and incline their heads. Rather than words, they send us waves of gratitude and hospitality. They're impressed by how fast my sister caught on to brain-talk. They indicate they're about to bound, then in a flash they're gone, leaving us alone with Mira.

"How'd you do that?" Marco asks my sister.

She shrugs. "I just gave it a whirl, and it worked. You should try."

"Next time the green guys show up, maybe I will."

"I knew you'd be a natural," I say to Addy. "You and I have been communicating without words since before you could talk."

Mira clasps her hands in front of her chest. *Come! I'll show you around.*

Her smile is wide, and she radiates happiness. I know she's

glad to see me, but it's more than that. For the first time, she's able to talk to all of my pod mates, not just me. Her connection with them is expanding, just like we hope will happen with the connection between Earth and the Youli.

I squeeze her hand. *Let's go!*

With the Youli gone, I can relax and look around. The room we're in is indeed cavernous. Bright light from the suns streams in, casting tall shadows around the room. The columns are spaced in a pattern, so the shadows reach across the room in long parallel lines. In the streaks of sunlight, tiny dust motes dance.

When we first arrived, I thought the columns held up the ceiling, and they probably do, but now I see they're also lattices to support the vines. Thick green stems wrap around each column, climbing to the ceiling above. Wide leaves reach like open palms, each angled slightly to catch the rays of the suns. Together they seem to pulse with that same subtle heartbeat.

"The Youli like plants, huh?" Marco asks.

The sparkly, bubbly sensation that I've come to know as Mira's laughter fills my mind. Addy and my pod mates bristle. They don't know what to make of brain-talk yet. Their reaction makes her laugh even more. It's cool that we're all connected now, but I can't push away the pang of jealousy that's batting at me. Brain-talk was Mira's and my special thing.

MONICA TESLER

Our communication was secret, just for us. Now that the Youli expanded our circle, can the others hear everything I say to her?

Mira's gotten even better at decoding my thoughts, because she answers my question without me having to ask. *Find the door and close it. See?* First, I feel like a curtain is sliding across my brain, leaving a mental space that's quiet and contained. Then the curtain opens, and I'm aware of the subtle mental self-chatter that must be the others.

I grab the mental curtain and yank it shut. *Just us?* I ask Mira.

She tips her eyes to me and smiles. *Just us.*

Now that I'm thinking about it, this isn't the first time I've sensed the mental curtain. When we were in the rift with the Youli, Mira used that same trick to shut *me* out. How did she know how to do that back then?

Mira squeezes my hand. *Just us*, she says again.

Right. Just us. And Mira's ability to read my thoughts. I could press her about the rift or savor our connection. It's an easy choice, at least for now. *I've missed you.*

*Me, too.*

I feel her brain against mine and close my eyes. "Missed" is such an understatement. It's like she took a part of me with her that I'm finally getting back.

Leave it to Marco to annihilate the moment. "Hey, uh, Mira? How is this brain-talk supposed to work? I've been shouting at

Addy for the last two minutes, and she hasn't responded."

"That's because I'm ignoring you," Addy says from the other side of the room. She has one hand on a vine and the other on a giant leaf.

"Serves him right," Lucy says, linking her arm with Mira's. "Sweetie, why don't we work on brain-talk later? Can you just tell us the plan? I'm tired and my feet are killing me."

"Maybe if you didn't wear those spiky heels they'd feel better," Marco says.

Lucy glares at him and snuggles closer to Mira. "Please?"

"I don't understand how to do it," Cole says, his face scrunched up in frustration. "Do we form words and send them through a link? Can you please give us step-by-step instructions?"

"I think Lucy's right," I say. "We need to rest. And I'm sure there will be time to practice brain-talk later."

*Now I'll show you to your room,* Mira says. *Join hands, and I'll bound you there.*

"How?" Cole asks. "Free bounding requires personal knowledge of the destination or use of a BPS."

"Mira has personal knowledge," I say.

"Yes, but we don't," Cole says through gritted teeth. If there's one thing that stresses Cole out, it's not understanding how things work. So far, this trip is proving to be pretty challenging for our *Evolution of Combat* expert.

I try to make my voice sound quiet and soothing. "Cole,

their technology is more advanced. Mira can link with us and direct the bound."

Cole shakes his head in tiny, jerky movements.

"Umm . . . I'm not a fan of that idea," Lucy says. "Can't we just walk?"

*That's not how it . . . works . . . here,* Mira explains. *There aren't hallways or elevators. We just bound where we need to go.*

Wow. The only way to get around is by bounding? That's both amazing and terrifying at the same time.

"So, let's do it," Addy says. She grabs Mira's free hand and extends her other to Marco. Lucy shrugs and takes Marco's hand. Cole doesn't move. I reach over and clasp his palm. With a final shake of his head, he lets Lucy take his other hand. Before anyone can change their mind, Mira bounds us out.

We land smoothly, still hand in hand, in an extremely familiar room, one that I was in earlier this week, in fact. How did we end up in our pod room? Did Mira bound us off the planet? Are we actually at the space station? I turn in a circle, taking everything in, trying to figure out what just happened. "Is this really our pod room?"

*No, it's—*

"Oh no, uh-uh," Lucy says, shaking her head. "I am *not* staying in another VR prison cell."

"VR!" Cole says, intrigue now trumping frustration. "Of course!"

"I agree with the Fresh Face of Earth Force," Marco says. "No thanks. Don't you have a hotel or a bed-and-breakfast or something?" He heads for the door, which, if what Mira told us about bounding is true, is probably a door to nowhere.

There's a ripple of anguish through our mental circle. Mira is upset. Her emotions are strong enough that even my pod mates immediately sense it. Marco backs away from the door. Lucy puts her arm around Mira.

Addy, who's been walking around the room, waving her fingers at the lava lamps and studying the starry ceiling, stops and turns to Mira. *You made this space special for us, didn't you?*

*For you. And for me.* Mira sends pictures—memories—through our mental link of her time on the Youli planet. Most of the pictures make little sense, but the emotions behind them have a common theme: loneliness. Then she shows us mental pictures of our pod room, or, rather, this replica of our pod room. She's still lonely, but there's an element of familiarity that wasn't present in the other memories. This room brings her comfort. Her memories flash by quickly, like a roll of vintage film on fast-forward. For a second, I think I catch a glimpse of a second person in this room, but then it's gone.

This room is her safe place. It's where she comes to remember home.

Lucy hugs her tight. "Of course we'll stay here, sweetie."

Mira stares at the green grassy carpet, but the twist of a smile raises her lips.

"I'm starving," Marco says. "Any chance we can get some food?"

Mira pulls free of Lucy and shows us to a side room with a small eating area. It has orange tables just like the ones in the space station. She tells us she'll arrange for food to be delivered.

My stomach growls. I'm hungry, too, but I have a bad feeling about what's to come. "So the food's VR?"

Mira glances up at me with an apologetic look on her face. *It's either that or chlorophyll.*

"As long as it's not snake venom, we'll deal," Addy says, referencing our less-than-ideal stay on Alkalinia.

"You mean those plants?" Cole asks. "They're the Youli's food?"

*They're the Youli's everything.*

Mira raises her hands to bound, cutting off Cole's thousand follow-up questions about the plants.

*Wait!* I shout, shutting the mental curtain like she taught me. *Can I come with you?* I extend my hand, hoping she'll take me on the bound.

She lightly brushes her fingers against my hand. *I'll see you soon. I promise.*

In a flash, she's gone.

**I'M SPRAWLED OUT ON A PURPLE BEANBAG**
while my pod mates are busy checking out our room, not that
there's much to check out. It's pretty much identical to our
pod room. There's the separate eating room, and then there's
a bunk room with five beds. So Mira isn't staying with us.
That bummed me out and obliterated my curiosity about the
rest of the fake pod room.

"Hey, J." Addy waves a hand in front of my face.

"What's up, Ads?"

She plops down on the beanbag next to me. "You know
those pictures Mira showed us? Those are memories, right?"

I feel guilty about my pity party, remembering how lonely

Mira's memories were. "Yes, but they weren't just pictures. They were full sensory memories, including feelings."

"I got that," she says. "What I didn't get is why you were in one of them."

I try to replay Mira's memories in my mind. For a moment, I thought I'd spotted a second person in one of them, but we only saw it for a flash. It's like Mira flipped by that one extra fast.

"I think I saw someone, too," I tell her. "I don't think it was a Youli, but it went by so quickly I couldn't tell who it was. It wasn't me, though. I've never been here before."

"Yeah, but it *felt* like you."

"Umm . . . really? What do I feel like?"

Addy laughs. "I can't explain. It just had an unmistakable Jasper feel to it."

"*O-kay,*" I say, drawing the word out. I have no idea what my sister's talking about. "Maybe Mira confused one of her memories from our actual pod room with this virtual one."

Addy shrugs. "Maybe."

Marco throws himself on the ground next to Addy. "Maybe what?"

"Nothing," I say.

"Just Jasper having a starring role in Mira's memories."

"Oh! Do tell!" Lucy says from behind. I had no clue she'd been listening. "Jasper's going to need a major pep talk when it comes to Mira!"

I sit up. "Absolutely not." I've got to find a way out of this conversation, and I might as well jump on the fact that we're all getting along, at least for now. "Hey, Cole! Come here. Join us."

Unlike me, Cole has spent every second inspecting the virtual pod room. He exits the bunk room and crosses to our corner. When I wave at the turquoise beanbag, he sits, rod straight, exactly how he always used to sit in our actual pod room.

"What did you find out about our fake pod room?" Lucy asks him.

He shoots a glance at Marco and Addy. "Nothing of significance."

"Really, Wiki?" Marco asks. "Are we going back to party lines? Keeping secrets? Just when I thought we were starting to feel like a pod again."

"First, Marco," Cole says, "there's nothing to tell. For all intents and purposes, this room is practically identical to our other pod room, minus the obvious additions of the kitchen and bunk room. Variations are immaterial and likely due to imperfections in Mira's photographic recollection of the room. Second, of course we're back to party lines. I'm an Earth Force officer, and you are . . . not."

"We can't be that rigid, Cole," I say. "In fact, the future of Earth might depend on the five of us getting along and moving things forward."

Addy sits up on her beanbag. "Jasper's right. This isn't just the Earth Force hierarchy or the Resistance leadership structure anymore. We're planetary ambassadors. All of us. We have a duty to our planet to work together for the greater good."

Cole wrings his hands together. He doesn't like this. He likes order and rules, not blurred gray lines. Still, the fact that he's sitting here and listening at all is progress.

"There *is* something different about this virtual pod room," he says.

We all stare at him, waiting for him to deliver what's sure to be something important.

A hint of a smile pulls at his lips. "Mira has equipped it with *Evolution of Combat.*"

After we've had a chance to rest, play several intense rounds of *Evolution,* and eat (tater tots and tofu dogs, just like the Earth Force mess hall—come on, Mira, tofu dogs? Really? If we have to eat virtual food, can't you at least give us something good?), there's a glimmer in the middle of the pod room. The next second, Mira appears.

She's dressed in the same white gown she wore earlier, but her hair is different. Her long blond braid is gone. Instead, her hair falls in waves down her back and tiny, twinkling lights are woven in the strands.

"You look like an angel," Addy tells her.

I think so, too, but I wouldn't have said it out loud. Of course, what's the difference since she can read my mind?

Mira smiles. *Come with me*, she says to all of us. After her words, she fills our minds with music like nothing I've ever heard.

"What is that sound?" Cole asks.

Mira smiles even wider and offers Cole her hand.

We gather around and link up. Mira closes her eyes for a moment, then bounds us out. When my feet feel solid ground, I open my eyes. We're standing in a small, white, windowless room. The floor, walls, and ceiling all look to be made from the reflective marble-like substance of the grand hall where we arrived.

The air is filled with music. It's not the same song Mira shared earlier, but it's similar.

Mira leads us from the white room to the entrance of an enormous pavilion. It might be the same grand room where we arrived, or it could be another one like it. The floor is the same white marble. The walls are windows, and the interior is filled with columns stretching skyward and wrapped with vines.

What's definitely different from our arrival is that there are Youli everywhere. They're sitting cross-legged in small groups, sprawled on cushions in pairs, leaning alone against columns.

"There's so many." Lucy's words are a fear-laced whisper, but the sound is unwanted. Its tone interrupts the glorious music that seems to emanate from every particle in the place.

*Brain-talk*, Addy says.

It's not just the floor that's crowded. What I thought were dust motes earlier are actually tiny crystals, and there are millions of them. They hang suspended in the air. Some of them seem to dance. As we walk into the room, they part for us.

*It's like a disco,* Marco says.

Addy shoots him a nasty look. *Try fairyland.*

*Shhh!* I shush them. Even their brain-talk is way too loud.

Fragrance drifts in the subtle air current. It's not the overwhelming smell of roses like in Lucy's office, or even the spicy scent of Nev and Dev's salon. It smells of lavender and hot tea, like how peace itself would smell if it had a scent. I inhale deeply.

As we weave our way through the room, we have to dodge and duck vines. Their offshoots have broken free from the columns and sway in time to the music. The music grows even louder, and it seems to resonate from everywhere. I'm with Addy. This place is magical.

*What is this?* I ask Mira, opening my mind to all my pod mates.

Mira flicks her eyes at me with a smile. *Union Song. Come. Sit.*

She leads us through the crowded pavilion. The Youli part to let us through. There's a subtle chattering at the edges of my mind as we pass. Greetings. One for me and my pod mates, another, more formal greeting for Mira. It must be some kind of ritual. As Mira passes, the Youli incline their heads, then turn away.

Mira finds a free spot on the crowded floor. It's just big enough for the six of us. Thick, colorful pillows form a small nesting area. Mira sits, and we sink to the ground next to her. The pillows mold around me. Their satin is soft against my skin.

When we're all seated, Mira sends us a memory. We're on the Paleo Planet. She raises her gloved hands and conjures a complex melody to lull the wildeboars and quell the stampede. That day we instinctively knew how to join her song.

There's no mistaking that the music we're immersed in now is emanating from the Youli. Mira closes her eyes and gently touches our mental circle. When she senses we're all tuned in, she adds her voice to the communal song. At first, her voice can be heard distinctly. It's not a singing voice. It's more like the brassy tones of a piano mixed with the tinkling of high notes on a vibraphone merged with what I imagine Mira's actual voice would sound like. Her song begins to blend with the larger song all around us.

Once her harmony is established, she opens her eyes. *Join*, she says to all of us.

Cole shoots me a glance and shakes his head.

"Oh, come on," Addy whispers. "Give it a try!"

Marco eyes her sideways. "Yeah?"

She lifts a finger to her lips, reminding him to whisper so

he doesn't disturb the Youli. "Since when do you shy away from trying something new and potentially embarrassing?"

Marco nods. "Good point."

My sister closes her eyes in concentration. I hear the first sounds she adds to the song. They're just single notes, far from complex, but they're beautiful, like the heart-piercing tones of her violin.

I concentrate on the music, feeling the melody and its many harmonies wind through my mind and my body. Soon, I'm swaying and tapping my fingers against the ground. My own notes rise up from somewhere deep inside. They mingle and entwine with the sounds all around me.

When I'm confident I can sustain my music, I open my eyes. Addy smiles at me and nods. Her face tells me everything I need to know. She's loving this. She's holding Marco's hand. His eyes are closed, but his lips are moving, almost like he's singing. Lucy is sitting cross-legged and rocking back and forth. Cole . . . well . . . he's trying. In fact, even as I watch him, he seems to relax and settle into the music.

I sense Mira next to me and pull our mental curtain. *This is amazing.*

She places her hand on top of mine and leans her head against my shoulder.

Time stops meaning anything as we fully give ourselves to Union Song. Crystals dance before our eyes. Vines snake across the ground and twist in the air. The music burrows beneath our skin and fills our very bodies. When the melody lifts in triumph, we all swell with pride. When the song turns melancholy, we slide into sadness. The longer I stay connected to the song, the more my awareness widens. Without even using my gloves, I can sense the greater world around me. My awareness stretches far beyond our small network. I'm acutely aware of all the Youli in the room. Then I'm aware of the Youli beyond this room, knowing with complete certainty that we're joined in song by every Youli in every crystalline tower on this vast planet.

It's not as if I sense each Youli individually, or even that I sense them collectively.

What I sense is our interconnectedness, our union.

I lose myself in the song. Five minutes may have passed, or it may have been five hours. If someone told me I'd been sitting here lending voice to this song for five days, I'd probably believe them. Still, the music could go on for five more days and I wouldn't want it to end.

Except I'd probably be hungry. And my legs might fall asleep. But those are logistical problems.

The point is, I love everything about Union Song. And what I love most is sharing it with Mira. When I focus, I can find her voice among the millions of strands of music. I weave my notes with hers. Together, we blend in harmony.

More time passes, and Mira lifts her head. She takes a deep breath and pushes up on her knees, clearly preparing to stand.

I grab her hand. *Not yet, please.*

She gently frees her palm. *We need to go.*

My pod mates look up, and I realize I've been talking into our wider communication circle. Heat rises to my cheeks. I shouldn't have tried to make Mira stay, or thought that our harmony was anything more than two voices among many.

Our visit to the Youli home world is temporary. Odds are, whatever passes between Mira and me while we're here is also temporary. It's going to end, just like this song. Even if I convince her to return to Earth, she probably will never see me as more than a friend.

I pull myself away from the melody. I gesture at my pod mates to stand and follow Mira, who's already weaving through the crowd.

"That was awesome!" Marco says, hopping to his feet.

"Quiet!" Lucy whispers. "You'll disturb the song."

Marco gives a thumbs-up followed by a zipping motion across his lips.

We quietly trail after Mira across the massive pavilion filled with Youli.

As we go, the Youli watch us. I'm again aware of the mental chatter as we pass. The Youli nod at Mira and turn away. Some of them eye us inquisitively (I mean, we *are* aliens. I'd stare, too, if I saw a Youli on Earth), but most of them seem to be looking at Mira.

We finally make it to the other side of the wide room. We reach an archway sealed with golden doors. A Youli stands to either side. They appear to be guards, although they don't carry weapons.

Mira stands before them. She bends her chin to her chest. Both Youli bow. When they stand, they wave their hands before the doors. The golden panels swing wide.

After a final glance back at us, Mira steps into the room. We follow.

The room we enter is a perfect circle. My first thought is that it reminds me of the Forgotten Shrine on Alkalinia. There's something special, almost reverent, about the room. Detailed scenes woven into rich tapestries cover the walls. Modern sculptures and mobiles adorn the space, and the room is filled with dancing crystals. The smell of lavender is present here, too, but it's stronger and laced with something rich and warm like cinnamon. Union Song has not diminished within the walls of this room. If anything, it swells even stronger.

Of course, this room is really nothing like the Forgotten Shrine, because where the shrine's ceiling was low and made for slithering snakes like Serena, this ceiling is high like the pavilion. The edge of the circle is covered in cushions of gold, silver, and bronze.

MONICA TESLER

Roughly a dozen Youli are seated on the cushions. Their hands are folded serenely on their laps, and their bodies sway gently in time to the music. There's no doubt these Youli are fully immersed in Union Song.

Once the six of us have entered the room, the Youli guards seal the golden doors. The walls of the room pulse with the intensity of the song, and I begin to see that the tapestries are here to absorb and contain some of the sound. As I'd guessed when we entered, the intensity of song in this room alone is more immense than the music filling the pavilion.

The seated Youli don't break from the song, but I can sense them bringing us into their awareness. I reach out with my mind for the edges of their consciousnesses, just as I do with Mira. But when my awareness rubs up against theirs, I pull back. There's something different in the quality of the collective awareness in this room. It hums with a wisdom and depth far beyond anything I've known.

Mira gestures for us to sit on some of the open cushions scattered around the room. I take a seat between two Youli. Without the security of my friends beside me, I'm very aware of the aliens' presence. Still, the song is seductive. I let down my guard and close my eyes. Taking a deep breath, I reach out for the melody and add my voice to the song.

I'm not sure how long we sing. My mind goes someplace else, or maybe no place at all. It simply empties of everything other than our song and the collective presence of the other voices. I'm vaguely aware of being hungry and tired, but those sensations are at the periphery of my consciousness, and certainly not strong enough to distract me from the music. More time passes still, and even though my mind is nearing exhaustion, I don't want the song to end, even if it means singing myself to sleep right here on this cushion.

Something in the song shifts. The music swells and narrows until there's a final tone blended in harmony across many octaves. The note builds and resonates until the crystals in the air vibrate with light. The entire crystalline tower vibrates. The vessels carrying my blood vibrate.

And then there is silence.

After all that music, the silence is immense. It's so heavy I want to shout or cry out or do something, anything, to fill the quiet. I catch Marco's eyes across the room. He's visibly shaking. Knowing Marco, it's taking every ounce of self-control he has to stay quiet. I don't know what's supposed to happen next, but I'm pretty sure it's not Marco or me blabbing about how great the tunes are.

I take a deep breath and blow it out slowly as I start to adjust to the silence. Around the room, the Youli are taking their time coming back to consciousness. Gradually, they settle into their physical bodies.

And when they do, almost every Youli's eyes focus on me.

**THEY'RE ALL STARING AT ME. ALL THE**
Youli in the room.

Wait a second. . . . Am I imagining things? Maybe it just
feels like they're looking at me because their eyes are so big.
Maybe all of my pod mates feel the same way, like the Youli
are looking at them.

I sneak a glance at Addy. She's staring at me, too. When she
meets my gaze, her eyebrows raise. She wants to know what's
going on as much as me.

I focus on Mira across the room and close our mental privacy curtain. *Mira, why is everyone staring at me?*

She hears me. I know she does because I feel her mind shift

as she starts to answer, but then she abruptly stops and throws open the curtain.

The next thing I know, an unfamiliar voice rings through my mind. The tone is rich, uplifting, and reminiscent of Union Song.

*Young ones, we are most delighted to host you on our home world. The Travelers welcome you.*

The Youli's chatter, which has come to feel like static at the edges of my mind, expands to fill almost all the space. In words of greeting, I recognize the voices of the Youli we met in the rift, Wind Chimes and friends. But it's not only words that crowd my brain. It's more like sensations. Honestly, it feels like fireworks are going off in my head.

That's quite a welcome, a sensory overload–inducing welcome.

Cole is clutching his head with his hands. Lucy's biting her lip. Even Addy and Marco look like they're about to explode. I sympathize. After all, I'm at least used to brain-talk. They're not.

Given my pod mates' current status and general inexperience with brain-talk, not to mention that I'm supposed to be the neutral spokesperson, I figure it's up to me to reply. I take a deep breath and expand my mental reach as far as I can. *Thank you. We are happy to be here on behalf of Earth. We look forward to learning more about your people before the Intragalactic Summit.*

One of the Youli crosses the room to stand before me. This Youli is small but radiates wisdom and serenity. I know at once that she's the speaker. *Welcome, Jasper Adams. We are glad to see you again. We hope you come with a willingness to learn, and that you will in turn impart lessons to your own people.*

The words have the ring of finality, like we're being dismissed. *It's time to leave,* Mira tells us, nodding at the golden doors.

I stand and give an awkward wave. *Thank you.* My pod mates try their best to imitate me. Only Addy manages a fully formed *thank you*, but the sentiment is still there.

When we're at the door, Mira jerks to a stop. She turns around. The small Youli who spoke with us is looking at Mira. It's clear they're communicating, though it isn't shared with me. Mira's face falls. She gives a small nod, then turns to the doors.

We follow Mira from the room. The pavilion where we spent the first half of Union Song is now empty, and the light is fading. The space is cavernous and cold without the warmth of the music and sunlight.

"Was that a Youli leadership group?" Cole asks.

*In a way,* she replies, leading us across the pavilion to the small mirrored alcove where we arrived.

"What are Travelers?" Lucy asks.

"How often do you sing?" Addy asks.

"Can we do it again?" Marco asks.

Mira doesn't answer their questions. *Later,* she says. She sounds sad, but she's probably just tired. I'm exhausted. *Time to go.*

My pod mates' questions are good ones. Mira must be planning to fill us in back in our pod room. I'm saving my questions to ask her privately. Why were all the Youli staring at me? And why did the small Youli say they were glad to see me *again*? More than any answer she can give me, though, what I really want is her time. There is nothing in the world I want more than time with Mira.

We link hands so we can bound back to the pod room. Even though we know the location, we still need Mira's help to navigate the security safeguards the Youli have in place.

Once we arrive, I open my eyes. It's just the five of us. Mira didn't come.

The next morning, I wake to the smell of waffles. Mira's VR game is definitely improving. It was probably a good thing that she didn't hang out last night. We were all so tired from Union Song that we were in bed fifteen minutes after bounding back.

Now, though, I'm ready to eat, explore the Youli planet, and spend time with Mira.

Much to my very pleasant surprise, she's already in the pod

room when I head out from my bunk. Better yet, she's battling Cole in *Evolution*. I had no clue Mira knew how to play, but she seems to be giving the game master a real battle.

*Good morning.* Her words reach me before she sees me. Our brain connection is so strong here, she senses me. I've missed that. I watch them play. I make fun of Cole when Mira tricks his troops into an ambush during the American War for Independence. Just when I think she may actually take him out, he overpowers her for a grand victory.

"Maybe the next gen of *Evolution* will be Earth versus Youli," I say.

"We're here to resolve that conflict, remember?" Cole says. "Although I admit it would be cool, especially if we could use our gloves to play."

Marco vaults the couch and plops down beside me. "Gloves? Playtime? I'm in! Seriously, Mira, are the Youli going to teach us glove tricks today? That's the main reason I agreed to come."

"No, it's not," Cole says. "You represent Earth on a diplomatic mission."

"Fine, Wiki, you're factually correct, as usual. But glove fun is on the agenda today, right?"

Mira confirms brain-to-brain.

Marco covers his head with his hands. "I'm never going to get used to that."

"First on the agenda is food." I hop up from the couch and head into the mini mess hall. Lucy is sitting at the table, painting her nails.

"I didn't know you were up," I tell her as I pile my plate with virtual waffles.

"Oh, I've been up for ages," she says. "I need to make sure I look my best. We're ambassadors for our planet, you know."

"There aren't any cameras here, Lucy," I say. "Don't work too hard on your signature look."

She shoots me an evil glare, then goes back to applying the bright pink paint to her fingers.

After breakfast, Mira gathers us together in the pod room to prepare for a bound. She won't give us any details about where we're headed other than to say *you'll see* with enough sparkle that I know she's excited and thinks we're going to like it.

Once we link, she bounds us out, and we land on some sort of open-air platform in the middle of the clouds. It's kind of like the launch deck at the Americana East aeroport, but it's even bigger—I'd say the size of four futbol fields at least—and it's completely immersed in the clouds. Except the clouds curiously aren't in the airspace directly above the platform. The result is that we have this totally private, hidden training deck.

"Is this a contained atmosphere?" Cole asks.

*Something like that,* Mira says. *Come.* She holds her gloved hands out in front of her and leaps into the air.

My jaw drops. Mira is flying without a blast pack.

*How?* I shout through our brain connection.

*Use your packs for now,* she says. *I'll teach you.*

I loosen the sensor straps from the sides of my pack and take off. Marco and Addy are already airborne. It feels amazing. I haven't had a chance to fly like this in way too long. I zoom across the platform, flying low to the ground, then looping up and nearly touching the cloud layer.

Mira hovers at the other end. I squeeze the sensors and accelerate. When I reach her, she takes off, flying hard for the other end. We chase each other through a few more laps. When she finally lets me catch up, I'm out of breath. *How are you doing that? Flying without a pack?*

She smiles. *I'm manipulating matter, just like in bounding or controlling objects. Now I'm using my gloves to control the air particles all around me. They're keeping me aloft and propelling me forward.*

*Okay,* I say, making sure our privacy curtain is closed, *and how are you doing* that?

*What?*

*All that brain-talk. Before, you communicated with me, but more with pictures. Your words were limited. Now you won't shut up!*

Mira's laughter sparkles in my brain.

*Seriously, Mira, what changed?*

Her face hardens, and she doesn't answer at first. Finally, she says, *I've spent a lot of time with the Youli.*

*And?* I ask.

*The way I communicate with them has grown more complex. I guess it's changed the way* you *experience my communication.*

*What do you mean?*

She scrunches her face in thought. *You say I'm using more words, but that's not how it works in my mind. I think what I want you to know, and then you know.*

That's a lot to get my head around. *I don't get it.*

She smiles and touches my arm. *You don't need to. And don't worry, I can still think in pictures.* She sends me an image of me chasing her across the deck, both of us flying without a pack. *Let's go!*

Now *that's* something I get, and I'm totally on board. I follow her to the center of the deck along with the others. Mira tells them what she explained to me about controlling the air.

*It sounds really hard,* Lucy says.

Mira injects positivity into our communication circle. *I'll show you. I don't think you need to focus on flying without your packs right away. That can be a long-term goal. For now, I think you can concentrate on staying aloft and using a single glove. That leaves your other hand free to use as you choose.*

Marco nods. "So if we're fighting or something, we can

drop the straps of our packs, use one hand to stay in the air, and use another to attack or defend. Is that what you mean?"

Something flickers behind Mira's eyes. *Let's say we're skill building.* She smiles at Marco. *Want to try first?*

We spend the next hour practicing with our gloves. I catch on fairly quickly, which is a relief. I figured I'd be decent since I'm overall pretty good with the gloves, but I'll never be able to shake the humiliation I went through with the blast pack during our first tour of duty while we were still using the conventional straps. Regis never let me live it down.

Regis. Thinking of him makes me lose focus, and I plummet toward the platform, catching myself with my gloves a split second before crashing. Maybe if we'd known how to fly and fight at the same time a few weeks ago, we could have pushed back Earth Force on Gulaga. Maybe Regis would still be alive.

I shake off the memories and launch. Once I'm nearly at the clouds, I drop my straps. With my left hand, I stabilize my weight in the air around me. With my right, I focus all my attention on Cole. Sure enough, I'm able to freeze him midair.

*Hi, Cole,* I say through the communication circle.

"Let me go!" he shouts.

*Not until you say please, brain-to-brain.*

He struggles against my grasp, but I've got him good. My left hand keeps me aloft at the same time. "Jasper! Let me go!"

*Say please.*

Grumbles erupt in my mental link. Then Cole's voice: *Jasper! Now!*

*Close enough*, I say, letting go of Cole. He falls to the ground.

A second later, he's on his feet, then in the air and gunning for me. He chases me across the platform. He starts out mad, but as we dip and duck and spin and soar, I can sense the anger melting away. Flying is fun, and it's hard to stay mad when you're having a good time.

Mira eventually calls us back to the center. I'm sweaty and out of breath by the time I touch down. From the look of the others, practice has gone well for everyone. Even Lucy looks like she had a good time.

*What's next, sweetie?* she asks Mira.

*Remember the Tundra Trials, when we raced against the other pods for one of the final tokens?*

How could I forget? Regis punched me in the face.

Marco answers. *You mean the time you used your magic powers to boost Jasper so our pod snagged the token?*

Mira flashes her palms at the ground and lifts into the air so that she's hovering right above us. *It wasn't magic. I'm going to teach you how to do it.*

BY LUNCHTIME, WE'VE GOT A SOLID handle on boosting. According to Mira, it's the first step in learning how to pool our power. I'm able to send Marco somersaulting through the air the full width of the training deck. Cole has trouble sustaining a boost, but he can generate a whip-sharp surge. When he hits me with it, I bullet so high, I cross into the clouds. Luckily, I'm wearing my gloves, because Cole's control fades, and I have to slow myself down to avoid landing like a pancake on the training deck.

Mira takes us back to our room to eat. I beg her to stay, but she says she has to take care of some things before she sees us this afternoon. I don't press her too hard because I'm starving and smell pizza.

The five of us sit around the orange table filling up on slices and orange soda and talking about the training session.

"This morning was awesome!" I say. "We learned more in a few hours than Earth Force could have taught us in a year."

Surprisingly, Cole agrees. "Before now, we had no idea of the scope of the glove technology."

Addy's face is scrunched in confusion. "What I can't figure out, though, is why the Youli didn't train us?"

"Why does that matter?" Cole asks.

"I thought the whole point was that the Youli would help us train with the gloves as a gesture of welcome and good faith before the Intragalactic Summit," Addy says. "So far, we've mostly interacted with Mira."

"There are Youli everywhere!" Marco says. "Are you forgetting Union Song?"

"No," Addy says. "It's just—"

I cut her off. "What's your issue with Mira? The Youli obviously sent her because she can communicate with us the best. And she knows how to use the gloves!"

"I don't have an issue with Mira!" Her tone is sharp. She's not happy I interrupted her. "She's great, but she's not a Youli!"

Lucy turns to Addy with a patronizing smile. "Jasper's

right. Mira is teaching us on behalf of the Youli. It makes things far less . . . alien. And don't you worry, I'm sure we'll see plenty of Youli before the Intragalactic Summit."

"I'm not . . . forget it. I'm going to the bunk room to read." She shoves back her chair and exits the mini mess hall.

"Remember," Lucy says once Addy has left the room. "She's not part of our pod."

I'm about to defend my sister, but Lucy's right, Addy wasn't an original member of our pod. Plus, I don't like her saying negative things about Mira, although I'm not sure she actually did. The truth is, I don't want to think too hard about the fact that my gut says maybe Addy is onto something.

I grab another slice of virtual pizza and decide not to worry about what's real, at least not right now.

Not long after lunch, Mira arrives and bounds us to one of the large Youli halls, where Wind Chimes and his two Youli friends are waiting to give us a highlight tour of their home world. A smug *I told you so* feeling fills my chest, and I shoot Addy a triumphant smile. See? There's no reason to be so skeptical.

Once we're assembled, something happens, I assume we bound, but it's more than that. We're no longer in the hall. We're outside, floating in the air inside one of the bubbles like the one that encapsulated our tiny capsule when we first arrived.

"Whoa!" Marco says.

"That was unexpected," Cole says.

"How about a heads-up next time?" Lucy asks.

My mind sparkles with laughter. It's more than just Mira's. In fact, it's so loud that all of us Earth kids (except for Mira) cover our ears (as if that would help). That only brings on more sparkles from the Youli.

*Turn down the volume,* I tell Mira.

She smiles. *As long as all of you promise to brain-talk. At least try.*

Our bubble starts to glide. As we slip past the first crystal tower, a swoop of purple flashes by our bubble. Then another, this one orange. And another, teal blue.

*Are those . . . birds?* Addy asks.

A swoop of yellow flies by. It kind of looks like a bird, but it doesn't have any feathers. Instead, it has colorful, flat arms that extend to the sides like a hang glider, supporting a small, bulbous body in the center.

*Similar,* Mira says. She sends us images: birds, bats, phosphorescent sea creatures from the ocean depths.

Our bubble picks up speed, and we weave between crystal towers, tightly wound with semitranslucent green vines. They go on as far as the eye can see, like we're floating amid a grand crystal forest in the sky. Everything pulses in time to the beating hearts in the Youli's chests, even the small bulb bodies of the birdlike fliers.

*It's like everything is alive!* Addy says.

The Youli radiate positive energy. *Yes, child!* Wind Chimes says. *You're beginning to understand. Everything is connected. Everything learns. Everything lives.*

I'm not sure how long we float, but soon I'm totally relaxed. Even though I'm standing, my body feels supported by the bubble. There's a sense of something that's hard to put into words. I start to feel . . . bigger . . . than I am. Broader. More expansive, like maybe I'm part of everyone in this bubble, everything on this planet, everything in the galaxy.

Everything.

It's the same feeling I had the first time I used the gloves.

*What's that?* Marco asks, breaking my trance.

Lucy grips my forearm. Addy gasps. I scan around me, searching for what they've spotted.

Up ahead, there's a trio of crystal towers that look different from the rest. The vines that circle their shafts are brown and leafless. The crystals pulse, but so faint it's hard to tell. Where all around us there is life, these towers show decay.

The Youli fill with sadness and a touch of something harsher. It's not anger exactly, but it's close. Maybe bitterness? Resentment?

Mira bites her lip like she's about to cry. Where the bitterness tugs at the Youli, Mira wrestles with shame and remorse.

*What happened here?* I ask.

She steels herself and stands up straight. *The degradation patch.*

What? My mind flashes back to the Youli ship at the last Intragalactic Summit. Earth Force staged a stealth attack. While the Force distracted the Youli at the perimeter of the space axel, our pod bounded to the Youli ship and planted a degradation patch in their tech systems room. The Youli used our brain patches to track Mira and me back to Gulaga. They counterattacked and destroyed the Gulagan space elevator.

"*Our* degradation patch?" Marco says.

"It worked!" Cole says. "Amazing!"

The Youli bristle at Cole's words. They obviously understand us, even if we don't talk brain-to-brain.

Lucy elbows Cole hard in the ribs.

"Earth Force did this?" Addy asks.

I look at my sister. "*We* did this."

When we bound back to our room, I'm relieved to see that Mira is still with us. At first, no one has much to say. I think we're all still processing what we've seen, the living interconnectedness of the Youli world alongside the rotting remains of the degradation patch damage.

Finally, Marco breaks the silence. "I don't really understand. I thought the degradation patch we planted affected the Youli systems. How did it kill all those vines and take out those crystal towers?"

Mira flutters her fingers at the ceiling, and the air above us is soon filled with thousands of tiny, twinkling stars. It's just like the time she did that in our real pod room during our first tour of duty, the first time we began to understand that the only people we could truly trust were one another.

*Earth and its peoples are like these stars,* she says. *Sometimes, we think of us together, like the night sky. But even so, each of us remains a single star, separate, distinct, alone among the cosmos. The Youli have evolved beyond separateness.* She waves her hand, and the stars swirl and blur until they are a single sun.

"So they're like a hive mind?" Lucy asks.

*No, they maintain their individuality, but not in a way I have words to explain. They are many. And they are one.*

"Yeah, that's like a wizard riddle, Magic Mira," Marco says. "And while your special effects are cool and all, you didn't answer my question. What happened to the towers with the dead vines?"

*The degradation patch was . . . primitive . . . by Youli standards. It targeted an isolated system. All of the Youli systems are integrated. They operate with the same oneness as the Youli themselves. Somehow, the patch acted like a needle picking at a single thread in a tapestry. Eventually, it pulled loose, and when it did, all the threads began to unravel. The result was so unexpected and so removed from the Youli's current stage of progress that they nearly failed to arrest it before it led to a full system collapse. Healing has begun, but it has a long way to go.*

"So," Addy starts. She shakes her head and tries again with brain-talk. *So the damage to the towers and the vines was a direct result of an Earth Force attack?*

Mira confirms.

The Youli in the rift told us that the degradation patch had caused grave damage and that their people were divided over what to do. *It's all starting to make sense,* I say. *No wonder there was a division within the Youli ranks. Some of them wanted to get revenge for our attack.*

"They did," Cole says. "Don't you remember the Battle of the Alkalinian Seat? They tried to annihilate us. Since then, the Youli have hit dozens of Earth Force outposts. Don't get distracted with this *we are one* messaging. This is war. This is what happens."

"We're trying to move past that," Lucy says. "Plus, we started this."

"No, we did not," Cole says. "The degradation patch is simply one stop on our long history of conflict stretching back to before we were born. Or did you forget the Incident at Bounding Base 51?"

"Fair point, Wiki," Marco says.

Mira stands. *I need to go. Enjoy your dinner and get some sleep. We have a full morning of training tomorrow.*

*Wait!* I say, scrambling to my feet. I wave her to the bunk room. When I'm sure we're alone, I take her hands. *Can't you stay a little longer?*

She shakes her head. *I've already stayed too long.*

*Says who? I want to spend time with you. There are so many things I want to talk about. And I have so many questions. You said you would help me understand when I came.*

She closes her eyes. *I know, but I can't. Not tonight.*

Anger builds in my chest. I know she senses it. I don't know how long we have together here, and I don't know what she'll do when we leave for the summit. The last thing I want to do is waste our time being mad.

Mira reaches up and strokes my cheek. *Tomorrow. I promise.*

If that's all she can give, it's enough.

She hugs me, builds her port, and bounds away.

I find my pod mates in the mess hall eating tacos. Mira definitely took a page out of the Alks' playbook with the menu since we complained about the day-one tofu dogs. The tacos smell delicious, and they even lift my spirits a bit, but not enough to drag me back from the world of grumpiness that Mira's departure pushed me into.

What's the deal? Why can't she stay? Why does everything have to be so mysterious?

"So?" Lucy asks. "How are things in the world of romance?"

"Shut up, Lucy," I say. "I'm not in the mood."

Addy snorts. "Well, you're clearly in some sort of mood."

I glare at my sister. What does she know about it? She and

Marco get to enjoy their cute little crush all they want while the girl I like has to live on an alien planet. "I assume you're satisfied now?" I ask her.

"About what?" Addy asks.

"Mira, obviously, and the whole invitation-to-the-Youli-world thing you were freaking out about this morning."

"First of all, I was not freaking out. And second of all, no, I'm not satisfied."

I raise my eyebrows and stare at her.

"Are *you*?" she asks. "I mean, what kind of tour was that? We didn't see any Youli children; we don't know anything about their business enterprises; we haven't seen where they eat or sleep. In fact, we haven't seen anything other than a quick bubble ride around the outside of their buildings and an up-close-and-personal look at the damage we caused. That doesn't exactly say *let's be friends*."

"I think it does," Cole says. "It's a clear act of diplomacy that unambiguously conveys they're willing to discuss peace despite our acts of aggression."

"I have to side with Wiki on this," Marco says. "Why would they show us all that stuff you talked about? Would you give away your secrets to the enemy?"

"Exactly," Cole says.

Cole and Marco agreeing on something? Wow. Maybe we're actually starting to function like a pod again. Still, I can't fully dismiss what Addy said. It's not that I think the Youli are lying to us. It's that there's something more, something we're missing.

Marco slaps the table. "Hey, so, we're all here, and we're leaving for the summit soon, and there's something I want to talk about." He looks at my sister. Addy nods.

He leans forward, waiting until he has our complete attention. "Bounders' rights."

Lucy laughs. "Can we all say *non sequitur*?"

"Non *what*?" Marco asks.

"*Non sequitur*," Cole says. "It means something that doesn't follow logically from a previous statement."

Marco's annoyed. "Well, I'll tell you what doesn't follow logically—"

Addy raises her palm to interrupt him. "What Marco's trying to say is that we think we should talk about Bounders' rights among ourselves before we head to the Intragalactic Summit, and this seems like the ideal time."

I already know where this is headed. Addy and Marco talked to me about Bounders' rights when I was last on Gulaga. I even gave Lucy a heads-up when we were in Eurasia West. Their points are important, and I hope that Cole and Lucy listen.

"So talk," Cole says.

Marco crosses his arms on the orange table. "The bottom line is this: if Earth Force reaches a peace deal with the Youli and the Resistance, they have no more need for Bounders. While we're looking out for Earth's interests, someone has to look out for *our* interests."

"What do you mean, they have no more need for us?" Lucy asks.

"We were bred to be soldiers," Addy answers. "No war, no need for soldiers."

Cole tips his head to the side. "Bounders have demonstrated their value independent of their military skill."

"*We* agree with you," Marco says, "but do you think the rest of Earth Force will? Do you think Admiral Eames will?"

Cole clasps his hands and stares at the table.

"Let's not sugarcoat it," Addy says. "They didn't want us. They made sure no one with our genes was ever born. Before the Bounder Baby Breeding program, we were extinct."

Cole lifts his gaze and takes a deep breath. "No."

"What do you mean, 'no'?" I ask.

"No, I don't think Admiral Eames will value the Bounders if we're not at war."

Wow. That's a *huge* admission, plainly and factually stated as only Cole can.

"Where does Waters stand on all of this?" I ask.

"Waters's days are numbered," Marco says.

I look from Marco to Addy then back to Marco. "What do you mean?"

"I mean he's on the outs," Marco says. "He runs the Resistance like he's this great mastermind, which sometimes he is, but his ends rarely justify the means."

"Meaning . . . ?" Cole nudges when Marco stops talking.

Marco glances at my sister. I'm sure they're both hesitant to say too much in front of Cole and Lucy, even now. If I had to guess, I'd say their faith in Waters finally cracked after the way he handled the battle on Gulaga. The only reason they didn't end up dead is that Denver and I managed to salvage Waters's flawed plans and convince Admiral Eames to agree to a cease-fire.

"Meaning it's time for new leadership," Addy says. "Waters has said so himself countless times. Not to mention, we all know that part of the terms of Earth's entry into the Intragalactic Council will be Gulagan independence. Last time I checked, Waters wasn't a Tunneler. The Gulagan people won't want him interfering in their affairs."

"Did he ever find out who was leaking information?" I ask. "Who tipped off Earth Force about the Resistance attack at the rally and the Alks about our arrival at Nos Redna?"

Marco shakes his head. "Nope. Let's just say that not everyone supports Waters, and those leaks prove it."

"In a few days, it shouldn't matter," Addy says. "Earth's entry into the Intragalactic Council and our domestic negotiations should change everything."

"Which brings us back to the beginning of this little chat,"

Lucy says. "Let's talk about us. When all those decisions get made, we need a voice."

"Right," I say. "We have a chance to shape the future here. What do we do?"

Marco and Addy outline their concerns about Bounders' rights in more detail as well as their plan for making sure our needs are met in the negotiations and beyond. In short, it comes down to two main points: First, the only ones capable of protecting Bounders' interests are Bounders. And second, we need to be part of planetary governance going forward. Without a voice at the table where decisions get made, Bounders have no chance of fair representation.

We talk late into the night. We're going to be tired at training tomorrow, but it feels great to finally be connecting as a pod. Everyone has their own perspective, and we may not always see eye to eye, but we're respectful, and our opinions are better mashed together than they usually are on their own, kind of like the swirling stars on the ceiling.

"There's something else before we head to the Intragalactic Summit," I tell them when our Bounders' rights discussion seems to be winding down. "Lucy?"

She squirms and picks at her pink fingernails. At first, I think she's going to pretend not to know what I'm talking about, but then she huffs and blurts it out. "I think Admiral Eames might be up to something."

Addy squints. "What kind of something?"

Marco looks from Lucy, to me, to Cole. He must be thinking what I first thought when Lucy told me about her suspicions: if anyone knows what the admiral is up to, it's Cole.

Cole straightens in his seat, giving the illusion of being a whole head taller than the rest of us. His nostrils flare as he eyes Lucy. "What exactly are you talking about?"

Lucy shrinks in her seat. "I'm not sure. I'm not in the know anymore. I just have a hunch that she's going to break the truce with the Resistance."

Cole shoots to his feet. "Absolutely not! I can't believe you'd suggest that! Lucy, you're an Earth Force officer! It's treasonous!"

She reaches out her hand. "Cole, I—"

"I've heard enough!" He stomps out of the mini mess hall all the way to the bunk room, slamming the door behind him.

So much for positive pod relations.

**THE NEXT MORNING, MIRA BOUNDS US TO**
a new place to train. Instead of one giant deck, she brings us
to a tiered training space. There are probably a dozen circular
decks layered among the clouds.

*Today we leave the packs on the deck*, she tells us.

Hmm . . . This should be interesting.

Marco swings his blast pack off his shoulders and flings it
to the ground. "Let's go!" Then he immediately face-plants
on the deck.

Addy bursts out laughing. She wipes her gloved hands on
her training uniform. "Serves you right, hotshot!"

"You asked for it!" he says.

Addy shoots into the air with her blast pack and guns for the tier above. Marco picks up his pack and chases after her.

"Can you go ahead and show us, sweetie?" Lucy asks Mira. "I'm not waiting around for that duo to come back."

Sparkly energy ripples through my brain. *Let's practice pair boosting for now.*

"Pairs?" Lucy asks, looking from Mira to me and Cole.

"I'll work with Jasper," Cole says.

Lucy shakes her head. "Oh no, you won't. Jasper will pair up with Mira. You're stuck with me." She grabs Cole's arm and drags him to the other side of the deck, shooting me a glare over her shoulder that clearly says *you owe me.*

She's right—I definitely do. Pairing up with Cole after their fight last night can't have been easy. They may end up in a full-on glove war.

I turn my back on Cole and Lucy. They can sort out their own issues. I may not have many more moments with Mira here on the Youli home world—and I'm not sure what comes next—so I'm going to enjoy them while I can.

Mira lifts her eyes to mine. I smile. *Where should we start?*

*Sense the connection?* She lifts her hand and reaches out with her mind. Our connection is so strong already, I feel her touch instantly.

I raise my own hand and press back. Usually, there's a distinct barrier where I end and Mira begins, but as we both push into our power, the barrier blurs, and we start to blend. It's a glimpse of what I felt when we were alone on the bounding deck a month ago.

Her cheeks color pink. *Access your power, and I'll amplify it.* She nods at my blast pack, discarded on the ground.

I grab hold of the pack with the power of my gloves and start to lift. Mira begins to infuse her own power into my neural stream. Suddenly, I'm back in the Ezone, lifting the practice chair with Mira feeding me her energy. How did she know how to do this all the way back then?

*I just know.* I feel her smile at my back. She's obviously eavesdropping on my memories, but I don't care. I open my mind and let her in. Her power surges through me, and my blast pack rockets through the clouds.

I let go of control.

Mira drops our connection. I feel her brain scrambling. I spin around, and her hands are lifted. Seconds later, my blast pack lowers to the deck. She shoots me an annoyed look. *You can't just drop it! I don't want to have to search the whole planet for your blast pack!*

I rub my forehead. *I thought it would just fall back down.*

*That's not how it works here.* She waves away her annoyance. *Switch! You boost me now.*

She grabs my blast pack and sends it into the air. This time, instead of tossing it on a linear path, she spins it through the air in the shape of an infinity symbol. I reach out with my mind, sense her source of power, and feed her my own. My blast pack accelerates at startling speed. Soon, I can hardly keep track of it with my eyes. It's just a whirling blur before us.

"Incoming!" Addy shouts. Marco and my sister gun from above.

Mira jerks, and the pack falls to the deck and skids across the surface. *Careful!* she lectures Addy and Marco. *That pack was spinning so fast, we'd be scraping your guts off the deck if you'd collided with it.*

"Nice visual, Magic Mira. We're back."

*Obviously*, I say, annoyed that my one-on-one time with Mira is over.

She draws closed our mental curtain. *Later, I promise.*

Yeah, I definitely don't mind her eavesdropping.

The next few hours, we focus on networked power boosting and flying without packs, although Mira is always quick to remind us that we're not really flying, we're manipulating matter to move and stay aloft. In other words: flying.

Soon, we're leaping from deck to deck and gliding back down, all with the power of our gloves. When we add networked power, the results are simply amazing. With the aid of my pod mates, I can bullet through every deck layer in a second while suspending all of our blast packs in the air. And I've only touched the surface of our joint power. Our combined strength is so immense, I'm pretty sure we could toss a bounding ship in the air, or drag a space station off its anchor, or rip through a force field.

Speaking of force fields, Mira teaches us this neat trick where we can invert our networked power to maintain a shield. Nothing outside the shield can reach our atoms or physically penetrate. It's like having our own personal force field and occludium shield rolled into one.

We want to keep practicing our new skills, but we're also starving. Virtual nachos never sounded so good.

*One more thing,* Mira says. *You can use your mental communication circle now, even when I'm not there. With his brain patch, Jasper is strong enough to hold the connection.*

"You mean we'll still be able to brain-talk once we leave the Youli planet?" Cole asks. When Mira nods, he adds, "That's incredible!"

"Why would we ever talk to one another like this once we leave?" Marco asks.

*You never know when you may need to talk privately.*

"You and your girlfriend can whisper sweet love notes, brain-to-brain," Lucy teases Marco.

Lucy's crack clearly digs at Addy, too, but my sister doesn't flinch. She looks at Mira with a tilt of her head. *When do you think we'll need to communicate in secret?*

I recognize the look on Addy's face. She thinks Mira's

withholding something again. *Drop it, Addy. It's time for lunch.*

Addy keeps eyeing Mira, waiting for a response, but Mira doesn't answer. Instead, she projects an image of a huge spread of delicious food complete with enticing aromas directly into our brains. Like Pavlov's dogs, we rush to her side to head back to the copycat pod room. In a flash, we bound.

I feel solid ground beneath my feet and open my eyes. I'm not in the pod room. The others are gone. It's just me and Mira.

We're in a small room. It has a pallet on one side layered with white cloth. There is a small table attached to the wall with a crystal on top. On the floor is a white rug woven from the same white cloth. There are billowing white sheets hung by a window that looks out over a central courtyard.

Mira pulls the curtains and sits down on the floor.

I sit beside her. *Is this your room?*

She nods. *I know you're hungry, but this was a chance for us to talk.*

She thinks I'd rather eat than spend time with her alone? *I'm not hungry.*

She gives me the side-eye.

*Okay, fine, I'm a little bit hungry.*

*I could get you some chlorophyll.*

I practically gag on the saliva that's been pooling in my mouth. *Uh, no. Don't you remember my food issues? If you ever want to torture me, just send me to Gulaga.*

*BERF.*

*Barf. Seriously, Mira, don't worry about food. This is where I want to be. With you.*

She smiles. A familiar melody fills my mind. "Heart and Soul." We played it on the piano together on Alkalinia. I sang it in her mind when the Youli attacked. It's how I kept her awake as we raced to take down the occludium shield.

So much has happened since then—the rift, the Lost Heroes Homecoming Tour, the Earth Force invasion of Gulaga—but not much has happened with *us*, Mira and me. Since we escaped the rift, thanks to the Youli, the only times we've been together were a month ago at the bounding base and the days we've spent here on the Youli planet. *How are you?*

She doesn't answer with words. Like before, a wave of emotion rushes out of her. Happiness. Despair. Hope. Regret. The emotions are so intense, they threaten to pull me under. I close my eyes and open my mind, allowing her to fill me with her feelings, without judgment, without interpretation.

It would be impossible for me to decipher what it all means, but when the flow slows to a trickle, and I open my eyes, Mira is staring back expectantly.

I don't know what to say. I don't know how to brain dump my feelings like that. Plus, all I really want to say is *I've missed you*. And all I want to know is why she left and whether she's coming back. But I'm scared of the answer, and I don't want everything to be all doom and gloom between us.

So I try to keep it light. *Union Song was awesome!*

She lifts her lips in a small smile. *Yes.*

She sends me a memory. We're in our pod room, our *real* pod room, with our pod mates. She fills the room with twinkling lights and music, and we dance together in the starlight, finding a moment of peace and fun even after learning the truth about why Earth Force needed the Bounders.

I smile back and generate my own memory to share. We're at the space station, in the music room down the hall from the sensory gym. Mira's playing the piano, and I'm playing my clarinet. Our first duet.

Mira slips inside my mind, right into my memory. She lassos the music in my mind, pulls it into the present moment, and sets it on a loop. The music—which a moment ago existed only in my mind—plays in her room all by itself. Before long, the song starts to evolve, more instruments and tones are added, the melody becomes more complex, and the harmonies grow more sophisticated.

*Amazing! How did you do that?*

Mira shrugs. She waves her hands and multicolored lights appear. They dance around the room in time to our song.

*How was Earth?* she asks.

Keeping it light seems to be working. I tell her funny

stories about the Lost Heroes Homecoming Tour. She loves hearing about Nev and Dev and their golden boy (me!). And her brain sparkles when I tell her that Florine Statton is now a hotel command system voice-over specialist.

Time slips by so easily. My stomach's not even grumbling anymore. I feel like I could sit with Mira, right here in this room, forever.

*You leave tomorrow,* she says.

I can tell she doesn't want this to end, either. *You're coming.*

*Yes, but it will be different.*

*How?*

Mira starts to answer, but then there's a flash, and suddenly Wind Chimes is standing beside us. I push back against the wall. There's not room in the small space for all three of us.

Mira jumps to her feet and slams closed a mental door that shuts me out.

Something is wrong. I don't know what they're saying to each other, but Mira is upset. So is Wind Chimes. And there's no doubt in my mind that it has something to do with me.

My mental door flies open. *You need to go back to your room,* Mira says. Her voice feels nervous and deeply upset.

*Okay, what's—*

There's another flash. Then a bound.

When I open my eyes, I'm standing in the pod room with Wind Chimes by my side.

*Where's Mira?* I demand of the Youli.

Before Wind Chimes can answer, Lucy starts talking. "Where have you *been*, Jasper? We've been worried sick! We thought something happened to you! And you . . . you . . . you Youli . . . This is our room! You can't just pop in here like that! You nearly scared us to death!"

Wind Chimes surges into our mental circle. *Come, young ones. I'm taking you to the surface.*

My questions about Mira are ignored as Wind Chimes gathers us together. My pod mates shoot me questioning looks, but all I can do is shake my head. I have no idea what's going on. A minute later, we bound.

We emerge inside a small bubble, like the one we used to tour the planet yesterday. Only, today, we appear to be on the surface of a planet. Although this can't possibly be the Youli planet.

It's a world without color. Everything is gray or grayer. Decrepit towers lay in crumbled ruins on the ground. The land is cracked and dry and devoid of life.

The only color near the surface is the green of the Youli who seem to be working. They're covered from head to toe in protective suits. Many of them hold equipment. They appear to be doing something to the soil.

"What is this place?" Marco asks.

*This is our planet,* Wind Chimes says.

Above us, storm clouds churn. They're purple and black, like bruises in the sky. Electric charges strike, ripping the sky like knives.

"I don't understand," Lucy says.

Wind Chimes sighs. It feels like steam along the edge of my mind. *You've been above. This is below.*

**"THIS PLACE IS . . . DEAD." ADDY'S FACE IS**
scrunched up in disgust. She repeats the words in our mental
circle. *This place is dead.*

Wind Chimes raises a hand and rests it against the side
of the bubble. I'm no expert on Youli facial expressions, but
Wind Chimes looks distraught. *You're not wrong.*

"I want to make sure I understand," Cole says. "This is the
same planet we've been on the last few days?"

*Yes.*

*So those clouds . . .* I point at the sky. *They're the same ones
we see when we're up there looking down?*

Wind Chimes's hand drops. *Yes.*

"Has it always been like this?" Lucy asks.

*No. Oh no.* In our minds, the Youli paints a picture of a beautiful city rising from a planet bathed in greens and blues and majestic purples, nothing like the bruised purple clouds above. Lush, verdant farmlands spread as far as the eye can see. Birds like we saw yesterday above the clouds swoop across the sky, and six-legged beasts of all shapes and sizes freely roam.

Youli are everywhere, sitting on benches, strolling along streets, reclined on the green ground.

This can't be the same place. I close my eyes and focus on a landmark in Wind Chimes's mental image, a mountain in the distance. When I open my eyes, I can spot the mountain in the desolate landscape. It's the only thing that looks remotely the same, but it's enough to confirm what Wind Chimes is saying. The ruins around us were once the gorgeous city in my mind.

*What happened?* I ask.

I'm glad it's Wind Chimes who tells us the story of the Youli. Wind Chimes's lyrical tone softens the horror in a way that makes it easier to hear all at once. We listen to the history of the Youli, their people, and their rise to power. Their intellect was unsurpassed, their technology was unrivaled, their dominance was unquestioned, and their greed was known across the galaxy.

*We, the Youli people, were on an unquenchable quest for*

more—more planets to exploit, more ore to mine, more, more, more. When we wanted something, we took it. Still, it wasn't enough. It was never enough.

The pictures Wind Chimes streams into our minds start to shift. The shiny buildings seem to tarnish as the lens turns down and we zoom in on Youli workers toiling on the surface.

*In the eyes of our ancestors,* Wind Chimes continues, *not all Youli were created equal. In order to sustain our epic growth, the Youli elite relied on the labor of the underclass. As our technology evolved from external to biologically based, we maintained a division: the technological elite and the workers.*

The images Wind Chimes sends us aren't just visual, they're steeped in feeling: fatigue, frustration, fury. We see the Youli descending into mines and nearly collapsing on their feet as they're forced to work countless hours building and maintaining to keep the upper class in luxury.

*When the Youli birth rates couldn't keep up with the demand for labor, we forced aliens from other planets to keep the pace.* The pictures in my mind speed up. More labor, more building, more want, more oppression. As the Youli's dominance stretches across the galaxy, they bend lesser developed planets to their will, forcing aliens to strip their own land of ore and taking their people far from home to spend their lives laboring for the Youli. In every image, there is despair. If I could close my eyes to stop from seeing, I would, but there's no way to shut off my brain.

Fortunately, Wind Chimes jars us back to the moment by abruptly cutting us off from the mental link. My eyes flash open. I glance at Addy. Her lips are pursed in a tight line, and her eyes are filled with tears.

We look at Wind Chimes, needing to know what happened next. How did those images morph into the decayed world beyond the bubble?

The Youli stares out at the barren landscape and seems to struggle to summon the will to go on.

*Young ones,* Wind Chimes finally says, *there is a general sense of fairness and justice that permeates the galaxy. When you stray too far from the acceptable, a course correction is inevitable, no matter how long it takes.*

Wind Chimes once again turns inward, withdrawing from our minds. Just when I fear the Youli won't continue, Wind Chimes lets out a deep sigh and picks up where the story left off.

*The workers grew weary and angry. The Youli elite did not expect the uprising on its own soil, and they did not think through their response. They counterattacked swiftly, but they hadn't imagined that other planets who had long been at their mercy would jump at the chance to fuel a revolution.*

Images of war flash in my mind. The workers rise in rebellion, walking off work sites, destroying machinery, seizing weapons, and demanding a voice. The conflict quickly escalates. Before the Youli elite understands the magnitude of what's happening, the planets they'd dominated for years join together and use the Youli's own spacecraft and artillery against them. My mind whirls as ships fire upon each other, raining sparks and debris in an astral fireworks display.

*Like a strong wind striking a house of cards, soon the whole galaxy was at war. Not every planet opposed us. Some, like the Alkalinians, played both sides. But before long, we began to strain under the weight of so much opposition.*

*There were voices of reason within the Youli elite,* Wind Chimes continues. *They urged the people to negotiate, to end their reliance on other planets for labor and materials, to use their superior intellect and technology to develop organic power sources that could replace the laboring workforce and the imported ore.*

*Our ancestors faced a choice that should have been straight-forward: charge ahead with a battle that would destroy our planet, or change our ways. But our people were stubborn, arrogant. In the eyes of the Youli elite, choosing change was choosing defeat.*

"So their choice left the planet like this?" Marco asks, gesturing at the world around us.

*Yes. And no.*

We wait expectantly for Wind Chimes to explain what "yes and no" means. Instead, the Youli jumps ahead in the story.

*At long last, we opened our eyes. From the ashes, we rebuilt, guided by utopic ideals. We set our intellect to work and built a city above the clouds fueled by organic matter. Our class*

*distinction was banished, and biotechnology was given to all. We
reached beyond our orbit to build just alliances with other planets, determined to be an ethical and model citizen of the galaxy.*

*The allied planets formed the Intragalactic Council.*

*We, the Youli, survived and came to thrive.*

*But while we created beauty and benevolence in the wake of
destruction, we had lost the surface of our beloved planet. It will
take a millennium before it's restored.*

"But *what happened*?" Lucy demands. "What did you
mean, 'yes and no'?"

It's a long time before Wind Chimes decides to answer.
Cole bounces on his toes. I can even sense Addy's impatience
through our mental connection.

*"Yes* then *no" is perhaps a better answer,* the Youli finally
says. *We did destroy our planet. We were on the cusp of destroying
the entire galaxy. The Travelers saved it.*

That word again: Travelers. They must be the missing link.
*Who are the Travelers?* I ask.

*We were scientists,* Wind Chimes tells us, *part of the Youli
elite but not part of the powerful. We discovered the rift by acci-
dent when we were testing alternative power sources.*

The rift? What does the rift have to do with this?

*We were working in another sector of the galaxy,* Wind
Chimes says, *and when our radars picked up the cataclysmic
explosion, we knew instantly what had happened.*

Wind Chimes pauses and presses his palm against the bubble again. In his green chest, his heart seems to glow a bit deeper than before.

"You can't keep leaving us hanging like this, Green Man," Marco says. "Tell us what happened!"

Wind Chimes's voice sounds miles away. *Our enemies pooled their resources and launched a final attack. They used the ore they'd once mined in our name to stop us from ever exploiting other planets again.*

*Our planet . . . this planet . . . exploded. Debris was hurtling through the galaxy, leaving a trail of wreckage. The world as we knew it had ended. But see . . . there was a chance . . . just a sliver of hope . . . that we could prevent it from ever happening. I gathered our team together, and we bounded to the rift.*

*We had no idea what we were doing. It was all trial and error in the beginning. We'd bound in and out, attaching ourselves to different temporal strands. The practice was so new that some of us didn't make it. They'd get out but be unable to get back. Or they'd land somewhere long ago and immediately be killed by hostile conditions or predators. We rarely knew what happened to those who didn't make it out of the rift.*

"You were using the rift to travel through time," Cole says, a note of awe in his voice.

He's right. Wind Chimes is a Traveler—a *time* traveler.

*Yes, when we finally understood the basics of how to navigate the linear timeline through the rift, we developed a plan. But first we discussed the rules. We knew we would be manipulating events that should never be disturbed. We aren't gods, after all. So we all agreed. We can only use the rift to alter the timeline to avoid cataclysmic results. Our alterations have to be as limited as possible. The decision to intervene has to be unanimous. And perhaps the hardest to follow, we cannot rejoin society, not in the true way. We can share our wisdom and help with the ethical leadership of the galaxy, but it must be from the outside.*

The first night during Union Song, Mira led us into a separate room filled with Youli, including Wind Chimes and the others who rescued us from the rift. I remember the wisdom and depth that were present. It was more enlightened than anything I'd ever experienced. Those Youli must be the Travelers.

"I don't understand," Lucy says. "Why can't you just go back to living among your people?"

*Many reasons. We are changed. We do not age. Something about repeatedly traveling through the rift has altered our own timelines, altered the very fabric of our DNA. We don't wish to be tempted to use the rift for our benefit or material gain. We do not understand what the possible ramifications are of degrading the timeline. So we must be careful.*

*Most of the time we live completely apart from society, emerging only to share our history with the new generations and to remind our people why all must take their turn toiling on the surface.*

*But in times like this, when the very heart of the galaxy is at risk, we step forward to offer our wisdom.*

*You're talking about Earth, aren't you?* Addy asks, her voice laced with despair. *Do you really think we're headed for a similar fate?*

*We do not judge you, young one, but we've traveled that path. We know where it leads. If only we'd had someone to show us, to turn our heads and make us see, things could have been so much different. We wouldn't have needed to end up here.* Wind Chimes gestures at the barren landscape beyond the bubble.

"I still don't understand," Cole says. "Why didn't you go back in time far enough to prevent all this devastation?"

*We tried many times, but it's difficult to change the course of history. We could convince our people to value peace and compromise, but only after they'd marched to the brink of destruction. Eventually, we accepted that this was the most we could do. And over time, we have come to believe it's a blessing that we couldn't save our planet's surface.*

"A blessing?" Lucy blurts out. "Why?"

Wind Chimes's eyes close. Moments pass as the Youli seems lost in memory, but then the tendrils of his mind stretch like the green vines growing above the clouds. *Because it means we can't forget.*

In my own memory, I'm transported to the underwater

world of Alkalinia. Serena coils around my feet and hisses into the voice box, "Remember or repeat!"

The surface of the Youli's planet is their Shrine of Remembrance.

It's late by the time we get back to our room. I haven't eaten anything since breakfast. I'm so famished, I think I might faint. So food first. But next comes the pod. We have to debrief about our visit to the surface. We leave for the Intragalactic Summit in the morning, and we have lots to talk about before we go.

"It's obvious now why the Youli asked for us to come early," Cole says once we're all gathered around the orange table with full plates. "They wanted to show us the ruins of their civilization so we'd help convince our people to stand down."

"It's like Serena said in the Shrine of Remembrance," Lucy says. "If we don't learn the lessons of the past, we're doomed to repeat the same mistakes."

Marco shoots a finger in the air. "Right! And we're lucky enough to learn from the Youli's past rather than our own mistakes. But time travel . . . whoa . . . Can you believe it?"

"I can't wait to tell Gedney," Cole says. "He was absolutely right about the rift."

Shockingly, it seems like Lucy, Cole, and Marco are actually getting along, or at least agreeing on the Youli's motivation in telling us about their history, which is a start. Addy has remained mysteriously silent.

"What do you think, Ads?" I ask her.

She looks up at the ceiling. "I'm not sure. There are still some unanswered questions."

More questions? I felt like we got a lot of answers from Wind Chimes. "You're so suspicious these days."

"Maybe, but why us?" she asks. "The Youli could have invited Waters and Eames to see their dead planet. That would have been a lot more straightforward."

Marco swings an arm around my sister. "That answer's easy. We're obviously far more intelligent and talented than our elders."

"And modest." She shrugs his arm off. "But seriously, they're staking a lot on our ability to convince our leaders to give up the fight. Unless the admiral has radically changed since I was in Earth Force, she's not too easy to persuade. And Jon Waters sure isn't, either."

"I never said I'd try to convince Waters," Marco says.

"What do you mean?" I ask. "You heard Wind Chimes. We're headed for a similar fate."

Marco crosses his leg over his knee. "Maybe, maybe not. Plus, there were holes in Wind Chimes's story. Like who were all those Youli on the surface today? I thought they got rid of their underclass."

"Wind Chimes told us that all their people have to take turns working on the surface, remember?" I say. Marco shrugs like he might not believe that. "What about you, Cole? What are you going to tell the admiral?"

Cole folds his arms across his chest. His face is cold and calculating. It's the face of Captain Cole Thompson, chief military strategist, not my friend Cole, *Evolution* game master. "The Youli said their elite were taken off guard, blindsided by the rebellion." He lifts his head and looks me square in the eye. "That won't happen to Earth Force. The situation is different."

"Maybe, but—"

"You know what I still don't get?" Addy interrupts. "Why Mira spent all that time training us with the gloves. If the purpose was to show us the surface, why train us at all? And if the training was supposed to be an offer of goodwill from the Youli, why weren't they around more to take credit?"

I'm not sure how many of us actually hear Addy's question. I do, and maybe Lucy does, but Cole and Marco seem to be in the middle of a stare down. Earth Force versus the Resistance. Whenever we start coming together as a pod, reconnecting as friends, the wedge keeping us apart just cuts deeper.

"We have an early morning tomorrow," Lucy says quietly, defusing some of the tension at the table. "I'm heading to bed."

Shortly after she leaves the table, Cole retreats to the bunk room. Marco soon follows, leaving my sister and me alone. Addy clears the dishes and stacks them on the counter. She pulls out the chair next to me and lays her head on her crossed arms. I kick my feet up on the table.

*I still think your pod is the answer,* Addy says, brain-to-brain. I know she can't actually read my mind like Mira, but she's always been good at knowing what I'm thinking.

*Maybe. Last night I thought we were getting on the same page, but today Cole and Marco seem miles apart on the issues that matter.*

*I'll work on Marco.*

*What about Cole? He's as committed as ever to the Earth Force agenda.*

Addy doesn't answer. Her silence tells me she has no idea what to do with Cole.

*You've been skeptical about Mira the whole time we've been here,* I say. *Be straight with me, Addy. What do you really think is going on?*

Addy lifts her head. *Honestly, I don't know. I think she's the reason we're here, but I'm not sure why.*

*Maybe it's that simple. Maybe the Youli picked us because Mira's part of our pod.*

My sister places her hand on my shoulder. *Mira will always be part of your pod, J, at least in your memories. But I don't get*

*the impression that she's going to jump back in and be one of us.*
*She's kept her distance, and she seems pretty settled here.*

My fiery emotions about Mira rage to the surface. I turn
on Addy, fingers balled into fists on my lap. *Pretty settled?*
*How can you say that? How could she be settled here? It's not her*
*planet! Her family's not here! Her friends aren't here! Well, we are*
*now, but we're not staying, and neither is she!*

Addy's face softens. She places her hand on top of mine
and leaves it there until my palms unclench.

"Time for bed, Jasper," Addy says. She stands up and offers
me her hand.

I let her help me up, and we walk together to the bunk
room. When we reach the door, I stop her. "Ads, tell me the
truth. Do you think Mira is coming back?"

I make a quick assessment in my head. If Addy answers
brain-to-brain, she's being honest. It's hard to lie with brain-
talk. If she talks out loud, then she's just telling me what I
want to hear. I bite my lip and wait for her response.

Addy looks at me and tips her head. A sad smile lifts the
corner of her lips. Then she shrugs. As I wait for something
more, my sister opens the door to the bunk room and ducks
inside.

**MONICA TESLER**

THE NEXT MORNING, JUST AFTER WE
stumble out of our bunks, Wind Chimes bounds into the
pod room.

Marco jumps. Lucy screams. The Youli doesn't appear to
notice.

*It's time, young ones,* the Youli says. *I've come to escort you.*

Addy glares at him. "Knocking really isn't a thing in your
world, is it?"

"*You* are taking us?" I ask. "What about Mira?"

*Mira is occupied with other matters. She will meet us at the
Intragalactic Summit. I will return for you in twenty Earth minutes.* Wind Chimes vanishes, leaving us alone once more.

I knew it. Mira is in trouble. I'll have to try to get some information out of Wind Chimes when the Youli returns. Or maybe that's a bad idea. I don't want to make it worse for Mira.

We scarf down some breakfast, then quickly dress—Lucy and Cole in their Earth Force uniforms, Addy and Marco in Gulagan tunics with an insignia in the center meant to represent the Resistance. I'm wearing a dress shirt and pants that I picked up during my brief visit to see my parents in Americana East before departing Earth. When I tried the outfit on for my mom, I stared at my reflection in the screen above our mantel. I couldn't break away. The person staring back wasn't me. When did I get so old? So tall? So tired?

"So handsome," Mom said, wrapping her arms around me from the side and leaning her head on my shoulder. I towered over her. "I remember when you first left for the EarthBound Academy," she said. "I thought you were so big *then*, but you only came up to my chin. Sometimes I wish I'd never let you go."

"Hey, Addy," I call to my sister, who's still in the bunk room with Lucy getting changed. "Do you think Mom was right in not letting us tell anyone we were Bounders?"

She laughs. "Are you serious? Of course not!"

"I'm not so sure anymore," I say. "With everything we've been through the past few years, now I'm kind of happy she gave us a chance to be normal while it was within her control."

"We *are* normal!" Lucy butts in. "How dare you say otherwise!"

"Actually, we're not," Addy says, walking out of the bunk room. "Be grateful. Normal is boring."

I raise my palms. The last thing I wanted was to start a fight. "I just meant everything changed as soon as we left for the EarthBound Academy. Sometimes I wish we could go back to before. Life was so much simpler then."

"Figure out how to navigate the rift, and you can," Addy says.

"I won't," I say.

Addy smiles. "I know."

In a flash, Wind Chimes returns. The Youli waves us over. We swing our blast packs over our shoulders and gather in a circle in the center of the room. I reach for Wind Chimes's hand, but the Youli immediately steps back. *We don't need to touch.*

Oh, right, how could I forget? The few times I've touched a Youli—on top of their ship on the Paleo Planet, right after we placed the degradation patch on their vessel, again in the rift—the experience sent both of us into shock. Human-Youli touch is like an express ticket to sensory overload. Just what I don't need before the Intragalactic Summit.

Wind Chimes raises his arms by his sides. The next thing I know, we're bounding.

When I open my eyes, we're on a large platform in the middle of the clouds. It looks exactly like the deck Mira brought us to for the first day of glove training. In fact, it may be that deck. Wind Chimes instructs us to stay put and goes to check on the departure status. I scan the area for any sign of Mira.

Next to me, Cole bounces on his toes. I swallow a laugh. He used to do that all the time, but now that he's the chief military strategist for Earth Force, he seems way too important to be so jumpy.

"What's with you?" I ask him.

"What do you mean?"

"You just seem . . . excited."

"Aren't you? I can't wait to see how they're going to get us off the planet."

"What do you mean, Wiki?" Marco asks. "Aren't we just going to get on a ship and bound?"

"Definitely not," Cole says. "The Youli would never risk revealing the location of their planet."

"Earth Force doesn't have bounding tracking capabilities," I say.

"No, but I'm sure other planets do," Cole says. "Remember how we got here? Not to mention, we might have the tech sooner than you think."

"What did you say?" Marco asks.

Cole jerks his head. I'm sure he didn't mean to let that slip in front of Marco and Addy.

"Seriously, Cole, what are you talking about?" I ask.

"It's just research, okay?" Cole says. "Everything's still in the development stage. Tracking isn't the main focus. Someday, the tech might make it possible for us to travel through the rift."

"No thanks," Lucy says. "There's no way I'm going to travel through time."

"What if you could rescue people trapped in the rift?" I ask. I'm kind of surprised Gedney agreed to do the tracking research for Earth Force, although I know he's intrigued by anything that might give us more information about the rift. Still, he's a Resistance operative, although I'm not sure Cole and Lucy know that. That kind of tracking tech would give Earth Force a lot of power.

"Over here!" Addy calls. She's lying on the rim of the deck, her head ducked over the edge.

She could fall. "Careful!" I shout, jogging over to her.

"Chill, J," she says, scooting back from the edge. "See for yourself."

I peer over the side. Beneath us is another deck, wider than this one, and then another beneath that. There are at least five additional decks beneath us, stacked like playing cards hovering in the clouds. Three decks down, the rim of a ship is visible. Most of the ship is blocked by the higher decks, but I can tell by how wide the rim is that it's enormous.

"I bet that's the one we're taking to the Summit," I say to my pod mates, who are now all standing at the edge of the deck.

"I bet you're right," Cole says. "That one looks to be about the same size as the Youli vessel at the last Intragalactic Summit."

A screeching noise like metal on metal sounds behind us, I turn around in time to see two small Youli ships bound in. They spin into saucers, then their boarding ramps unfurl. Youli exit both ships, carrying equipment. Around the same time, groups of Youli bound in without ships. A streak of white catches my eye. In the group farthest from us, I spot Mira.

I start toward her at once. She must sense me, because she turns. The groups of Youli bound away, maybe descending the platforms to board the ship. Mira raises her palm. My heart leaps. A second later, her group is gone.

I skid to a halt and rest my hands on my knees. Why is this happening? Where are they taking her? Why can't she just be with us? I have so much on my shoulders the next few days, I can't afford to get distracted with Mira. Still, if they'd let me talk to her, at least I'd know she's okay.

"Yo, J-Bird!" Marco calls from across the platform.

Wind Chimes is back. I jog over to the group and step right into the Youli's space. *Why won't you let me see her?*

Wind Chimes doesn't even pretend to be clueless. *Mira will be at the Summit. I'm sure you will see her there, Jasper Adams.*

*I want to see her now.*

*I'm afraid that's not possible.*

Addy squeezes my hand before I have a chance to protest more. "It's time to go, Jasper. Don't forget, we have a lot of work to do."

I nod and let my sister coax me into the bounding circle. Seconds later, we're standing at the ramp to the enormous Youli vessel a few decks down. It's definitely the same ship they took to the last Intragalactic Summit.

Wind Chimes leads us aboard. I look for Mira, but I don't see her anywhere. We wind through the orange halls to a private chamber. Wind Chimes asks Cole to place his palm on the wall. Before our eyes, the orange mush morphs into the familiar seats of an Earth Force passenger craft. The walls fade to brown, the floor sprouts carpet, and a window unfurls on the outer edge of the chamber.

"What kind of travel technology will we be using to get off the planet?" Cole asks the Youli.

*Before we bound to the Summit, our ship will be towed through the atmosphere and slung into orbit via a pin sphere. You can watch out the window.*

Once Wind Chimes leaves, Cole takes his seat and lights up like a kid on Christmas morning. He practically places his nose on the window glass. I lean back and close my eyes. Maybe I'll decide to watch the cool Youli tech in action, or maybe I'll spend a few quiet minutes wallowing in self-pity and missing Mira. Then I'll have to put on my neutral face and try to bridge the gap been Earth Force and the Resistance before we're called before the Intragalactic Council.

My pod mates appear to enjoy the trip. Me? Not so much. My breakfast nearly makes a repeat appearance as the large vessel is dragged up through the atmosphere then launched like a slingshot into the cosmos. Once we arrive at the pin sphere, which is much bigger than the one we traveled through to get to the Youli home world, a large chime sounds in the vessel. Then we spin faster than I thought possible under the laws of physics. I have no idea what happens to the ship or our Earth Force–look-alike cabin or even our bodies as we whirl into a sphere and then bound, but I consider it a miracle that I'm not covered in vomit by the time the vessel has spun itself back to its full size once again.

"Check it out, kids!" Marco says.

Out the window, in the distance, is the giant rotating axel dock erected just for the Intragalactic Summit. Cole asked Wind Chimes before we departed, and the Youli told us that only a few individuals know of the location of the Intragalactic Summit until a few days before the meeting is scheduled to begin. Admiral Eames paid a steep price to the Alks for the previous Summit's location data. Now I understand why.

The dock looks just as I remembered. There's a central sphere where the Council meets, like the axis of a bicycle tire. Spokes extend in a circle that rotates and revolves around the center. On the end of each spoke is a dock.

Security is mega amped up. Multiple shields circle the axel, and dozens of combat ships form barriers in between the shields. Earth Force may have penetrated the defenses with a surprise attack at the last Summit, but I doubt anyone's getting through all the redundant security this time around.

I count thirteen ships already docked. Some of the ships look similar to the Youli vessel, large, silver, and intimidating with obvious bounding capability, but others are radically different. There's a ship that's long and skinny like a baseball bat. There are three ships that are built in a classic aerodynamic shape. If those ships can bound, it's probably not in the same way as the Youli and Earth Force bounding ships. There's even a cube-shaped ship on the other side of the axel. Directly next to the cube, one of the new Earth Force passenger crafts is parked.

When we spot the Earth Force ship, my pod mates and I collectively exhale. I think on some level none of us were sure this would actually come together. All the delegates—half from Earth Force and half from the Resistance, all of whom pretty much hate one another—had to meet at a bounding base, board the ship, and travel to the Intragalactic Summit.

Together. Of course, all we know now is that the ship is docked. We don't know who's on board, but we might as well be optimistic.

Addy eventually puts words to our thoughts. "They made it."

"So far, so good." Lucy shoots me a glance. Maybe the fact that the Earth Force ship is here means Admiral Eames isn't up to anything.

I'll stick to her words. So far, so good.

**THEY LET US OUT WITHOUT ANY** instructions. I wanted to talk to Mira before we left, but I couldn't find her. As soon as the vessel cleared security and was towed into the dock, a Youli showed up to kick us out—out of the cabin, straight along the hall, and down the ramp, the door closing behind us.

"Thank you and you're welcome and all that fun stuff, green dudes," Marco says as the door to the Youli vessel seals shut.

"And there ends our days as ambassadors to the Youli," Cole says.

Lucy puts her hands on her hips. "You would think they'd have a farewell ceremony or something."

"You were really expecting a ceremony?" I ask.

She gives me the side-eye. "We deserved one."

"What now?" Addy asks.

Cole starts down the long axel dock leading to the central sphere. "Report for duty," he calls over his shoulder.

We take off after him.

The Earth Force vessel must see us coming, because we actually do get a bit of fanfare. When the ramp is lowered, Earth Force and Resistance guards stand at the ready for our arrival, and a group of midlevel officers from both camps greet us.

Thankfully, it sounds like everything is going as planned. Everybody's on board. Forcing physical proximity is probably a pretty good way to start negotiations.

Or maybe it's not, because from what I can tell from the guards, the only interactions between the senior members of the two delegations have been petty fights and lots of glares since they met up at the bounding base. I guess that means there's a lot of work to do before our planet is called before the Council tomorrow.

Soon, Cole and Lucy are escorted to one side of the ship, and Addy and Marco to the other. The others guards disperse until it's just me and a lone Earth Force guard I never saw until today. We nod at each other. I'm not about to hang with this guy, and I think he knows it. He suggests I pass the time in the main passenger cabin. He offers to take me there, but I wave him off. I can get there myself, thank you very much.

With my friends gone, it's just me and my pity party. Cole and Lucy have Earth Force. Addy and Marco have the Resistance. What am *I* supposed to do? Sit around and count stars until it's time for a joint session? I wouldn't even mind seeing Dev and Nev right now. Sure, they'd poke and prod me and activate their glam plan, but at least I'd have someone to talk to.

I slowly shuffle to the main cabin, feeling sorry for myself.

"Hey, kid, I thought you'd never get here!" Denver Reddy is sitting in the dead center of the cabin with his feet kicked up on the seat in front of him. He has a fancy drink with a pink parasol in one hand.

I smile. I totally forgot that Denver was going to be here.

"Come fill me in," he continues, waving me over. "I'm bored out of my mind trapped in this spaceship waiting around while the important people argue."

I head over and sink into a seat a few down from Denver. Now that I'm sitting, I realize I'm exhausted and still a bit queasy from the trip. I nod at his drink. "What's with the tropical beverage? Missing our Paleo Planet cruise?"

Denver laughs. "You look like you could use a drink. I'll make you one!" He jumps up and rushes over to the bar. Apparently, he was desperate for something to do. He must have really been bored.

"Don't worry," he calls from the bar, "it's nonalcoholic. We've got to stay fresh for our important roles as neutral facilitators in this planetary power meet-up, am I right?"

I lift up the seat dividers on either side of me and lay down. "I wasn't worried, Denver. Giving alcohol to a minor violates at least a dozen Earth Force regulations, and there are several senior officers on board." I chuckle to myself thinking about Admiral Eames cuffing Denver for trying to get me drunk. He'd probably call her Cora and end up with the cuffs so tight they cut off his circulation. "How are things with Earth Force and the Resistance going?"

"Ha!" Denver shouts. "There haven't been any fistfights, but that's about the only positive thing I can say. The vibe is more grade school feud than planetary leaders meeting to discuss a treaty." He rushes back from the bar and hands me a glass filled with fizzy purple liquid and capped with an orange umbrella.

I swing my feet down and sit up. "What is this?"

He grins. "Pomagranana juice."

I shove the glass back at him. "No thanks. Don't you remember what that stuff does to your insides? I'm already nauseous."

Denver pushes my glass back. "Kidding, kid, it's seltzer mixed with blackberry syrup. A couple rounds of poma-granana juice could add a bit of humor to these peace talks, though, don't you think?" He puts on his best Admiral Eames voice. "Captain Reddy, what is that smell?"

The drink is a perfect mix of tart and sweet. It makes me pucker but tastes like candy on the way down. "You know how you were hoping to reinvent yourself when this is over? Maybe you should take up bartending."

We both kick our feet up and fill in the blanks about what's been going on the last few days. I tell him about the Youli planet—the cool towers with their crystals and vines and the dark reality beneath the clouds revealing the consequences of the Youli's bad decisions a millennium ago.

"Oh, so it's the whole *we speak from experience* thing, huh?"

"I guess. Their story was kind of scary." I tell him about the rift and the Travelers.

"Really? So those guys who showed up to rescue us were time travelers. Interesting. Now let's get to the good stuff. How's Mira?"

We've never actually talked about it, but he's spent enough time with me to guess about my feelings for her. I shrug. "I'm not sure. There are moments when things are great. Our connection is stronger than ever. But there are also moments when she's so distant that she feels a lifetime away."

"Have you asked her about her plans after the Summit?"

I shake my head. "I couldn't find the right moment." When things were going well with us, the last thing I wanted to do was ask a downer question. And no other time felt right. Now I have no idea when I'll see her next.

"I don't know what you're waiting for, kid."

Several nonalcoholic beverages later, after Denver and I have watched old EFAN vids and made fun of Florine Statton for what seems like an eternity, Addy shows up.

"Why aren't you guys at the meeting?" she asks.

I straighten up in my seat. "What meeting?"

"The joint caucus."

"Shoot!" Denver says. "What time is it?"

"Time for the joint caucus meeting," my sister says pointedly.

"We're coming, we're coming." Denver hops to his feet.

"Hurry up," Addy says. "It's cold as ice in there." She gives me a look that lets me know things are not off to a good start before rushing out of the passenger cabin.

I stand up and stretch. "Nice of you to give me a heads-up about this meeting, Denver. We could have spent time preparing rather than watching *In the Flo* reruns."

"I don't need to practice being a referee," he says, "and you have to admit my *Flo* riffs were priceless. Who actually watches that drivel?"

"We do, apparently."

I follow Denver to the rear of the craft. There's a long, narrow conference room that stretches much of the length of the vessel. Floor-to-ceiling windows look out over the dock leading back to the central axel and beyond. Nearly the entire structure of the Intragalactic Summit is visible, where now almost every dock is filled with an alien craft. It's an excellent location for our prep meetings. With all those ships constructed with superior technology staring back at us, it's hard to forget what's at stake.

Everyone is already assembled around the table. On one side is the Earth Force team: Admiral Eames, Captain Ridders, Cole, Lucy, and a few other officers I don't know well. The Resistance has the other side: Waters, Marco, Addy, and a few other former Earth Force officers who defected during the time I was trapped in the rift. Barrick is seated to Waters's right. Even though he's a Tunneler, Waters insisted he be present, both as the second-highest-ranking member of the Resistance and also as a representative of the Gulagan people and their interests.

Denver walks to the head of the table on the left side and gestures for me to take a seat on the far right. So basically we're the bookends of this festive gathering. As we take our seats, all eyes are on us, and no one says a word.

"Nice of you to join us," Admiral Eames finally says.

It's a dig at us being late, and Denver knows it. He smiles at Eames. "Thank you, *Admiral*." He puts lots of emphasis on her title, making a point that he's not calling her Cora while also highlighting that he finds her title a bit ridiculous given their history.

*Kleek Arrr. Arrr. Kitt. Blerk,* Barrick growls. His voice box translates: "Let's get on with it."

Waters leans back and crosses his arms against his chest.

Admiral Eames nods at Ridders, who clears his throat and starts to talk. It's kind of like an opening statement. Earth Force protects the planet, we represent all Earth's people, our mission is . . . blah, blah, blah. I lean back and try not to yawn.

It's weird to be sitting here in the middle of all this. It wasn't too long ago that Waters was our pod leader. Admiral Eames is a legend, and Denver Reddy is probably the most famous aeronaut of all time. And here we are—my pod—sitting at the same negotiating table with them. That's mind-blowing.

When Ridders finally finishes, everyone looks at Waters. Presumably, it's the Resistance's turn for an introduction.

Waters folds his hands together on the table. "I'm not going to waste our time with a long-winded soliloquy about the Resistance. We all know who we are and what we stand for. This discussion should be simple, mostly because what we want is in line with what the Council will require from Earth. Withdraw your presence from all alien planets. That, of course, means immediately ceasing occludium mining and the use of alien labor."

Waters isn't much off the mark. Everyone should be anticipating that the Council will require us to stop interfering with lesser-developed planets and alien species. It's one of their main rules. I'm assuming my pod mates told their camps all about Wind Chimes's tour of the surface of the Youli planet. They were nearly destroyed by their exploitation of other planets. Now, as self-appointed Guardians of the Galaxy, there's no way the Youli—and especially the Travelers—would allow Earth to continue on the same track.

Denver slaps the table. "Great, we got that out of the way. Now let's see how we can meet in the middle."

"Perhaps we could agree to a staged reduction—" Ridders starts.

Admiral Eames lifts her hand, silencing Ridders. She looks at Denver. "No one appointed you mediator." Then she turns her gaze to Waters. "We won't agree to your demands."

Waters returns her stare. "I wasn't finished." He leans forward and directs all of his remarks to the admiral. "The Resistance won't sign any treaty that doesn't specifically provide for the public acknowledgment of our rebellion, a disclosure of the accurate history of Earth's relations with Gulaga and the Youli, and the complete disbandment of Earth Force." He sits back and clasps his hands behind his head. "Today's the day, folks. It's time to usher in a new era."

Admiral Eames rises. "We won't dignify your absurd

demands with a response." She marches toward the door, obviously expecting her team to follow.

Cole slowly pushes to standing. Marco and Addy exchange glances. Lucy shoots me a knowing look. Maybe this is what the admiral planned all along.

"Wait!" I shoot to my feet. "Didn't you hear what happened to the Youli? They destroyed their planet! It's clear they think we're headed for the same fate. Something needs to change. If we don't agree here, today, among ourselves, the Intragalactic Council is going to make us comply." I wave my hands at the window. "Look out there! We can't fight all of them! They'd annihilate us!"

The admiral pauses, her hand on the door latch, and for the briefest of moments I think I may have gotten through to her.

I soften my voice. "Can't we all just talk?"

From across the room, Denver pleads, "Come on, Cora."

It was the wrong thing to say. Admiral Eames's face turns to steel. She twists the handle and exits the room. The rest of her team slowly follows her lead.

# 20

**I'M PACKED INTO A RIDICULOUSLY SMALL**
single bunk room aboard the Earth Force ship, and I can't
sleep. The blanket is flimsy. I'm not cold, I just need something heavy to keep my body from feeling jumpy. Maybe nothing would work for me tonight. My mind is racing. I feel like
there's something I should be doing, but the truth is that I can't
stop the train wreck we're heading toward—not on my own.

How come it feels like my pod mates and I just keep getting shuffled from one group of adults to the next, all with
their own agendas? Tonight was the worst. I wasn't even able
to talk to my friends after that joke of a joint caucus. Both
sides have remained behind closed doors.

If tomorrow morning goes as poorly as tonight, we're going to walk into the Summit as fools. They'll be forced to make us comply, and I'm sure that won't be pretty.

Even if we do miraculously reach some kind of compromise, how different is it really going to be? Waters talks about building something new, but when he talks, all I hear is a recycled version of what we already have, packaged with a pretty new bow but with the same rotten stuff inside.

Regis said the Bounders would be the ones who end this. It sure doesn't feel like it. I mean, what good did we do today? Nothing. Zero. Zip.

Tomorrow is the Intragalactic Summit. Change is going to come one way or another. I just wish we could be part of the solution and not the problem the whole galaxy is glaring at.

At least I might see Mira tomorrow.

I curl into a ball beneath my blanket and try to let that thought carry me into sleep.


It's a shock, but things are looking up in the morning. I may not have reached Admiral Eames in the moment last night, but my words apparently had a lingering effect. Not to mention, I definitely motivated my pod mates to push back on their teams.

By the time I make it to breakfast, my pod mates have been up for hours negotiating. It turns out both Earth Force and the Resistance are open to a staged reduction in Earth Force presence on other planets. That's a good enough start to appear before the Council.

"What about all that other stuff?" I ask. "The public statements and the disbanding of Earth Force and all?"

"Those are domestic matters," Cole says. "The Council has no business in our planet's internal affairs."

"We have a long way to go on those issues," Addy says, "but we need to keep the Council as the primary focus for the sake of the planet. We can negotiate once Earth has been admitted to the Council."

Denver pipes up from the other side of the conference room, where he's devouring a stack of pancakes. "I'll work on Cora!" He tagged along with me this morning because he had no one to eat with.

"How'd that go yesterday?" I holler back at him. I partially blame Denver and his "Cora" slipup for derailing our talks last night.

"No one asked you," Lucy says to him. Ever since the Lost Heroes Homecoming Tour, when she realized Denver wasn't interested in romance, she's soured on him entirely.

Denver just smiles and keeps eating. When Denver has syrup, Denver is happy.

Before long, the room starts to fill up. Aside from our pod, Earth Force keeps to one side of the table and the Resistance stays on the other. Still, there isn't any bickering or even any nasty looks.

I check my watch. We're scheduled to leave for the Summit in twenty minutes. "It's almost go time," I say to my pod mates.

Waters is here—he's over in the corner talking with Barrick—but there's still no sign of Eames. We need to firm up our position, and we need to do it now. I eye Denver across the room. Since he's the senior neutral in the room, I'll let him take the lead.

Denver reluctantly sets down his fork on his fourth plate of pancakes. He swipes a napkin across his mouth, then clears his throat. "Good morning, Jon," he calls to Waters.

Waters crosses his arms against his chest. "Denver."

Denver leans back in his chair. "The kids tell me there's been some shuttle diplomacy, and that apparently Earth Force and the Resistance are in agreement."

Waters eyes Addy. She nods. "That's right. We're ready to go."

Denver turns to Ridders, who's sitting with the rest of the Earth Force team. "Where's your fearless leader?"

"I'm authorized to speak on Admiral Eames's behalf," Ridders says. "The admiral's been busy with other matters this morning, but she's ready to attend the Summit. Earth Force stands by the strategy outlined by Captain Thompson and agreed to by the Resistance earlier this morning."

"Just to make sure," I say to my pod mates, "we're all on the same page, right? Whatever Cole told Ridders is final?"

When they agree, I clap my hands together. "Let's do this!"

As we stand at the threshold of the Intragalactic Council chamber, Waters and Eames (who finally decided to show) at the front of the group, we actually feel like an alliance. It's easy to understand why. This place is super intimidating, and it's better to face it as an allied front.

We saw the chamber from a distance when we arrived, but up close is a different story. For starters, it's enormous. The chamber sits in the exact center of the axel structure. It looks like a huge silver globe freely floating in the middle of a spherical track. It rotates and revolves in a random pattern and casts sharp glares across the dock when the light strikes its glossy surface.

"Fascinating," Cole whispers beside me as we wait to enter.

The sphere stills, and a loading plank extends from the end of the dock where we stand. When the plank reaches the chamber, part of the sphere's walls melt away to form an open archway.

Wind Chimes walks out of the sphere. *Welcome, young ones. Please extend my greetings to your people. Come this way.*

My pod mates and I exchange glances. Addy nods at me.

"Uh . . . the Youli says hello and invites us in," I say to the group. "So let's go." I take a deep breath and walk the plank.

Wind Chimes steps aside to let us enter. Our group heads through the archway onto a wide platform. Since I'm first in, the others crowd behind me. I freeze. It's the exact sensation I had the first time I entered the open pit in Gulagaven. One step more, and I'm sure I'll tumble to my death.

The inside of the chamber is enormous and dark and hollow. There's no floor or ceiling. Like the pin sphere where we landed before heading to the Youli planet, gravity seems to be anchored to the rim of the sphere and on the dozens of floating platforms, most of which are currently flush against the edges.

The sphere is filled with every variety of humanoids I've seen or imagined, even more than at the crowded space bar on Nos Redna. I clasp my hands to stop them from shaking. It's hard to take it all in, and this is just a small fraction of the diversity in the galaxy. The aliens in this chamber are only those admitted to the Council, the ones who have reached the threshold level of advancement.

The archway seals behind us, and the platform we're standing on sails forward. Lucy clutches my arm. Next to me, Denver catches his breath.

"Be cool," I say.

"Always, kid," he whispers.

*This is your planet's dais,* Wind Chimes tells us. The platform shifts, and the material beneath our feet molds around us so that we're all sitting down. *Your seat before the Council.*

"This is Earth's platform," I tell the others. "Our dais, the Youli call it."

As our dais glides to the center, two others rise to meet us, one of which is filled with Youli. And Mira.

I swallow hard. *Hi,* I say to her.

*Quiet,* she says. *Listen.*

There's so much I want to say, but I know she's right. I need to put my planet first and pay attention. Wind Chimes steps from our dais onto the second one that's risen. It's staffed by half a dozen aliens that are roughly three meters tall but only twenty centimeters wide. They have cyborg limbs like the Alks, except they have eight of them. One of the aliens hands Wind Chimes an armful of silver discs suspended on cords.

Wind Chimes nods at the tall, skinny aliens, and their dais returns to the edge of the sphere. The Youli hands out the silver discs. *Translation devices,* Wind Chimes tells me.

"They're voice boxes," I whisper to the others, slipping one of the cords around my neck.

Once the discs are distributed, Wind Chimes crosses to the Youli dais, which starts to glide away.

*Wait!* I call to Mira. *You're from Earth. You belong here with us.*

She doesn't reply. I squeeze my eyes shut and tell myself to let it go. Now is not the time to focus on Mira.

Our dais shifts, and I nearly lose my balance. As it tips and reorients, I have to grab on to Denver for support. Logically, it feels like we should be tumbling off, but instead gravity adjusts around us. Our dais sails across the sphere in an arc and then slowly lowers to the edge. This is such a strange sensation. It's like sitting in a crowded stadium, but the stadium is inside of an enormous beach ball.

There's a long period of silence when nothing seems to be happening, nothing other than every single alien in the entire sphere staring at us.

Addy kicks my foot. When I glance over, she raises an eyebrow. *What's going on?*

I can't help but smile. I'd totally forgotten that we can still talk brain-to-brain. I shrug. *No clue.*

As soon as the words leave my mind, a dais rises from the edge of the sphere. Several Youli are assembled on the dais. I'm not sure who they are, but I'm confident they're Travelers. Their dais rotates and revolves on a course around the sphere so that the Travelers come in visual contact with everyone in the chamber.

Around us, there's a rumbling, a stirring, a shifting in seats. When the Traveler's voice reaches my mind, I recognize it instantly: it's the Youli who spoke to us in the Traveler's chamber during Union Song. She's small in stature but mammoth in presence. Our voice boxes kick in. For me and my pod mates, the voice is an echo. We first hear the words in our minds, and then they're translated by our voice boxes, exactly how it was for Mira and me the day we discovered Waters and Barrick meeting with the Youli in the underground Wacky headquarters on Gulaga. The other Earthlings on our dais—the non-Bounders—hear only the translation.

The voice, both in my mind and in translation, is lilting in tone, pleasant even. But there's nothing pleasant about the actual words.

"Citizens of Planet Earth, you have been called today before the Intragalactic Council to answer for your violations. You have been warned that continued breach of the Intragalactic Treaty would result in action by the Council. Today is your final opportunity, or we will be forced to act against you in accordance with the laws of the galaxy."

**AS THE YOULI CONTINUES TO SPEAK, OUR**
dais rises to meet the Travelers. We face one another, circling
and spinning in the center of the sphere. Between us, the air
fills with a holographic image of Earth.

"Do you acknowledge that prior to this Council meeting
you were aware of the Intragalactic Treaty and its contents
and also that you were provided with a list of Earth's violations of that treaty as determined by the Council?"

Admiral Eames sets back her shoulders and stands as
tall as her small frame will allow. "We acknowledge that
we were provided with them." Her voice is powerful and
commanding, yet respectful. There's a ripple through the

sphere as her words are translated into dozens of alien languages.

Before we left our ship and crossed the dock to the Summit chamber, Admiral Eames signed off on the strategy we'd agreed on for the Summit. The negotiated arrangement between Earth Force and the Resistance should go far enough to get us admitted to the Council and also allow us more time to finalize our domestic treaty. It was a compromise everyone could live with. Somewhat surprisingly, Admiral Eames agreed immediately when Ridders summarized the discussions. I assume their team must have been updating her as the talks progressed.

The admiral only insisted on one thing: she wanted to be the spokesperson—the only spokesperson—for Earth in front of the Council. Waters made out like that was a huge concession, but I know it was all an act. Waters cares about a lot of things, but being the front man isn't one of them as long as he's able to pull the strings. Sure, he'll take up the helm if necessary, like he has with the Resistance, but he's more of a behind-the-scenes operator.

The Youli continues, "The individual violations are too numerous to name in this setting; however, they can be summarized as follows: (1) interference with lesser-developed alien species and their planets, including interference with natural technological development; (2) forced labor of lesser-developed alien humanoids; (3) theft of organic and inorganic materials from planets inhabited by lesser-developed alien species; and (4) repeated and sustained acts of aggression against other aliens and their planets. All of these acts, both as summarized and in their individual capacities, are clear violations of the Intragalactic Treaty."

The Youli keeps talking, outlining the demands, which include keeping off alien planets, no longer using Tunnelers for free labor, and halting our occludium mining. I barely slept last night, and it's starting to catch up with me. As I hear the Youli in my head and on the voice box, the words blend and all start to sound like gibberish. Before me, the holographic globe spins. I remember the first time I saw Earth from space. It was the day we left for the EarthBound Academy. I cried. There, out the window, was my planet, my home. I had no idea what to expect as I left it behind.

Only a few weeks later, I discovered what being a Bounder really meant. I learned that Earth Force had been lying to us our whole lives. I found out that I was born to fight the Youli, and then I *did* fight them on the Paleo Planet.

After the battle, on our journey home to Earth, I saw the Paleo Planet out the window. Yes, it looked like Earth, but it looked like the Earth we see in storybooks or in history shows, with healthy hues of green and blue. Our Earth today is dying. We're destroying it.

If something doesn't change, Earth will look exactly like the surface of the Youli planet. Even though the Travelers managed to save their world from total destruction, the Youli have been cleaning up their mess for a thousand years and have a thousand more to go.

The Council isn't punishing Earth by making it comply with their treaty. They're saving us, or at least giving us a chance to save ourselves.

Addy's voice breaks into my mind. *This is it. She'd better not blow it.*

Everyone in the sphere is still looking at us. But more precisely, they're looking at Admiral Eames, waiting for her response.

Even in this room filled with powerful aliens from across the galaxy, it's amazing how much authority Admiral Cora Eames can command. She is a force. We may not always see eye to eye, but in this moment, I'm glad to have her represent me. That is, like Addy said, if she doesn't blow it.

The admiral insisted on being the spokesperson. Now is her moment of truth.

Admiral Eames scans the sphere, letting her gaze fall on all the groups of delegates. Finally, her focus comes to rest on the Youli in front of us.

She inclines her head. "We are honored to be here before the Intragalactic Council."

I exhale. So far, so good.

"Earth is young compared to many of you," she continues. "We have much to learn. As you mentioned, we have gone through an era of internal discord. That era has ended. A month ago, we executed a cease-fire treaty, and we have begun the process of putting our differences aside. We understand your demands, and we will meet them. We have already tentatively agreed among ourselves to a staged withdrawal from Gulaga, including the ultimate cessation of all occludium mining operations."

Okay, this is sounding good. It's exactly what we discussed.

"We are very close to finalizing our internal peace treaty. With all due respect to the Council, we humbly ask that you excuse the Earth delegation from the remainder of today's session. We will use our best efforts to reach our own agreement and present our domestic treaty to the Council tomorrow, at which time we will be prepared to enter the Council as planetary members, subject to your jurisdiction, and in full compliance with the treaty."

"Break until tomorrow?" Waters whispers. "We didn't agree to this."

Barrick growls. Fortunately, his voice box doesn't pick it up.

"What are you doing, Cora?" Denver asks quietly.

I get why they're annoyed, but her proposal seems reasonable. We're going to need to work pretty hard to hammer out all the specifics of the domestic treaty under such a tight deadline, but another day won't make a difference in our whole citizens-of-the-galaxy plan. And we might as well get it done while we're all here and ready to roll.

The Travelers confer, then the small Youli replies. *Earth, your request in granted. Your attendance is expected tomorrow morning at 0900.*

As soon as the translation comes through, our dais arcs away from the center of the sphere and retracts to the exit. The silver wall molds into an archway again. Outside, the plank extends from the dock.

Admiral Eames turns and, without a glance back, walks off the dais and onto the plank. After a moment, we chase after her.

The admiral has already crossed the plank by the time the rest of us have exited the Council chamber.

"Admiral!" Waters calls after her. "What was that all about? We expected those demands, and we were prepared to answer today. Why did you ask for more time?"

"Why not get it all tied up with a pretty bow while we're here, Jon?" she replies, speed walking along the dock. "The Council will be more than satisfied if we present them with a complete domestic treaty resolving our internal differences at the same time that we formally join the Council and agree to be subject to the Intragalactic Treaty."

"You should have told us that was your plan," Denver tells her. "You aren't the leader in this. We're a team."

She swipes her finger across her com link, then picks up her pace. "Well, then, I'm sure teamwork will get that treaty finished in no time."

I have to run to keep up with them, but I don't want to miss anything.

"Fine," Waters says. "Then let's wrap this up right away, as soon as we get back to the ship."

Ridders nods. "I agree. Let's meet in the conference room. We can have a working lunch."

"I'll leave you to it," Admiral Eames calls over her shoulder. "I have other matters that need my attention this afternoon."

"Stop!" Waters grabs her arm. "You need to participate. You're the one who asked for more time!"

She skids to a halt and shakes off his hand. "You managed without me this morning." She lowers her voice. It's quiet and cold. "And Jon? Don't you ever touch me again."

She spins on her heels and practically sprints the rest of the way back to the ship.

"Cora!" Denver calls after her, but even he seems to know it's a lost cause.

"This is ridiculous," Waters says. "Are you going to tolerate this?" he asks Ridders. Then to Cole, "What about you?"

Denver puts a hand on Waters's shoulder and steers him to the side. "It's fine, Jon. Let Cora have her break. We have until tomorrow morning."

Ridders and Cole race to catch the admiral. Barrick and Waters aren't far behind.

Denver runs a hand through his hair and takes a deep breath. He looks troubled.

"You okay?" I ask.

"Huh?" he says, like I broke his concentration. "Yeah, fine. It's just . . . Everything's fine. She needed a break, that's all." He turns and runs up the dock toward the Earth Force ship.

I fall back and walk with the rest of my pod mates, too tired to dwell on Denver's odd reaction.

"Why aren't you up there with the other Earth Force officers?" I ask Lucy.

She shrugs. "If they need me, they'll let me know. Last night I started brainstorming the post-Summit narrative. I was up super late working on it, and I'm exhausted today. It took all my energy to keep my eyes open while we were twirling around the dark sphere. I'm too pooped to chase after that crew."

"Hopefully not too pooped to entertain us with your signature style, Drama Queen," Marco says.

"Shut up," Lucy says.

"Really, shut up," Addy says to Marco. "We're all tired. The last thing we need is to deal with your annoying jokes."

"Oof," I say. "You got burned, my friend."

Part of me feels like telling Lucy that for my part in the negotiations, I'm going to insist that there be no more narrative. Not now. Not ever. But I don't have the energy to get into that right now. I'm just as exhausted as Lucy.

So when we reach the ship and discover that Waters and Ridders agreed to a one-hour break before resuming negotiations, I don't complain. Instead, I beeline to my bunk.

Just like last night, my mind races. I keep seeing Mira drifting away on her dais. When my wristlet buzzes to wake me up, I feel like I just dozed off.

By the time I make it to the conference room, most of the negotiating team is already there. Barrick is barking about occludium production, and Ridders is asking questions. I fill my plate with food and take a seat next to Addy.

*You okay?* she asks.

*Tired*, I say, fighting back a yawn. *It's going to be a long afternoon.*

I try to pay attention to Barrick. The next few hours are going to be a constant internal battle between me and my attention span.

In fact, I start to zone out. Then a buzzer sounds, jarring me back to the present.

"Someone forget to turn off their alarm?" Marco asks.

Another alarm sounds.

Waters looks around the room. "If this is someone's idea of a joke, it isn't funny."

A second later, Mira bounds into the room.

# 22

**"MIRA!" WATERS CRIES.**

I rush to her side. "What are you doing here?"

The alarms keep sounding. Ridders runs out of the conference room with Cole close on his heels. Marco leaps to his feet, then dashes out after them.

"Something's happening!" Addy shouts, looking out the window. Several of the guard ships are crossing the shield perimeter.

Waters is yelling, and Barrick is barking into his com link.

I barely pay attention to them. Mira's in my mind. Her words come at me in a flurry. *It's happening! It's happening! We need to act now!*

*Slow down, Mira. What's happening?*

She searches for words—*tried, destroy, stop, please, Earth, attack*—but everything dumps out of her brain in a jumbled mess.

I grab her hands. *Slow. Breathe.*

She closes her eyes and inhales. When she opens them, they're as wide as saucers and filled with panic. This time, she sends me pictures.

*Bounding ships. The Paleo Planet. Admiral Eames. The Bounders.*

She takes another breath and squeezes her eyes shut.

More images: *The Youli Planet. Earth.*

Then the pictures stop coming, and the stream from Mira is pure emotion.

*Death. Destruction.*

"I don't understand!" I tell her. "What are you trying to tell me?"

Marco bursts into the conference room. "Admiral Eames is gone!"

"What do you mean she's gone?" Waters says.

"I heard Ridders say it. She left on a shuttle with her honor guard. The log says they left as soon as we got back from the Council chamber."

Waters lets loose a string of swear words. "That's why the bound detection alarms are sounding! She must have rendez-voused with a bounding ship. She probably thought she was outside of the range."

"What does that mean?" Addy says. "Where did she go?"

Marco slaps my shoulder. "What did Mira say?"

Mira places her hands on the back of a conference room chair. She steadies her mind, then opens it to the communication circle so that all my pod mates can hear. *Admiral Eames betrayed you. She's left for the Paleo Planet. Earth Force is about to launch an attack on the Youli home world.*

"But that's not possible," Lucy says. "Earth Force doesn't even know the location of the Youli home world."

"Youli home world? What's happening?" Waters demands. "What has Mira told you?"

Wait a second . . . Cole said Gedney was working on new tracking technology. "Where's Cole?"

Addy turns to Waters and Barrick. "According to Mira, Admiral Eames bounded to the Paleo Planet and is preparing to launch an attack on the Youli home world."

Barrick growls and barks.

Waters runs his hands through his hair. "How does Mira know? Is she sure?"

"Cole!" I shout again.

Cole and Ridders emerge at the doorway.

Waters crosses his arms against his chest. "Well?"

"Admiral Eames has left the ship," Ridders says. He delivers this information calmly, but his eyes dart around the room, betraying his anxiety.

I storm up to Cole. "Does she know the location of the Youli home world? We need the truth, Cole!"

Cole looks to Ridders. At first Ridders does nothing, but then he tucks his chin in a nearly imperceptible nod. "Yes," Cole says, "she knows."

"What?" Waters shouts. "How?"

"They tracked Jasper's brain patch," Cole explains, "similar to how the Youli tracked Jasper and Mira back to the Gulagan space elevator."

"Since when—" Waters starts.

"You said Gedney was still working on the tech, that it wasn't ready! You lied to us!" The gears in my brain start to shift. "Were you in on this?"

"No!" Cole shakes his hands like he's flinging off water. "I didn't lie, Jasper, I swear. I don't think Gedney even knew the tech was ready. Desmond must have finished the research on his own."

I flashback to Desmond in the Ezone before we left. He had no reason to be there. No reason other than . . . "Desmond scanned my brain patch before we left! He said he was just testing stuff, but he must have activated the tracking tech!"

"I'm sure he thought it was a just a test ordered by the admiral," Cole says. "Desmond would never outright lie about—"

Before Cole can finish the thought, Barrick launches himself at Ridders. Marco and I jump in and try to hold him back. It's not easy. The Tunneler may be old, but he's fierce!

"Stop it, Barrick!" Waters says. "That's not going to get us anywhere. If we have any chance of salvaging this, we need to act fast."

"Salvaging what?" Lucy cries. "It's done! We've betrayed the Youli!"

"At least we can try to block her attack on the Youli home world," Waters says. "Addy, Marco, reach out to Gulagaven, mobilize the Resistance. Every ship needs to be airborne within the next twenty minutes."

*Wait!* Mira shouts in my mind. *Please! We need to go! We need to go now!*

I grab my sister's shoulder. "Hold on a sec!"

Mira's mind crackles with anxiety. She's barely holding it together. I turn to face her and take her hands. *Focus. Slow. What do you need us to know?*

*The pod. Network. Bound. Now.*

Waters steps between us. "There's no time, Jasper. What is she saying?"

I pull back from Mira. Everyone is looking at me. "She says our pod needs to bound. I think she has a plan that involves us."

Waters shakes his head. "No way. We need all the help we can get here." He swipes a finger across his tablet and activates his com link.

"It's not up to you, Mr. Waters," I say. "And don't forget, you were the one who implanted the brain patches. We have you to thank for all of this."

Waters shouts something at me, but I block him out.

Mira shakes with impatience. *Jasper, please! They are going to destroy Earth.*

I try to process her words. *Who?*

*The Youli.* What she's saying seems so extreme, yet it feels true, almost like it's already happened.

I turn to my pod mates. "Mira's right. We need to go now. Team up, and she'll bound us out. Please, guys, you have to trust me."

Marco studies me for a moment, then steps to my side. "Whatever you say, J."

"Count me in," Addy says.

Lucy looks from Mira to me, then takes Mira's free hand.

We need to leave now. "Cole?"

He takes a step back. "No."

"Come on, Wiki!" Marco says. "Jasper says we have to go."

"I'm staying." Cole eyes Ridders. "I support the admiral's decision."

Lucy puts her hands on her hips. "I don't believe that for

a second, Cole Thompson. The admiral didn't even tell you what she planned."

Cole looks at his toes. "I didn't say that."

"We all know it's true!" I say to him. "You're a horrible liar."

"She must have her reasons." Cole's voice shakes. "I . . . I . . . I trust my superior officer."

"She obviously doesn't trust you," Addy says, "or she would have clued you in on her plan."

"I'm not going," he says with resolve. "I'm staying here and awaiting further instructions."

"Leave him!" Marco says.

*It has to be all of us!* Mira says. Cole flinches when her words touch his mind.

"Come on, Cole!" Lucy pleads. "I'm in Earth Force, too, but I'm going. It's all about the pod!"

"Who do you trust more," Addy asks, "the admiral or us?"

"There's no time for this." I turn to Mira. "Show him."

Mira closes her eyes and fills our minds with pictures. The Youli bound outside the Earth's atmosphere. They link and generate a power greater than anything we've ever seen. They target our planet. I'm not sure what the images are. The Youli's plans? Her grave predictions? All I know is it's terrifying. And if there's anything we can do to stop it, we must.

Cole's face is pale, his eyes trying to blink away the images. Then he clenches his fists, steps into our circle, and takes my hand.

The bound feels weird, like we're being stretched apart and then pushed back together in a way that makes my bones ache and my brain feel bloated. I land on my hands and knees on the mushy ground.

"Where are we?" Marco pushes up beside me.

At first, I think that Mira brought us to the Youli ship and that we've landed in the cantaloupe VR template. But when I open my eyes, everything is dark and foggy and—much to my horror—familiar. I jump to my feet.

I know exactly where we are. "Why did you bring us to the rift?" I shout at Mira. "How are we going to get out?"

"So this is the rift," Addy says. "You were right, J. It's gloomy."

*I know how to get us out*, Mira says.

"Fine, you know how," I say, angry at Mira and annoyed that no one else seems to understand how bad this is. "You've spent the last few months with your Youli pals learning how to bound in and out of the rift, is that it? Answer me this, then: What are we supposed to do when you bound us out and all that time has passed? Time isn't the same in here. By the time we get out, the battle will be over!"

*The rift has many different gateways. Here, time stands still.*

Okay, well, that's new. I take a deep breath and try to calm down. Everyone's watching me, and it's not just because I freaked out a second ago. They expect me to do something, make a decision, give a pep talk, stand tall and lead.

I never signed up to be the leader. Don't they get that? Not today! Not at the Academy! Not ever!

But that doesn't matter now, does it? If Mira's right, everything—our planet, our lives, the very existence of our species—is at stake. To have even a small chance of fixing things, we're going to need a leader. Since the admiral betrayed us and Waters isn't any better, I guess I'm just as good as the next guy.

So focus, Jasper. Get it together and lead.

I take a deep breath and slowly blow it out. Then I open my mind to my pod mates, look at Mira, and say as calmly as I can, *Tell us why you brought us here.*

Tears stream down Mira's cheeks. She doesn't respond at first. In her I sense a reaching, a summoning of strength to endure what comes next.

She wipes her tears and pinches her lips together. *I need to show you.*

Mira closes her eyes and slips into our brains. She exhales and releases something deep inside. Her mind pinpoints a trove of images and uncorks it. The pictures come rushing at us.

It's like a tidal wave. I cover my eyes with my hands as my brain swells with the new information. I don't feel like I'm in the rift anymore. It's like I'm in Mira's mind, living through her shared experience.

I hover in the clouds in the Youli home world. Crystal towers rise all around me. Maybe I'm on a training platform? That part's not clear. The next thing I know, Earth Force bounding ships manifest all around. They target the towers and start firing. Some of the towers crack and crumble before the Youli have a chance to meet Earth Force in battle.

Then the Youli emerge. They smash the Earth Force ships like they're ants underfoot. It's as easy as manipulating atoms. In fact it *is* manipulating atoms, just on a grander scale, like Mira taught us. Earth Force's defeat is swift and complete.

We always said the Youli probably had the technology to annihilate us if they wanted. Well, if this image is anything close to the truth, we were right. They've been holding back all these years to *protect* us.

The image of the Youli home world fades, and I'm transported across the galaxy. I'm suspended in space staring at my own planet. I sense my pod mates all around me as we collectively witness Mira's mind fill with pictures similar to the ones she showed us before bounding here. But now our view is strange, enhanced. Somehow we can see the whole planet, all its sides, at once. It's surrounded by Youli ships.

They fire. A million rays of light leave their ships with a single bull's-eye. Earth.

Our planet explodes.

A brilliant ball of light, then a billion shattered pieces of home hurtle through the cosmos.

That's it. What more could there be?

I open my eyes. Mira isn't the only one crying. There isn't a dry eye among us.

"That's what you think will happen if we don't end this?" Addy whispers.

*Yes,* Mira says.

Cole throws his arms in the air. "How can we know that? You can't be sure! We can't fight our own people on a worst-case-scenario hunch!"

*I know because it happened before. It will happen again. You are Earth's only chance.*

"Huh?" Marco says. "No more riddles, Mira. Give it to us straight."

She nods and seems to brace herself. *Those images aren't predictions. They're my memories.*

A shiver runs along my spine. *What do you mean, Mira?*

She pulls our mental curtain closed. *I'm sorry, Jasper. I wanted to tell you before.*

**MIRA SENDS US ALL ON ANOTHER DEEP**
dive through her mind.

Mira and I are standing in the rift. We're with the lost aeronauts and the Youli Travelers seconds before they rescue us and bound us to the Ezone.

Wait a second . . . These events actually happened. They're memories, like she said. They could even be my own.

Then my story changes, although it feels just as real as my actual memories. The Youli bound us out of the rift, but this time, I don't land in the Ezone. They take Mira and me to the Youli home world. Images fly at us. Mira and me in the grand hall. Mira and me in the virtual pod room. Mira and me at Union Song.

Mira and me holding hands, blending harmonies, happy.

I break free of our communication circle. "What is this? These things never happened!"

"Shhh!" Lucy says. "Mira said there's not much time."

*Please, Jasper*, Mira says. *Just watch.*

The scene shifts. Images fly through my mind, one after the next. Mira and I meet with the Travelers. They show us our planet. Earth Force is gathering strength. So is the Resistance. They're fighting. Violence spreads across Earth. Fighting breaks out on Gulaga. The Youli are frustrated, still angry about the degradation patch. Earth isn't worth the risk, they say. Give them another chance, the Travelers tell them, hoping that Earth will join the Intragalactic Council. Earth Force defeats Waters and the Tunnelers. They draw down the occludium stores. They develop tracking technology. They reject an invitation to the Intragalactic Council. Earth tracks a bounding ship to the Youli home world. They attack.

Mira and I watch as the Youli annihilate Earth Force. Then they blow up Earth.

It all comes at us so fast, it feels like I've been hit by debris when the explosion fills my brain.

Addy gasps.

Lucy screams.

"No more hypotheticals!" Cole shouts. "Get us out of here!"

What does it all mean? I don't understand! "Why was I in those images, Mira? We both know that's not what happened!"

Mira falls to her knees sobbing. *It* is *what happened, Jasper! It's not hypothetical. Earth was destroyed.*

"Mira?" Addy whispers. "We don't understand. What are you saying?"

Mira sucks in a deep breath, then another. She lifts her head and steels herself for what she has to say. *It took everything we had, but we convinced the Travelers to give us a second chance.*

Lucy kneels beside Mira and strokes her hair. "But what does that mean, sweetie?"

Mira drags her fingers through her long, blond hair. She gasps for breath, swallowing her sobs. *We knew our pod had the strength to stop this, but only if one of us continued in the original timeline and coaxed things along.*

"That doesn't make sense!" Marco shouts. "What are you talking about?"

Something twists in my stomach. She's telling the truth. And I'm pretty sure I've been running from this truth ever since Mira and I were last in the rift.

*The Travelers agreed to help us,* she explains, *but we had to comply with their rules. The only way it could work was for me to continue with the Travelers and for Jasper to be intercepted in the original timeline. I would live through both timelines. Jasper, though, would only live through the second. It would be as if the original timeline never existed for him. This was the only way to give Earth another chance.*

I crouch down in front of Mira. *You mean . . . what you showed us . . . it actually happened?*

I look up at Addy. She's biting her lip. All of my pod mates are watching me, waiting for my reaction. We're all weighed down by Mira's words.

"It was like a game reset in *Evolution*," Cole says. "You went back to the last saved setting to try again."

Mira nods. *We watched them destroy our planet, Jasper. This was our only chance to save it. I know you don't remember, but we made the choice together. You had to be the one to reunite the pod.*

Mira looks up at me, her bottomless brown eyes filled with tears. *You're the glue, Jasper. It had to be you. It's always been you.*

Those words . . . those were her words from the rift, the words I've gone over in my mind a million times. The pieces shift and fit together. It's amazing, really, how something so mindboggling can suddenly make perfect sense.

*So in the rift,* I say, *when it seemed like something happened to you, that's when you bounded back from the original timeline?*

*Yes.*

*But there was a moment when you simply weren't there.*

*When the Youli arrived,* Mira explains, *the timeline shifted. I bounded into the rift seconds later.*

*From the future?*

*Yes.*

*So you lived that time twice. For me, though, since I didn't come back, it's like I never lived that alternative timeline?*

*Yes, but you did, Jasper.*

I push to my feet and pace around the mushy gray ground. I can't process this. "I don't understand. What happened to the Jasper that's living that other timeline? Where am I?"

*I don't know. No one knows what happens to those threads.*

"What if I'm out there in some parallel universe all alone? You abandoned me!"

Mira buries her head in her hands. *This wasn't just* my *decision, Jasper. This was* our *decision.*

"Yes, but—" I start.

"Enough!" Addy shouts. She positions herself in front of me and grabs me by the shoulders. "Snap out of it, J! There's no time for your existential crisis. You asked us to trust you. Now it's your turn! Trust Mira! Trust the decision the two of you made! Save our planet!"

I shake my head and try to pull free of Addy's grasp. I don't want to do this. I can't do this. They're asking too much from me! It's not fair!

Addy tightens her grip on my shoulders. "Stay with me, J."

All of these feelings fight to the surface, followed by a flood of memories. I'm back on Alkalinia, struggling to bring the shield down. Mira drags me out with her mind and bounds us to the rift. The Youli show up, and something happens to Mira. She tells me she's leaving with the Youli. She says it's her choice.

All this time I thought she was choosing them over me. But in truth, we were both choosing Earth.

A lone tear snakes its way down my cheek. It drips off my chin and falls to the ground. Addy's right. There's no time for this. I have my whole life to relive those moments in the rift, at least in my mind. But now I need to live in the present. I need to be the person they imagine me to be, the person Mira must have imagined me to be when we decided I would be the one to stay back.

I nod at my sister. She smooths my shoulders and steps to my side. Then I turn to Mira. *Tell me how to save our planet.*

Mira clutches her hands to her heart. Her mind melts with relief. At least, that's what it feels like through our connection. *You have to stop the attack on the Youli home world. You need to make sure Admiral Eames and her envoy never leave the Paleo Planet. After that, everything needs to change. Earth cannot be allowed to continue on the same path.*

I'm willing to lead, but there's so much to process: the prior destruction of Earth; Mira's explanation about the timelines; what needs to be done to save our planet. Like she said, everything needs to change. Where to begin? My mind is reeling.

Cole starts unbuttoning his uniform. "I don't know what to make of what Mira said. All we can do right now is accept it as true and assume our planet is in jeopardy. The risk is too great to proceed in any other way." He strips off his Earth Force jacket and carefully lays it on the ground. He looks much younger in his crisp white T-shirt, but he still commands authority when he says, "I formally denounce Earth Force. My actions now lie with the protection of my planet."

Wow. I never thought I'd hear him say that. It gives me fuel to step up. "Thanks, Cole." I pat him on the back. "Our planet is lucky to have a military mastermind like you fighting for it."

"Definitely, Wiki," Marco says, "because stopping Admiral Eames is not going to be easy."

"We're going to need an army," I say.

"We need Bounders," Addy says. "They've been trained to fight, and they can get there fast. The Resistance Bounders should be easy recruits once they learn that Marco and I are on board."

"Definitely," Marco says, "and since we'll be fighting against Earth Force, I'm sure Waters will bring the rest of the

Resistance to the party, even if it's on his own terms."

"We'll take whatever help we can get," I say, "at least for the battle."

"I can convince the Earth Force Bounders to join us," Lucy says. "Learning that Cole has defected should be enough to persuade them. He's earned their respect and loyalty. They know he wouldn't turn his back on the admiral unless he has a really good reason."

"You cool with that?" I ask Cole.

"I have to be." His words are matter-of-fact. He moves on to stage two. "After we reach out to the other Bounders, we'll need to get the shield down on the Paleo Planet so we can bound in and assemble."

"I bet Ryan will do it," I say. "The admiral already sent Ryan, Meggi, and most of the Bounders to the Paleo Planet. If we can reach Ryan directly, I'm sure we can get him to help from the surface and deactivate the shield." Now I get why the admiral sent them to the Paleo Planet. Why didn't I ask more questions about that at the space station? I might have figured out what the admiral was up to a week ago.

Marco claps his hands. "We've got a plan! We get the other Bounders, bound to the surface, and kick some butt!"

"Wait!" Lucy says. "We need to think about what comes after. What about public relations? We can't risk beating Eames on the ground only to have her broadcast lies about us. We might never persuade the people of Earth that we're fighting for them."

"That's true," I say. "Words have power. I can't believe I'm saying this, but we need to take control of the narrative."

"We can blast a broadcast through Earth's web channels directly from Gulaga," Addy says. "Everything's still set up from a month ago when Waters tried to get you and Denver to renounce Earth Force in front of the cameras."

"Great!" I say. "Who knows how to work them?"

"Neeka," Marco says.

"And Jayne," Lucy adds.

That's right. Jayne's on Gulaga now. I haven't seen her since the rally in Americana East. I can't say I'm excited to see her, but that's beside the point. If she can help with our cause, we need her.

"It's settled, then," I say. "First, we bound to Gulaga."

"Wait a second, Ace," Marco says. "The planet is shielded."

"Is the communications system at the space elevator still operational?" Cole asks.

"It should be," I say. "They're running a salvage operation from there."

"Then that's where we bound," Cole says. "From there we can contact the other Bounders. We can convince someone on the surface to lower the shield."

"Let's go!" I say.

"Wait!" Lucy says. "What about the battle? How do you

expect us to defeat Admiral Eames? She'll have weapons, ships, soldiers."

"Isn't it obvious?" Addy smiles and puts her arm around Mira. "That's why we were invited to the Youli home world, so Mira could train us to fight Admiral Eames. Together, we'll be able to boost the power of all the Bounders."

My sister's right. All that fun with the gloves stuff on the Youli home world was actually military exercises. Mira was preparing us to fight Earth Force. She knew where this was headed all along.

I look at Mira. *Can you bound us out?*

Mira grabs my hand. *I can get you out. But I can't go with you.*

"Why?"

*It's against the rules.*

"What rules?"

*Don't you understand, Jasper?* Mira shakes her head. Her brown eyes spill over with tears. *I'm a Traveler. I can't come back.*

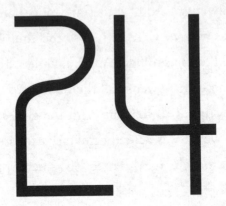

# 24

**I HATE THE GULAGAN SPACE ELEVATOR**
station even more now than before the Youli snapped the elevator shaft in two. The clear floor of the main systems room sends me into a sensory panic. The surface of Gulaga spreads out beneath us. With every step, I have to remind myself that I'm not going to plummet through space straight to the frigid tundra below. Actually, I'd probably get burned up in the atmosphere entry before being flattened on the surface.

"It's not so bad," Lucy says beside me. "I think the pin sphere was worse."

"I guess," I say. At least my sensory overstimulation is distracting me from thinking about Mira. So she's a Traveler.

What does that mean, exactly? I try to recall what Wind Chimes told us, but all I remember are Mira's words: *I can't come back.*

Addy kicks my shoe. "You with us?"

I nod and wedge in between Cole and Marco. "Did you get the com link system online?"

"Almost," Cole says, inputting code and tinkering with the switches. "There, got it!" He presses a button and leans toward the microphone.

"No!" Addy knocks Cole aside. "We don't want everyone in the Resistance to know our plan. I'll take it from here."

She activates a secondary screen and punches in some numbers.

Nothing happens.

I frown. "What are you waiting f—"

Addy holds her finger in the air, silencing me.

Then the board flashes green. She pumps her fist and leans toward the microphone. "Neeka, it's Addy. Shhh! Don't say anything! Get somewhere you can talk privately."

A minute passes, then there's an excited bark over the com, followed by a voice box translation. "Oh! Oh! I was so worried! No one's telling us anything, but we know something's gone terribly wrong."

"I'll fill you in, I promise," Addy says, "but you've got to do something for me first."

"Oh! Anything!"

Addy shoots me a look. "You've got to take the occludium shield around the planet down."

Neeka doesn't respond right away. "Oh! Addy!" she finally says. "I don't know. Are you sure that's wise? We heard there might be fighting. What if Gulaga is attacked?"

Neeka's father, Commander Krag, was killed in the Youli attack on the Gulagan space elevator, and she lost friends in the recent battle with Earth Force. It's understandable that she'd be nervous. I grab the mic. "Neeka, it's Jasper. We're up at the space elevator station, and we have to get down to the surface. The only way is to bound. I promise you're not under attack. Please, Neeka. The shield only has to be down for a minute."

Silence.

"Give me that." Lucy takes the mic from my hand. "Hi, sweetie! I can't wait to see you!"

"Oh! Lucy! Is that you?"

"Yes, and I've missed you terribly!"

"Oh! Oh! Me, too! Give me five minutes. I'll get the shield down. Bound to the Nest. I'll meet you there."

"Thanks, sweetie! And bring Jayne with you!"

Lucy sets down the mic and smiles at the rest of us.

"Nice work," Addy says. "You have the magic touch."

"Lucy and Neeka were separated at birth," I tell my sister.

Marco shakes his head. "That's an odd image, Ace."

MONICA TESLER

Lucy winks. "Let's say we're soul sisters."

We stare at the planet through the transparent floor, waiting for the shield to be deactivated. Minutes pass. My palms start to sweat. Finally, the silvery gauze that floats above Gulaga vanishes.

"Shield's down. Let's go!" Marco says. He opens his port and bounds.

With a last look at the planet beneath us, I bound beneath its crust, straight to the Nest.

As soon as I land, I scramble back and climb onto the bench. The floor is crawling with bugs, and furious barks fill the air.

I swat at the bugs wriggling near my shoes and scan the room.

Neeka's friend Grok is sitting on the moldy carpet. His voice box kicks in.

"Don't you guys ever knock? There should be some rule against bounding in unannounced."

Marco slaps him five.

Addy arrives. "Hey, Grok! Argotok!"

When Cole and Lucy arrive, Grok surges to his feet with a snarl.

"Cool it, Grok," Marco says.

"What are they doing here?" He's obviously not too happy to see them.

"Long story," I say. "What's with the bugs?"

He grabs a handful and stuffs them in his mouth. "Snack time."

My stomach seizes. I press my hand to my mouth, hoping breakfast doesn't come rushing back up.

"Want some bugs? Or a BERF bar?" He points to the bench, where a few boxes of bars are stacked.

The Nest is completely trashed. The carpet is littered with BERF bar wrappers, and everything's crawling with bugs.

Marco shakes his head. "Grok, this place is a dump!"

"We've talked about this, Grok," Addy says. "You can't come in here if you're going to treat it this way!"

"Since when are Tunnelers even allowed in the Nest?" Cole asks.

Grok growls at Cole. "This is our planet! You're lucky *we* allow *you* anywhere here."

Marco steps between them.

"Cool it, guys!" I say. "We're not here to cause trouble, but we *are* in a hurry." Mira estimated that Earth Force would be battle-ready in less than two hours, so we need to execute our plan *now*.

Fortunately, Jayne and Neeka rush in at that exact moment.

Neeka snarls at Grok. He grumbles back. After stuffing another handful of bugs into his mouth, he barks something at the rest of us and hurries out of the bathhouse.

"What's with Grok?" Addy asks. "He's super grumpy."

Neeka shakes her head. "He's not happy that we're negotiating with Earth Force, and I'm sure he's mad that you kicked him out of his hangout."

"*His* hangout?" Marco asks.

"Drop it," Addy says. "Even though Admiral Eames might think she has surprise on her side, we have to move fast. If we don't get to the Paleo Planet before she leaves for the Youli home world, none of this matters."

Yes, we need to get to work, but I'm tongue-tied. I haven't seen Jayne since the Resistance staged its attack at the Americana East rally. I knew she made it to Gulaga, but I was so worried that Earth Force would capture and torture her once they discovered she was the mole. I have to admit, I'm glad to see her. She looks good in the emerald-green tunic with the Resistance insignia. It suits her.

She touches my arm. "Hey."

"How are you?" I ask.

"Great." She looks up at me with her purple eyes. "It's hard being so far from the action, but it's good to be back with my friends."

"Your *real* friends." I didn't mean to go there, but the words just slipped out.

She doesn't take the bait. "I'm happy to see you, Jasper."

Part of me wants to take another stab at her, shout about how she led me on and pretended we were close just so I'd join the Resistance, but that's about the furthest thing from what we came here to do.

"We need your help," I tell her.

I let Cole run through the plan. Jayne and Neeka already knew that something had gone wrong at the Summit. Barrick transmitted a vague update instructing the Resistance to mobilize, prepare for battle, and await orders.

"I'll need to contact Ryan Walsh," Cole says. "He's on the Paleo Planet."

"If you know his com link signature, we can make that happen." Jayne says. "We know how to navigate the Earth Force communications systems without detection."

Lucy scoffs. "I hope so. You had plenty of practice at it."

I was wondering when Lucy was going to take a shot at Jayne. She has as much reason as me to be angry. Jayne was Lucy's assistant, the person poised to take her place as the fresh face of Earth Force if something happened to Lucy. Even if she wasn't the kindest mentor, Lucy gave Jayne a ton of opportunities. And Jayne betrayed her.

It's Neeka who soothes Lucy. "Oh! Jayne is a dear. This is war, Lucy. We have to do what's called for."

Lucy looks from Jayne to her Tunneler friend. "If you say so." She squeezes Neeka's palm. "It was so hard being on the other side of this battle from you." Neeka snuggles up against Lucy's shoulder.

"Knock it off with the BFF fest," Marco says. "Keep going, Wiki."

Cole confirms that Jayne can rally the Resistance Bounders. "The key is they agree to report to Marco and Addy, not to Waters. And they need to bound to the rendezvous point immediately. Can it be done?"

Jayne nods. "I've got it covered."

"So that leaves the broadcast," he says.

Lucy and I explain what we need to accomplish. The plan is to inform the public as simply as possible of the truth. No more narratives. We decide to prerecord the broadcast and set it to air after we depart Gulaga. That way, we can maintain our element of surprise while ensuring that our message gets out.

Jayne is on board with our plan. "Neeka and I will get the equipment and bring it back to the Nest. We can record the message here. We'll set the recording to broadcast in one hour."

"Sounds good," I say. "But remember, no one can know we're on Gulaga. We can't afford to delay, and we definitely can't get shut down. We need to do this whether Waters approves or not."

Jayne nods. As they make for the door, Lucy stops them. "Bring some makeup and a brush. I can't appear before the planet looking like this. I'm the face of Earth Force, after all."

"No, Lucy," I say. "You're the face of the Bounders now."

Addy, Marco, Lucy, and I work on the broadcast statement. We all toss out ideas, and Addy takes notes on her tablet. While Addy translates our notes into a draft, Jayne sets up the equipment. Neeka and Lucy disappear to the back room for Lucy to get camera-ready.

While Lucy is prepping, Cole and Jayne infiltrate the Earth Force communications system and reach Ryan. It doesn't take long to get Ryan on board with the plan. He guarantees he can get the shield down in ten minutes. He transfers Cole to Meggi's com link. Meggi promises to bring all the Bounders on the Paleo Planet up to speed. She'll meet us at the rendezvous point once they're mobilized.

After Lucy drafts the statement, I ask Jayne to read it, even though it annoys Lucy. Jayne worked in PR, too. Plus, she probably knows better than anyone how to appeal to both Earth Force and Resistance supporters.

When we're sure we have the text right, we get ready to film.

"Remember," I tell my pod mates. "As soon as Lucy finishes, we all bound to the Paleo Planet. Ryan promised Cole he'd have the shield down. Jayne will film the bound so that it goes out in the broadcast. Then she'll mobilize all the Bounders on Gulaga. Neeka, wait fifteen minutes and then inform the Resistance of our plan."

Jayne and Neeka do a final check on the cameras. The rest

of us gather behind Lucy, who is sitting behind a small table
we dragged in from the reception area of the baths.

"Okay," Jayne says. "You're on in three . . . two . . . one."
She points at Lucy.

"Hello. This is Lucy Dugan with a very important message.
There are many who wish to keep what I'm about to tell you
a secret, but we can't, not if we want to save our planet. For
many years, Earth Force has only told you what they want
you to know. The truth is, the Youli war isn't new. We've been
fighting this war my entire life. In fact, Earth Force had the
Bounder genes reintroduced into the population specifically
so we could grow up to fight the Youli.

"The Resistance you've been hearing rumors about? It's real.
The Resistance is a rebel group that's fed up with the Earth
Force's lies. And they're angry about how we've treated other
aliens. Some of those aliens are mad, too. The Resistance has
teamed up with the Tunnelers to fight Earth Force.

"That all sounds bad—and it is—but there is hope on the
horizon. Fellow citizens of Earth, the galaxy is far vaster than
you've been told. There's an Intragalactic Council made up of
lots of planets. They've asked Earth to join. All we have to do
is follow the rules.

"This week, representatives from our planet met with the
Intragalactic Council. We had a chance to enter a peace treaty
with the Youli, to agree to stop the fights between Earth Force

and the Resistance, and to join the Council with the other planets. Everything was moving in the right direction.

"But something has gone terribly wrong. Under the leadership of Admiral Eames, Earth Force betrayed our planet's delegation at the Intragalactic Summit. At this very moment, Earth Force is planning to launch an attack on the Youli home world.

"This must be stopped! These aliens are much older than us. They have much greater technology than us. And they have told us that our time is up. If Earth Force attacks them, the Youli will not only destroy Earth Force—they will also destroy our planet.

"Fellow citizens, we need your help. We need to stand up to Admiral Eames and the rest of Earth Force and tell them to stop fighting. We want peace. We definitely do not want to provoke a far more powerful alien race.

"I used to be in Earth Force. I'm not anymore. Neither are the people standing around me. You recognize some of them. Cole Thompson, Earth Force's former chief military strategist. Jasper Adams, our hero who rescued the lost aeronauts from the rift.

"We aren't members of the Resistance, either.

"Who are we?

"We are Bounders. All of us.

"By the time this broadcast airs, we will be fighting for

you, our fellow citizens of Earth. We are about to bound to the Paleo Planet and force Admiral Eames to stand down. If we are successful, Earth will survive. If we are not . . . well, let's just hope we win.

"On behalf of Earth, this is Lucy Dugan, signing off."

Lucy pushes back from the table and lifts her gloved hands. Behind her, we step apart and open our ports. From beside the camera, Jayne nods, and Neeka raises her paw.

Together, we bound.

# 25

I LAND IN THE TALL GRASS TWENTY
meters west of the watering hole, sending a cloud of giant blue
bugs into the air. Thank goodness Ryan got the occludium
shield down. I didn't just sentence us all to death by failed
bound. My atoms are intact, not scattered across the galaxy.

Geez! The starlight is blinding. I shield my eyes with my
hand. I forgot how bright it is here. I should have dug up
some sunglasses on Gulaga before bounding.

"Over here!" Lucy calls.

I push up on my knees and scan the area. It looks like we
all made it. And fortunately, no one looks to have landed
right in front of an amphidile or sabre cat. But . . . what on

earth is *that*? The ridge where the Youli parked their space-ship the first time we were here is now half blown apart, and there's construction equipment everywhere.

I flatten into a pancake and crawl toward Lucy. Marco's already reached her, and Cole and Addy are heading our way.

"What are they building over there?" I ask Cole, pointing to the ridge.

"A new occludium mine," he replies.

"Thanks for the heads-up, Wiki," Marco says. "Bounding right in front of an Earth Force construction site wasn't the slickest choice."

Cole waves his hand. "It's staffed by Tunnelers. I'm sure the admiral called them back to the other site today. She'll want as much security as possible at the primary facility."

"First, we wait to see who shows up." There are so many things that have to fall into place for us to have a chance at stopping Admiral Eames. For starters, there's no way my pod can take her down on our own. We need an army. If the other Bounders in Earth Force and the Resistance aren't on board, we might as well wave a white flag now.

So for now, we wait. There's no sign of the mammoths or the wildeboars. They're probably scared away perma-nently thanks to the mine construction. Still, I can picture the wildeboar herd charging the last time we were here, the vibrations of their hooves radiating across the ground, the dirt rising above them and clouding the air. If it weren't for Mira and her music, we would have been trampled. From the beginning, it was always Mira who instinctively knew what to do. She knew how to use the gloves. She knew how to calm the wildeboars. She was behind my power boost on Gulaga during the Tundra Trials. She figured out how to link with me so I could eavesdrop on the Alkalinians, the only reason we knew the Youli were planning to attack.

Now Mira's gone for good. She's a Traveler. She can't come back.

Focus, Jasper. Do. Not. Think. About. Mira.

A cluster of orange kite bats dip low to drink at the watering hole. Their large leathery wings stretch more than a meter.

"Remember when I petted one of those the last time I was here?" Marco asks.

"Not like we could forget," Lucy says. "You nearly provoked those things into attacking us."

"I did not! I was only—"

"Shhh!" Addy says. "Focus!"

Fortunately, we don't have to wait long for backup. Jayne, Minjae, and the Bounders from the Resistance land a few meters away. As they scoot in our direction, Meggi, Annette, and Hakim bound in.

"Thanks for getting the shield down," I tell Meggi.

"It was Ryan and Randall," she says. "They're holding the

shield center now. They also deactivated the bound scramblers. They covered their tracks, so hopefully it will be some time before anyone realizes the shield isn't operational."

"What about the other Bounders?" I ask.

"They know what to do," she says. "They'll join the fight once we engage. Most of them stayed at their posts so we wouldn't raise suspicion."

"Neeka and the Resistance will send backup," Jayne says, "but it will take them at least an hour to get here at FTL."

"Thanks, everyone, for pulling together," I tell them before turning to Cole. "It's your time to shine. Show us all why you were named chief military strategist."

Cole nods. "I see most of you brought your blast packs. That's good. My pod didn't have time to get ours when we bounded away from the Summit, but we have different ways of fast travel."

Hakim raises his eyebrow. "Like what?"

"You'll see, hotshot," Marco replies. He may have learned to deal with Regis, but apparently he doesn't have much love for Regis's former sidekick.

Cole doesn't elaborate. "Are the tunnels open?" he asks Meggi.

When she nods, he launches into his plan. "The scramblers are off, but Earth Force has bounding detection sensors running throughout the connected areas of the base, the main mines, and the theme park, so no bounding within the perimeter before it's time. There's a tunnel system that runs underground so the Gulagans can work without going to the surface. We'll access the tunnels in the theme park and cross over to the base. So let's head out and meet on top of the ridge to the east. Everyone clear?"

"Theme park?" I ask.

"You'll see," Annette says. "It's hard to miss."

"And then?" Minjae asks.

Cole is quiet for a minute. He presses his lips together and surveys the landscape. Then he pushes to his feet. "The only way Earth Force can reach the Youli home world from here is by the bounding ships. We need to disable them. Let's go." He reaches out with his gloves, gets his bearings, and takes to the air like Mira taught us.

"See?" Marco says to Hakim. Instead of waiting for an answer, he races to catch Cole.

Soon, we're all airborne and heading for the ridge. I think I spot a sabre cat prowling at the edge of the field where the grass meets the pomagranana grove, but I can't be sure. Last time we were here, there were animals everywhere. All this development has definitely changed things.

When I crest the ridge, I can finally see the theme park that I apparently can't miss. It turns out Annette's words were the understatement of the year. I knew Earth Force was building a tourist center here, but this is outside anything I imagined.

The theme park is huge. It's secured with ten-meter fences. It's filled with rides and restaurants and a mock watering hole. On the front is a giant sign that reads PALEO PLANET in a classic Jurassic font. Close to the entrance is an enormous building that glitters in the light like it's made of gold.

"That's the hotel and spa," Annette tells me. "You, too, can have a golden holiday, if you can afford it."

"Gross," Addy says from my other side.

The central feature of the theme park is a replica of one of the planet's tall, steep mountains. A flume ride wraps around, then plummets from a waterfall near the summit. I shake my head in disbelief. I imagined that ride the last time I was here, but I'm dumbfounded they actually built it.

The theme park is heavily guarded. Several Earth Force officers walk the perimeter.

Cole watches their circuit, then lays out a plan. "We'll make for the entrance near the side of the hotel. My pod will take out the guard."

"How?" Lucy asks.

"Put our new skills into practice. If we pool our power, we can disarm him and carry him to the top of the flume mountain. By the time he figures out how to get down, we should be at the base."

"Here," Jayne says, tossing me a role of duct tape she fished from her blast pack. "Neeka gave it to me before I left. You never know when it may come in handy."

As our pod nears the fence, Cole puts his finger to his lips.

*Brain-talk, remember?* Addy says.

*Good call,* I say.

We kneel in a trench a few meters from the fence, and look to Cole for directions.

*At my count, we'll freeze him. Then Addy and I will open the fence, and Lucy will wave the others through. Once he's frozen, Jasper and Marco, do you think you can manage to haul him up to the top of flume mountain? The rest of us can boost you.*

Marco grins. *Need you ask? Let's go!*

*On my count. One, two, three, now!*

The five of us reach out with our gloves and seize hold of the guard's atoms, including his vocal cords. Together, we're just as powerful as the Youli who paralyzed me in the rift. Once he's frozen, it's easy for Marco and me to hold him. Addy and Cole rush forward, find his key card, and scan the security panel, opening the fence gate. Cole gives a thumbs-up, sending Lucy running back for the others.

*Ready?* I ask Marco.

*Always, Red Baron.*

I laugh through our brain link. He hasn't called me that in a long time. It's one of the nicknames I earned from my famed fall during our first blast pack lesson at the space station. I've come a long way since then.

Since Marco and I are already holding the guard's atoms, the only challenge now is to get him in the air. I sense Marco drop the hold with his left hand, so I drop with my right. He nods, and we both push off. As soon as we do, the others send us a boost and we shoot ahead, the guard wedged behind us.

We fly behind the golden hotel to maintain our cover, the guard suspended between us. The side of the fake mountain forms a border with one of the fences, so we're able stay under cover all the way to the top. When we get to the high ledge, Marco holds the guard while I secure his hands, feet, and mouth with the duct tape. Once he's taped up, we release him. The guy squirms and whines, but it doesn't do him any good.

"Shut up!" Marco shouts, giving the guard a shove. The guard staggers forward, trips on a fake rock, then tumbles over the ledge to the tier below.

"Oops," Marco says. "I didn't mean for that to happen."

We can tell by the guard's squeals and squirms that he wasn't hurt too bad.

I shake my head. "He's fine. Let's go!"

"Wait, check it out," Marco says, pointing to the flume track. We're partially obscured by the fake rocks, so the passengers can't see us. The log is packed with people—mostly older women in floral bathing suits. They reach the crest of the ride and raise their hands. Their screams pierce the air as they plunge over the waterfall. Their log splashes down and skims the surface of one of the many swimming pools that circle the mountain. Almost every lounge chair is filled. The Paleo Planet is packed with tourists!

"This place is absurd," I say, "but I'll admit that flume looks pretty awesome."

"Maybe after this is over we can come back for a ride," Marco says. "Before we go, let's check the peak. We might be able to see the base."

Sure enough, once we land on top of the fake mountain, we can see the whole valley, including the Earth Force base and the occludium mine. The metal buildings at the base still spread in a honeycomb pattern, but the size has at least tripled since we were here last. The base runs right up against a pomagranana grove on one side and a mountain range on the other. The other two sides are bordered by the theme park and the mine.

Between the base building and the theme park is an enormous bounding deck *filled* with ships. Even from up here, we can tell that the deck is buzzing with activity.

"Umm, Ace?" Marco says. "They have a lot of ships."

"Clearly. When did they build all those?"

He shakes his head. "No idea. Our intelligence told us they were manufacturing ships, but we weren't thinking anything on this scale."

"Am I imagining things? Or are those ships carrying warheads?" Before now, Earth Force had never built battle-ready bounding ships. Occludium is too unstable.

Marco shakes his head. "Looks like warheads *and* precision gunners."

Goose bumps spread across my forearms. "They have a whole fleet of hybrid, weaponized bounding ships, and they're about to attack the Youli home world."

"That about sums it up, Ace."

"Admiral Eames must have been planning this for a long time." I stare a moment longer then raise my gloved hands. "We've got to tell Cole what we learned."

Marco and I take a new route down the mountain, planning to enter the hotel through a different door and meet up with the others in the basement equipment room, where Cole says we'll find an entrance to the tunnels.

We land in a cluster of fake pomagranana trees. (I don't get it. Why would you want to vacation in the middle of all this artificial stuff when the real deal is just outside the fence?) All around are mechanized fake animals with long necks, big bellies, and four stout legs standing two stories high and munching on the spiky purple fruit.

"What on earth are these things?" Marco asks. "I never saw any of these creatures during our first trip here."

"I think they're dinosaurs," I tell him.

"Sure, that's what they look like, but they don't have dinosaurs on the Paleo Planet."

"Clearly that doesn't matter to the people who built this place."

We weave through the trees to a pedestrian walkway that separates the grove from the hotel. Marco points at a nondescript door labeled STAFF ONLY. It looks to be locked by a standard bolt, which shouldn't be a problem to break through with our gloves. "All we have to do is sprint across, and we're in."

Up the path is a group of tourists headed our way. They'll see me. Doesn't he know I'm one of the biggest celebrities on Earth? "We can't. They'll recognize—"

Of course Marco doesn't pay attention. He takes off across the path, blows the lock, and ducks inside the door, obviously expecting me to be on his heels.

Fine. Here goes nothing. I shield my face with my hand and bolt for the door.

As I reach for the handle, someone screams.

"Jasper Adams!"

# 26

**FOR A MOMENT, I FREEZE IN MY TRACKS.**
Charging toward me at an alarming speed is a herd of sweaty, screaming tourists. It's a stampede!

*"Jasper!"* Their cries hit me like a tidal wave.

I kick my feet into gear and take off. When I reach the hotel door, I dash inside. The door dumps me into a back room of what I'm guessing is the spa. There are shelves filled with plush white towels and hundreds of mini lotion bottles. I race through the room to another door and escape into a hallway, almost colliding with a large man in a bathrobe. He shouts at me. I backpedal and crash into a lemon-water dispenser that splashes to the ground.

I sprint down the hall as the crowd of tourists pours out of the supply closet behind me.

Where is Marco? I'm going to flatten him!

At the next corner, I hang a left and dodge into the first door I find. It's dark and takes a second for my eyes to focus. There's barking and screaming. I'm pretty sure I just busted in on a woman getting a massage. She's sitting up on a high table clinging to a towel. A very mad Tunneler in a white uniform snarls and shoos me out the back.

"Sorry!" I shout, spilling out the door into another room packed with people. A giant whirlpool is in the center. Before I can find an escape route, the herd crowds through a different door and spots me.

"Jasper!"

"I love you, Jasper!"

"Remember me? We met on the cruise!"

How could I forget that horrible cruise?

They descend on me like vultures, grabbing my clothes and stroking my hair.

I can't believe it. The fate of our planet is at stake, and I'm going to be taken out by rabid fans. I swat at the tourists like a cornered animal.

"Out of the way!" someone shouts. "I said move it!"

Next thing I know, strong arms loop beneath my armpits and haul me out of the mob all the way to a private dressing room. The bolt slides closed with a click. "You okay, Adams?"

I spin around to face my rescuer. Bai Liu is covered in mud from head to toe.

"Bai? What are you doing here?"

"What are *you* doing here? I thought you were with my boy, Denver, at the Intragalactic Summit."

"Long story. Can you help me ditch the crowd and get to the main electrical panel in the basement? I can fill you in on the way."

"Sure thing."

Bai routes us through a back door to a staff staircase that winds down to the basement. While we rush down the stairs, she explains that Florine Statton bribed the lost aeronauts with an all-expenses-paid vacation to the Paleo Planet if they agreed to do a few public appearances. She'd booked Sheek to show up, but apparently he bailed once he heard about the incident with the *diruo* fuse on our cruise ship.

I tell Bai about the admiral's betrayal and our plan to thwart her attack on the Youli planet.

"Count me in," she says when I've brought her up to speed.

"Really? You'll fight with us?" We could definitely use someone with her brawn and brains.

"I'll do one better. Once we find your friends, I'll go round up the other lost aeronauts. They'll follow Denver anywhere, and I know Denver has your back."

As we weave through the basement hallways, I finally hear Addy's voice up ahead. "Jasper!" She runs to meet me and wraps me up in a hug.

"What on earth happened, J-Bird?" Marco asks.

"You happened, Marco. If you hadn't bolted for that door, we wouldn't be in this mess."

Marco pinches his eyebrows together, probably searching for a witty comeback but obviously not clear on what I'm talking about.

"Forget about it. There's not time." Addy shoots a glance at Bai and sticks out her hand. "I'm Addy Adams, Jasper's sister, and I'm so thrilled to meet you! You're my all-time favorite aeronaut."

All-time favorite? What about the poster of Sheek that used to hang above her desk? Granted, that *was* before her protest days.

"Thanks." Bai shakes her hand. Addy's palm comes away covered in dirt. "Sorry. Mud baths."

"Where are the others?" I ask.

Addy explains that Cole led the other Bounders through the tunnels to the base. There's an equipment room where he's told us to meet. He hopes to scope out the base up close from there. I thank Bai for the escort, then follow Marco and Addy to the tunnel entrance.

"How'd they plan to get through undetected?" I ask them.

MONICA TESLER

"They didn't," Addy says. "They were just going to act like they belonged in the tunnels. Unless Earth Force sounds an alarm, none of the Tunnelers should be bothered by a group of Bounders, many of them in uniform, coming through."

"If it works for them, it should work for us, Ace," Marco says.

"We aren't wearing uniforms."

He shrugs and takes off. "Just follow my lead." Addy dashes after him.

The last time I followed his lead, I was almost trampled by a tourist mob. But seeing as I don't have much choice, I get moving.

The tunnels aren't crowded, and they aren't really tunnels. It's just a subterranean level that crosses beneath the theme park, base, and occludium mine. Tunnelers are super sensitive to light, so this environment must make things easier for them (and also help with their productivity, which I'm sure is why Earth Force had it constructed this way).

We jog by HVAC systems, water pipes, repair studios, and storage rooms. We pass Tunnelers at every turn, but they don't seem to notice us. We keep our cool, and they mind their business.

When I'm pretty sure we're close to the base, I get the feeling we're being followed. I keep spinning around, but no one's there. Finally, I'm fast enough to spot a small Tunneler tailing us.

The Tunneler acts like me catching him is an invitation to say hello. He scampers up to us and grabs Marco's shirtsleeve. His bark is high-pitched and hyper, kind of like Neeka's. "Oh! I know you!" his voice box translates.

"No. You don't," Marco says, pulling his sleeve free.

"Oh! Oh! Yes, I do!" The small Tunneler looks around the hallway and quietly barks. Unfortunately, his voice box doesn't have volume control. It booms out, "My name's Lok. You're Marco Romero! And you're Addy Adams! My cousin Grok told me all about you! You're Resistance leaders!"

"Shhh!" Marco says, throwing his arm around the Tunneler and rushing him into a vacant supply room. "Turn that thing down." Once we're all packed in there with the door closed, Marco adds, "Lok, it's great to meet you, dude, but you have to do me a huge favor. Don't tell anyone you saw us. Trust me, it's what Grok would want."

"Oh! You don't understand, Marco Romero. If you're here for the rebellion, I want to help!"

"We don't need your—"

Addy puts her hand on Marco's shoulder. "Wait a sec. Lok, what do you mean?"

"Oh! Grok told us all about the Resistance! Lok and his friends want to fight! We're ready! Say the word, and we are at your service."

Addy's on to something. If Lok and the Tunnelers will fight

with us, we should accept their help, even if there's a risk they'll tip off Earth Force. "So, Lok," I start, "are you saying that the Tunnelers here on the Paleo Planet support the Resistance?"

"One hundred percent!" Lok answers.

"And you want to help us, even though it's going to be dangerous?" I continue.

"Oh yes!"

I look at Addy. She nods. It's worth the gamble. "Listen up, Lok. You're right. We're here to fight Earth Force, and we need your help. Round up all your Tunneler friends and meet us at the bounding deck. And make sure Earth Force doesn't find out what you're up to. Got it?"

Lok hops up and down, shaking his paws. "Oh! I do! I do! Thank you!"

"Good work, Lok," Addy says. "Find me on the surface. I'll tell you and the rest of the Tunnelers what to do."

Lok swings his paw to his forehead. "Yes, sir, Addy Adams! Lok is reporting for duty!"

Marco slaps Lok on the shoulder and heads for the door, grabbing a few extra rolls of duct tape from the supply shelf. Once we exit, we break left. Lok spins right, gives another salute, then scurries away.

"You sure bringing him in was a good idea?" Marco asks my sister as we jog down the hall. "Seems kind of impulsive."

Addy bursts out laughing. "I can't believe you said that."

When we reach the next fork in the tunnels, we see a stair-case up ahead. That must be the way to the surface between the theme park and the base. A minute later, we're up two flights of stairs and running into the equipment room where the other Bounders are gathered around Cole.

"All good?" he asks when we burst into the circle.

"Better," I say. "We recruited." I tell him about Lok and the other Tunnelers.

"Great. Here's the plan."

Cole's plan is fairly simple: take out the guards, then take out the bounding ships. No ships, no attack on the Youli planet. The execution, though, is going to be a challenge.

We split into teams led by me, Addy, Marco, Lucy, and Cole, since we're trained on the advanced glove skills. There are at least twenty guards lining the wall between the theme park border and the bounding deck, and there's sure to be more along the two flanks. When the first guard cries out or calls for help on her com link, our element of surprise will be gone, and we should expect full battle engagement from Earth Force troops. Of course, that's also when the other Bounders plan to join the battle, so hopefully things will bal-ance out. And if we're extra lucky, Bai and the lost aeronauts and Lok and his Tunneler buddies will show up to fight. If we can hold out long enough for the Resistance fleet to get here, we have a shot at blocking Earth Force's attack on the Youli home world.

"They'll eventually sound the alarm," Cole says. "When they do, we'll need a diversion, something that will confuse the officers who respond to the backup call. Marco, you up for that?"

"Of course, boss." He grins. "Diversions are my specialty."

"Each team will target a predetermined stretch of the wall," Cole continues. "Once the guards have been immobilized, the team leader will boost the members over the wall. Everyone trained to pilot a bounding ship will board and bound, ditching the ships back by the watering hole so they're sufficiently out of range for non-Bounders to locate them and launch the attack before Resistance backup arrives. Then we free-bound back to the base. Anyone not piloting will provide cover. The first bound will trigger the bounding sensors, so even if we make it past the guards without an alarm sounding, we know it's only a matter of time."

Sounds simple enough, but once the fire fight starts, it will be chaos.

"Everyone clear on the plan?" Cole asks, making sure to look each of us in the eye.

When all of us have nodded, Cole stands up straight. His face hardens with the focus and quiet dignity of a true leader.

Then he claps his hands. "Bounders, we fight for each other. We fight for our planet. We fight for the future. Now let's do this!"

The tall grass looks practically technicolor under the bright light of the planet's sun, and the strong metallic smell from the occludium mine is nearly overpowering. I crouch with my team in the field between the theme park fence and the wall of the base. "This is it," I tell them. "I freeze the guard, Jayne tapes him up, we move on to the next. The rest of you know your roles as lookout and assist." I give the go sign, and we dart forward from our hiding spot, keeping low along the sub wall so we're out of the guards' line of sight. A pair of eight-legged rodents scurry out of our way and dive into a burrow beneath the wall as we pass.

The first guard spots us seconds before we descend. She opens her mouth to scream, but I reach out with my right glove and freeze her vocal cords. She goes for her gun, but by then my left hand's raised, and I seize control of all her atoms. Jayne wraps the guard's wrists and ankles in duct tape, then slaps a strip across her mouth.

Randall gives me a thumbs-up, meaning our route is clear and we can move on to the next guard. I grab the first guard's gun and slip it into the waistband of my pants. You never know when an old-fashioned weapon may come in handy, although I hate the idea of using it.

I tap into my pod mates' mental communication circle. *First guard down.*

A few seconds later, Marco, Addy, and Cole all confirm. I cross my fingers that Lucy has similar luck, but I go ahead and wave my team on to the next post. When we're just about to take out our second guard, Lucy lets us know that her first is immobilized.

So far, so good. Each team has four guards to go before we reach the second stage.

Our next two guards are easy. I wave my team on.

We're nearly at our fourth guard when one of the younger Bounders on my team trips. He goes down hard, and a loud yelp escapes his mouth when he hits the ground.

No! We're busted.

My team flattens to the ground, partially hidden by the high grass. We military crawl toward the next guard.

"Who's there?" the guard calls.

I lift my head. The guard is coming our way—another meter and he'll definitely see us. In one swift movement, I shove back on my knees and flash my gloves. The guard freezes in place.

A voice calls from behind the wall. "Everything okay over there?"

She must have heard the frozen guard call out. Jayne looks at me with her eyebrows raised. What do we do?

Before I can come up with a plan, Hakim shouts, "Just some tourists."

I brace for the response, focusing my energy on keeping the guard on our side of the wall frozen in place. I can see from his eyes that he's furious and straining with all his might against my hold.

For a moment, the only sound are the cries of the orange kite bats flying to their roosts in the pomagranana grove. Then the guard behind the wall laughs. "Tell 'em to go back to the pool!"

I flash Hakim a thumbs-up. Jayne secures the guard with duct tape, and I wave us on.

The fifth guard down the wall is easy. Once we immobilize her, we wait for my pod mates to check in.

"Good thinking back there," I whisper to Hakim. "Blaming the tourists, I mean. Creative and totally believable."

Hakim smiles. "Thanks, Jasper."

The others report in. Their guards are down. We're only waiting on Lucy.

I cross my fingers and try not to hold my breath. The silence stretches as I will her to give the signal across our brain link.

Come on, Lucy. We're so close. You've got this.

The silence is pierced by the wail of an alarm shrieking across the base.

**I LIFT A FINGER TO MY LIPS. "HOLD POSITION,"**
I whisper to my team.

The alarm is so loud, it's hard to focus.

*Up and over! Now!* Cole orders across our brain link.

"Go!" I shout.

My team bursts into action. Jayne flashes her gloves at the top of the wall. I boost her over. Randall's next, then the rest of my teammates. I'm last to go. I fly to the top of the wall.

From this height, I can see the bounding deck and the base. Officers spill out from the main building. I try to count how many of them are Bounders when a flash of light zips by my head. They're firing on me!

I jump off the wall and dash for the closest bounding ship. Hakim is already halfway up the scaffolding. "Watch out! We're under attack!" I manipulate the atmospheric particles closes to Hakim to function as a shield. I'm not strong enough alone to build anything big, but hopefully it's enough to protect him while he boards the bounding ship.

A few seconds later, he disappears inside while the rest of my team ducks behind another ship. The scaffolding falls back from Hakim's ship, and the spider crawlers *tick-tick-tick* away. The air around the ship flickers, and the port opens. It's like a beacon to Earth Force. Before we know it, all of their guns are trained on us, and we're under massive fire.

"Take cover!" I shout to my team.

Where's Marco and the diversion? *Marco!*

*On it!* he shouts.

The onslaught starts to thin, which probably means another team has activated a ship.

Hakim's ship pushes into its port and—*bam!*—it's gone.

Without the ship to hide behind, my team is totally exposed. "Run!" I shout. I target the first guard I see and toss him to the ground. I bolt to the right, where our team is working on the next bounding ship.

*Here I come!* Marco hollers as I shield a Resistance bounder climbing into the next ship.

A horn sounds. I scan the base for the source, but everything is blocked by bounding ships.

In our brain connection, Marco cackles. Instead of sparkles like Mira, his laughter sounds like popcorn. Through a gap up ahead, I spy an egg car weaving through the ships. Earth Force officers dive out of the way.

I laugh out loud. We saw the egg cars during our first trip to the Paleo Planet. The strange egg-shaped vehicles are used to haul occludium from the mines. An egg car's driver's compartment is built for a Tunneler—in other words, small. Marco's knees must be up to his armpits in that thing. He's a total goof! A total *genius* goof!

"Is that Marco?" Hakim asks beside me.

Hakim's already returned from the bound? "Yeah! And hey! You made it to the watering hole?"

"There and back. Two other ships landed before I returned. We're doing it, man!"

The port opens on our second ship. When it bounds away, we dash for the next one.

Shots rain all around us as we bolt across the deck. Jayne dives for cover behind the next bounding ship. Behind her, one of the Resistance Bounders jerks back and falls to the ground. I skid to a halt and throw up a shield. Shots batter the thin barrier as I kneel by the fallen Bounder. My shield starts to warp. I won't be able to hold it for long.

"Run, Jasper!" someone shouts.

I scan for the voice. Bounders from Earth Force surround a group of guards, engaging them in a fire fight. I check the pulse of the young Bounder on the deck. It's weak and fading, but there's nothing I can do. I can't drag her off the deck and hold the shield at the same time. I don't want to leave her, but the others are counting on me.

Hakim sprints from behind the bounding ship to my side. "You keep the shots away, and I'll pull. Deal?"

Nodding gratefully, I extend the shield to cover the three of us. Hakim loops his arms under the fallen Bounder's shoulders and starts to pull.

He manages to drag her behind the ship, but it doesn't buy us much cover. Earth Force officers seem to pour out from everywhere.

Even with the extra Bounders, we don't have the numbers. How many Bounders will die today? But if we fail, it's not just Bounders who will die—it's *everyone*.

"Cover me!" Jayne shouts, waving her arm at the closest ship.

We have to keep fighting. I boost Jayne to the top of the ship, then fly to her side and hold the shield.

"You know how to pilot these?" I ask her.

"I've done it once."

"Then get down. You're not trained!"

"Look around, Jasper! We need more pilots."

Jayne's right, even though I hate to admit it. I raise my left hand as a shield and use my right to open the hatch. She disappears inside. I hope she knows what she's doing. Before I jump down, I scan the base.

Our side of the bounding deck is clearing out, but nearly twice as many ships are left on the other half. And that's where Earth Force is targeting their attack.

Hakim bounds back to the deck from taking a second ship. I hop down beside him. "I've got to help out on the other side," I tell him. "You're in charge, okay?"

"Me?" he asks. When I raise my eyebrows, he nods. "Absolutely. I've got it covered."

I push off with my gloves and fly to the back wall. I skim along the rear of the deck and come in from the opposite side.

An Earth Force officer corners me. I spin in his direction and knock him to his knees.

"B-wad!" he shouts. I haven't heard that word in a long time.

I reach out with my gloves and lift him into the air. "You don't get to call me that!" I force my neural power into my fingertips and hurl him over the fence.

Up ahead, Addy and Cole are pinned behind two bounding ships. At least a dozen Earth Force officers close in. My sister grabs hold of one of the guards and spins him around.

The guard keeps firing, accidentally hitting two of his own. More Earth Force officers race from the compound and join the fight. I bolt to Cole's side.

*Where's Lucy?* I ask him.

*I don't know. She never checked in after the alarms sounded. Jasper, we're outgunned here. We've been holding them off, but they keep coming.*

*Pool our power.*

I feed my energy into Cole's neural stream. He reaches out with his gloves and grabs two guards at once. He flings them across the bounding deck. They land in a heap on the other side.

Still, Cole's right: there's just too many of them. We keep them from advancing on our side, but they're closing in on Addy. I switch my boost to help my sister, but I might be too late.

*Charge!* Marco's voice breaks into my brain. His egg car plows into the crowd, scattering the officers. Next thing I know, Earth Force is under attack by . . . flying pomagrananas?

Barks and growls fill the air as Lok shakes his arm and leads a small army of Tunnelers over the wall. They're armed with rocks and tools and, yes, spiky purple fruit. The Earth Force officers scatter, facing attack from every direction. Before they can regroup, Tunnelers from the base rush out and join their friends on the offensive.

*Got them on the run!* Marco shouts as the Earth Force officers retreat for the base.

We chase after them, shielding shots as we go. In my peripheral vision, I see Bai and the lost aeronauts dropping down from the wall at the back of the deck. I leave Marco, Cole, and Addy to tackle the guards and race to the back.

"What can we do, kid?" Bai asks when I reach her.

"You guys still know how to fly these things?" I ask.

"Are you kidding? We're the experts, remember?"

"Good. Split up, grab a ship, and bound it to the watering hole beyond the theme park. When you're done, head back and do it again."

Bai turns to instruct the aeronauts. She's the last person I need to hand hold through a battle. I shout my thanks and run to the other side of the deck, hoping to check on my team.

By the time I get there, even more bounding ships have disappeared. We must have removed 80 percent of the fleet. Earth Force is done for!

Lucy's voice reaches our circle in a panic. *Help!*

*Finally! Where are you?* Cole asks.

*In the center. Come quick. Admiral Eames is about to board one of the bounding ships.*

I race for the middle of the deck, meeting up with Cole and Addy on the way. Marco speeds by us in his egg car. Shots ricochet off the vehicle. Since it's made for hauling occludium, the thing is built like a tank!

*We have to stop the admiral!* I tell my pod mates. *Even if it's only one ship, if she reaches the Youli home world and drops those warheads, Earth is done for!*

Admiral Eames must know her original plan is ruined. So what on earth is she doing? Would she really attack the Youli with only one ship? That's a suicide mission! But it could still set off a chain reaction that would lead to the Youli destroying Earth.

An envoy of guards surrounds the ship and forms a human barrier all the way to the scaffolding of the bounding ship. A second group of guards escorts the admiral to the ship, firing at anything in their way.

Bounders target the guards, but they're under direct fire. If they don't hold their cover, they're dead.

*Over here!* Cole waves us to the side where we meet up with Lucy.

"We have to hold that ship!" he shouts when we reach him. "If the admiral bounds, nothing we did today matters!"

"What if we're not strong enough?" Lucy asks.

"Pool our power, like Mira taught us," I say. "We can do this! It's all about the pod!"

"Get in position!" Cole shouts. "Hold that ship!"

We spread out around the bounding ship and take cover. I duck behind a spider crawler midway between Addy and Cole and reach out with my gloves. By the time we're all in place, Admiral Eames is already inside the ship.

I seize hold of the connection and focus all my power at

the ship. At first, it's easy, but then something shifts. Someone inside must have activated the occludium membrane. The slippery outer coating vibrates, and my grip on the ship slips.

*Hold it!* Cole shouts.

I shake my head and focus. Jayne and Hakim slide in next to me. "Keep it up, Jasper," she says. "We'll hold off the guards." They spread out, trying to draw fire away from me.

A quick glance to my right reveals that more guards have joined the fight for Earth Force. Where do they keep coming from?

My distraction costs me. My gloves start to slip.

*Pay attention!* Addy yells.

The air around the ship shimmers. The pilot has activated the port. Another misstep, and that ship will bound across the galaxy.

She can't possibly be planning to fight the Youli. It makes no sense, not that it ever really did. Maybe she's just trying to escape, though it's not like Eames to admit defeat or run away from a fight. What if she really does intend to attack? Doesn't she see she'd be dooming Earth?

We can't risk letting her bound. I bite down on my lip and force all my focus into my gloves. Must. Hold. Ship.

Earth Force changes its tactics. They target the Bounders covering me and my pod mates. The admiral must have figured out we're the ones preventing the bound.

Other Bounders join the fight, but Earth Force is too strong. They're focusing all their fire power on the five of us. We can't keep this up much longer.

My hands shake. My grip is slipping.

*Just . . . keep . . . holding,* Cole says. His words come slow and broken up.

*What's the plan, Wiki?* Marco asks. *We can't hold her forever.*

*The Resistance will be here any second,* Addy says.

Well, they'd better get here soon. Cold sweat drips down my face. I can no longer feel my fingers. All I can do is focus on the ship and my neural connection.

"You've got this, Jasper!" Jayne shouts at my side.

Hakim hollers, "Over here!"

"What's happening?" I whisper through gritted teeth.

"The Resistance!" Jayne cries.

Tunnelers dressed in colorful tunics run past me to join the fight. A renewed energy surges through our ranks. The guards defend the Gulagan advance, giving us a break from the constant attack.

The hatch to the bounding ship flips open. Did we do it? Does Earth Force see they're outnumbered? Is Admiral Eames going to wave a white flag and give up?

*Keep holding that ship, no matter what!* Cole shouts. *It's still bound-ready!*

I summon up my remaining strength and focus every last

ounce on holding the ship. My gaze is locked on the open hatch.

Time slows. It's just me and my gloves and my pod mates in our connected neural circle. If we can just hold on a minute longer . . . gloves slipping . . . mind fading . . .

An Earth Force officer sticks her head out of the hatch. . . . Oh my God . . . I'm pretty sure . . . that's Admiral Eames!

The admiral looks down at the battle waging beneath her. She raises her gun. I'm sure she's about to drop it to the deck floor, declaring surrender.

Instead, she lifts the gun and levels it at my sister.

*Addy, move!* I shout.

*Hold the ship!* Cole shouts.

I know Addy. She won't move. She won't raise a shield against the admiral. There's no way she's going to drop her hold on the bounding ship.

"No!" I shout, hoping to draw the admiral's attention to me. I almost shift my gloves to shield my sister, but I don't think I have the energy to do it in time. And I know if I do, we'll lose our hold on the ship. My pod mates can't do it without me. And too much is at stake. The fate of our planet could be decided in the next few seconds.

Tears leak from the corners of my eyes, mingling with sweat as they slip down my cheeks. Please don't shoot. *Please!*

There's a hand on my back. The guard's gun I swiped earlier is pulled from my waistband.

Denver Reddy steps to my side, gun in hand. He lifts his arm and aims at the admiral.

"Cora, stop!"

Once the words leave his mouth, everything seems to freeze. The guards shift their aim to Denver, the Bounders hold their fire, time stands still.

Admiral Eames jerks her head in Denver's direction, but her target on Addy doesn't waver. "Get out of here, Captain Reddy!" she shouts. "You'll be caught in the cross fire."

"No one else needs to die today, Cora."

She glances at Denver again, but only for a moment. "You are so wrong, Denver. The devastation has just begun."

He takes a step forward, closer to the bounding ship. "You're not thinking straight, Cora. Look around. You've lost."

"Back off!" she shouts. "I've been waiting for this day since the Incident. The Youli destroyed my life, and I'm not about to stand down!"

"Cora! It's over! I'm *here*!" He takes a few more steps toward the admiral. "You don't need to avenge me." He carves his way through the guards, heading for the ship's scaffolding. "I'm back now, Cora. We can pick up where we left off."

Admiral Eames laughs, high-pitched and vicious. "How could we? I've aged fifteen years."

"That doesn't matter to me!"

"It matters to *me*!"

"Please, Cora, we're better than this. At least I know we can be. I don't want revenge!"

For the tiniest of seconds, the admiral closes her eyes. A flurry of thoughts runs through my head. Maybe I should drop my hold on the ship, grab her atoms, and fling her off the—

But before I decide on anything, her eyes flash open.

"I do," she says. Then she fires.

I drop my hold on the ship and throw a weak shield around my sister.

I'm too late.

Addy crumples to the ground.

A second shot rings out, and Admiral Eames tumbles off the top of the bounding ship.

# 28

**I DASH ACROSS THE BOUNDING DECK TO**
Addy. Marco reaches her before me. She's covered in blood
and shockingly pale, but she's conscious.

"Are you okay?" I ask. "Where were you hit?"

"My shoulder," she says through gritted teeth. "Get back
out there!"

"I'm not leaving you!"

Marco pulls my sister onto his lap and props her up. The way
he holds her is exactly the way my dad held my mom when
she was wounded at the Americana East rally. I shake off the
memory and strip off my sweatshirt. I press the cloth against her
shoulder, hoping it will stop the bleeding until we can get help.

I place my fingers against her neck. Her skin is cold and clammy, but her pulse is strong. That has to be a good sign.

"Ace!" Marco snaps his fingers in front of my face. "Check it out!"

I glance over my shoulder. Earth Force officers are lining up in front of the bounding ship we were just holding. Before joining the line, they lay down their weapons on the tarmac. A pair of Bounders guard the stockpile. Ridders and Cole stand in front shouting orders.

I spin back to my sister.

"Go!" she says.

"You sure you're okay?"

"I've got it under control, J-Bird," Marco says.

After pushing to my feet and wiping Addy's blood off my hands, I jog over to Cole.

"How is Addy?" he asks.

"She'll make it. What's going on?"

"It's over, Jasper," Ridders says.

Cole nods. "I've asked the Bounders to stand down."

I don't understand. "'Over' as in . . . ?"

"Admiral Eames is dead," Ridders says. "I've taken control of Earth Force and called an immediate cease-fire."

"And the Youli attack?" I ask.

"We stopped it, Jasper," Cole says.

"You're sure?" If the admiral's guards figured out where we stashed the bounding ships, they could still launch.

"Completely," Cole says. "Even if there are Eames loyalists still out there, we've raised the shield. No one's bounding off this planet."

"The threat died with the admiral," Ridders says. "Most Earth Force soldiers were just following orders—not that that's a full excuse, but plenty of them didn't even know what the admiral's plans were. They definitely didn't know what was at stake."

I look at Cole, then back to Ridders. "And you do?" How does Ridders know that the Youli would have destroyed Earth if Eames attacked their home world?

"Once we left for the Paleo Planet," Cole says, "word traveled fast."

Just then, I spot Neeka and Lucy chatting excitedly across the deck. Neeka knew our plans; of course the news spread fast.

I still don't understand how everything came together. "How'd you get here?" I ask Ridders.

"Once we found out what was happening, Denver contacted Bai. Then we filled Waters and Barrick in, and the four of us left the Summit on an Earth Force shuttle outside the bound detection range and transferred to Bai's bounding ship. A minute later, we were here on the Paleo Planet."

Bai must have taken one of the ships from here and

bounded it off the planet to pick up Denver. I don't know if I'm mad at her for not telling me or just impressed at her resourcefulness. Either way, it worked out.

I scan the deck. There are barely any ships left. We actually managed to clear most of them off the deck. The Bounders are by the wall, standing guard over the rest of the Earth Force officers. Over by the pomagranana grove, members of the Resistance talk with the Tunnelers stationed on the Paleo Planet. I can't be sure, but it looks like Grok is introducing Lok to Barrick and Waters.

Not all the sights on the deck are so positive. There are bodies strewn about, some Bounders, some Tunnelers, some Earth Force. Medics from the base check for vitals and move on, leaving the dead to be dealt with later. One of the twins from Addy's pod, I'm not sure if it's Orla or Aela, sobs over the broken body of her sister.

Next to the bounding ship my pod held with our pooled power, Denver sits on the ground, the admiral's body cradled in his lap. He strokes her hair and stares at her face. Tears fall from his eyes, and his shoulders heave. Even from here, I can hear him weeping.

"You okay?" Jayne touches my arm. I hadn't heard her approach.

I shake my gaze away from Denver and shrug. "Was it Denver who shot the admiral?"

Jayne nods, then slips her hand into mine. "Come with me, Jasper. Marco and the medics just brought Addy inside. I'll show you where they took her."

I let Jayne steer me away from the deck. My feet drag. I'm exhausted, and the adrenaline that's fueled me the last few hours is starting to fade. Still, I can't believe we did it. We stopped the attack on the Youli home world. I guess that means we saved our planet.

I don't remember—I'll never remember—but apparently Mira and I staked our own future on the hope of today. I guess it was worth it.

Any future that includes Earth is worth it.

Even if it has to be a future without Mira.

The rest of the day passed in a blur. The fighting was over, but there was a ton to do. Everyone had to be accounted for. All of the bounding ships had to be piloted back to the base. The resort guests needed to be evacuated. Ridders arranged to have the tourists shuttled back to Earth aboard their cruise ships, citing "safety concerns." Seeing as there was a battle waging on the other side of the wall yesterday, that isn't too far from the truth (although the concerns were a bit delayed since the battle was over). The first batch of guests left last night, and their rooms at the resort were reassigned to

Resistance fighters and anyone else who joined the battle and needed a place to sleep.

To say it was strange to wake up to Florine Statton's automated hotel voice in a room decorated like the Paleo Planet cruise ship complete with paw prints and a sabre cat bedspread after all that went down yesterday would be a colossal understatement.

Today the rest of the tourists are being shuttled off the planet. Since the medical facility at the Earth Force base is way beyond capacity with those wounded in battle, the staff doctors decided that the best way to deliver care would be to transport stable patients back to Earth aboard the second cruise ship leaving later this morning.

Addy is slated to be on board, and Jayne is going with her. She volunteered to help out the medics during the flight.

"I haven't seen my family in a long time," Jayne tells me as they prepare the patients for the trip to Earth. "I'm overdue for a visit."

I'm tempted to go along, too—I would love to be there when Mom and Dad finally reunite with Addy—but my work here isn't done. "What will you do next?" The question is vague, but Jayne knows what I'm asking. Now that there won't be a Resistance to support as an inside operative, Jayne's basically out of a job.

She shakes her head with a smile. "I don't know for sure. Maybe go back to school? Be a kid for a while? I never really got the chance."

We burst out laughing because we both know she'll never decide just to "be a kid."

Her smile softens. "Look me up, Jasper, the next time you're on Earth."

"Sure," I say, and I actually mean it. I'll never forget Jayne's betrayal back on the Lost Heroes Homecoming Tour, but I've forgiven her. I probably would have made the same choices in her shoes, particularly if I knew what was at stake.

"Is Addy over there?" I ask, pointing at the room in the back where the medics are setting up cots and IVs for transport.

She nods, and I head in that direction. Addy's in the corner making friends with some older Earth Force soldiers who were injured in the battle. Her cheeks are pink, which is a welcome sight after how ghostly pale she was yesterday.

"Hey," I say. "Ready to go?"

She thinks about it for a second. "Yeah, I am. It's going to be weird to be out of the action, but it's not like I'd be much help right now anyhow."

"Hopefully we're done with action for a while. How are you feeling?"

"I've been better, but I can't really complain. There are a lot of people here who have it much worse."

"Do Mom and Dad know you're coming?" I'm sure my parents are flipping out if they know my sister's on her way home. She hasn't been to Earth since my fake funeral more than a year ago. Plus, my parents thought Addy was dead, too, for most of that year.

"Not yet. I'm going to surprise them."

"Have you thought about what you'll do once your shoulder heals?"

She shrugs. "I was just shot yesterday, Jasper." Then she grins. "But I was thinking I might try to reach out to old connections in the protest movement, help do some grassroots organizing to get support for the new government, and start a solid campaign to make sure the government actually represents the planet's people—*all* the planet's people, including us Bounders. Got to keep everyone in check, you know?"

Of course she has it all planned out. It's Addy, after all. "What about Marco?"

"What about him?"

"I just thought—"

Addy cuts me off with a laugh. "He'll be fine on his own. We have our whole lives in front of us. If Marco and I are meant to be together, we will be. And if not, we'll always be friends. We've been through too much together not to be."

"I thought he would be here."

"He just left. He had to get to a meeting, so we said our good-byes early."

Oops. I think I'm supposed to be at that meeting, too, along with former Earth Force and Resistance leaders. We need to talk about what's next for Earth. At least for now, I'm part of those discussions.

"Love you, Ads." I give her an air hug so I don't hurt her shoulder. "Say hi to Mom and Dad."

She grabs me with her good arm and pulls me in close. "Take care of yourself, J. You deserve a break after saving the world."

By the time I make it to the meeting in the officers' briefing room at the base, they're halfway through the agenda. I slide into an open seat next to Lucy.

"Guess what happened!" she says to me. In classic Lucy fashion, she doesn't actually wait for me to guess before plowing forward. "You know how we recorded the message? Well, they blasted it over the webs just as we planned. And apparently, it's been running on a loop ever since. Just me and our message on repeat. Of course, it's all anyone on Earth can talk about, or so I've been told. So anyways, I got a call from my agent, and the most amazing thing has happened! They want to give me my own show! It's going to be called *In Your Face with Lucy Dugan*! I can set the format myself, but we're thinking about a show that really digs into the truth about things. I can get started as soon as we're back. Can you believe it? Isn't that incredible?" She grabs both my hands and squeezes.

I squeeze back. "That's amazing, Lucy."

Ridders clears his throat. Apparently, the rest of the room is waiting for us to pay attention. At least this time I can blame my distraction on Lucy.

"As I was saying," Ridders continues, "that brings us to the IGC. I contacted the Council leadership late yesterday and told them what happened. They agreed we could return to the Summit and finalize the terms for our entry into the IGC. Let's discuss the steps we'll need to take to bring Earth into compliance and what we should present at the Summit."

"Shouldn't we wait for Denver?" Waters asks.

"He's out," Bai says.

"What do you mean?" I ask.

"Denver's not going back to the IGC," Cole explains.

"Of course he is," Waters says. "He's part of the existing delegation."

Bai slaps the table. "Give the guy some space!"

"Well, then, we need to appoint—" Waters starts.

"You're not going, either," Marco says.

Waters leans forward. "Are you talking to me, Romero?"

"I sure am, *Waters*. You've been saying that it's time for a new generation of leaders ever since I joined the Resistance. The time is now. And your time is up."

"There's no need to get ahead of ourselves," Waters says. "There'll be time enough to work those things out after the IGC."

"It's already decided, Mr. Waters," Cole says. "You'll be returning to Earth tomorrow. I've instructed the space station to issue an immediate release for Dr. Gedney as well. He'll meet you at your labs."

"You all talked about this before the meeting?"

I'm wondering the same thing. Somehow I missed the memo on this, although I wouldn't say I disagree.

"It makes sense, Mr. Waters," Lucy says. "You and Gedney have to get to work developing alternative power sources now that we need to phase out our reliance on occludium."

"But the Resistance needs representation," Waters says.

"Not exactly," Neeka says through her voice box. "The Resistance is being disbanded since control of Gulaga is being returned to the Gulagans."

Waters looks at Barrick, disbelief painted on his face.

"Sorry, friend," Barrick barks. "It's nothing personal, but we don't want Earthlings involved in our affairs anymore." He nods at Neeka, and she nods back in solidarity. Barrick is heading up the new, independent Gulagan government. I heard earlier today that he asked Neeka to be his number two. I never would have guessed it when I first met her, but Neeka's really starting to follow in her father's footsteps. Commander Krag would be very proud.

Waters shakes his head, at a loss for words, maybe for the first time since I met him. I wouldn't say I'm proud that I'm enjoying this, but I can't stop a smile from sneaking across my lips. Denying Waters the chance to witness what he's been working for his whole life—Earth's entry into the IGC—somehow seems like the right kind of justice after all the bad decisions he made on his path to get here. If there's one thing I've learned from him, it's that the way you conduct yourself on the journey is as important as how you act once you reach the destination.

"You should go, Jon," Ridders says. "The other matters we're going to discuss don't involve you."

Waters nods at Bai. "Why does she get to stay?"

Bai stands and crosses her muscled arms against her chest. "Because I'm taking Denver's place at the IGC. Now get out of here before you say something you'll regret. You sound more like a child than the young people in this room."

Waters pushes back from the table and grabs his tablet. He scans the room with a look I know well, a look that says you're making a mistake. A few years ago, that look would probably have been enough to make me change my mind. Not anymore. Finally, Waters marches out, slamming the door behind him.

"That was unexpected," I whisper to Lucy.

"We would have told you," she says, "but we knew you were busy with Addy."

Although I think booting Waters was the right call, Lucy knows my opinion doesn't really matter. I've agreed to head back to the IGC, but then I'm out. I already told my pod mates that I need a break. I still haven't gotten a chance to process losing a year of my life in the rift, and now I have to get my head around the fact that I left another life behind for the chance to save Earth, even though I have no memory of it. And then there's Mira. I haven't even let myself think about her yet. Not really.

So I'm going to leave the picking-up-the-pieces part of this process to the other people in this room. I know them. I trust them. Our planet is lucky to have them paving the way.

And as for me? It's time to pave my own way.

# 29

I FIND DENVER ON TOP OF THE FAKE
mountain in the theme park after a couple of Tunnelers told
me they saw an Earthling trying to scale the rocks. "How'd
you get up here?"

"I climbed." His words sound rough, like he's losing his
voice. "Not everyone needs fancy gloves like you to get
around."

I sit down next to him. In the distance, a herd of mammoths approaches the watering hole. "You okay?"

He chokes out a harsh laugh. "No, kid, I'm definitely not
okay."

"I'm sorry . . . about the admiral, I mean."

Denver shakes his head. "I still can't believe that she's dead. That I killed her. How could this happen? I *loved* her." He takes a deep breath and swallows hard. "How did I not see this coming, kid? There must have been a way I could have stopped all this."

I remember what he said to me on the passenger craft when we brought Regis's body back to Earth. "You're not a god."

"No, I'm definitely not. I'm a man. An *old* man, even if I don't look it."

We're quiet for a while, watching the watering hole. Where are the humanoids who live here? What will happen to them once Earth packs up and leaves? Will the legends of our presence mold the development of their species? Will my ancestors someday welcome them to the Intragalactic Council?

"What's next?" I eventually ask.

He shrugs. "I was thinking of maybe traveling after this. Buying an old junker ship, heading to Nos Redna Space Port, and seeing where the stars lead me next. I could use a companion. You up for it?"

Traveling with Denver could be fun, but I'm not ready to decide anything yet. "Maybe. I have to get through the IGC first."

"That's fine, kid. I can wait."

"I'll let you know soon." Staring across the Paleo Planet, I wonder if I'll ever be back. It truly is a beautiful place. "I've got to go."

Denver nods. "See ya, kid."

I stand and pull on my gloves, preparing to build a port.

"Hey, Jasper, before you go, there's something I need to say." He takes a deep breath and swallows hard. "You're hoping to see Mira at the Summit, aren't you?"

I nod. There's no reason not to be honest with Denver.

"Make sure to tell her how you feel, kid. You never know when it might be too late."

After all the chaos of the last few days, I'm expecting there to be tons of drama at the Summit. Instead, everything goes smoothly. Representing your planet is a lot easier when members of your delegation actually share the same goals.

Earth is admitted as a full member of the Intragalactic Council. There's a lot we need to do to comply with the Intragalactic Treaty—like stop making aliens from other planets work for us and taking their occludium—but the IGC is giving us some time to make the changes. Plus, I think we *should* make the changes. It's not fair to take advantage of other planets and their people. We've also got to stop attacking people from other planets, which is basically a no-brainer. Since it means aliens can't attack us, either, it's really a win-win.

Now that Earth is a full galactic citizen, there are lots of perks, too. We can make cultural and technological exchanges with other member planets. I kind of wish Gedney had been with us to hear about the tech stuff. He would have flipped. Cole promised to fill him in by vid conference after the Summit. We get to trade and pool resources. Ridders said that will help us phase out our reliance on occludium while we're developing new power sources. And, of course, we'll get to send delegations to future Summits. I wouldn't mind being an IGC delegate someday (after a very long vacation).

While we've been at the Summit, we've also had a chance to talk about our planet's leadership. Our delegation agreed ahead of time that Earth Force will be disbanded, and a new planetary government and security organization will be created to replace it. Earth's people will need a voice in that process, but for now, the transfer of power will be managed by a three-person panel: Ridders, Cole, and Bai Liu. Bai was kind of a surprise, but now that I've got my head around it, I think it's a perfect choice.

We also agreed that Bounders need an ongoing, independent representative in our planetary government, and Marco volunteered for the job. I never thought I'd see him in a such a leadership role, but part of being a leader is passion and creativity, and Marco has more of that than anyone I know. He has a ton of work ahead of him. Bounders who served in Earth Force need help transitioning into new positions. Younger Bounders need support and education from people who understand them. The future of the Bounder

Baby Breeding Program has to be figured out. There aren't easy answers, but our delegation agreed unanimously that increasing the brain diversity of our planet is extremely important. If there's one thing we learned after bringing Earth to the brink of destruction, it's that in our differences lie our strengths.

Every member of our pod brought unique strengths to our circle. Despite our differences, we came together. We were so much stronger together than we ever were alone. If Mira hadn't taught us to work together and pool our power, we never could have saved Earth.

Mira. I can barely even think about her without getting choked up. The whole reason I agreed to come back to the IGC rather than pulling a Denver was so that I could see Mira.

But she's not here.

So I've kept to the sidelines. I've tried to pay attention during our delegation strategy sessions, but I can't keep my mind from drifting back to the rift and listening to Mira tell me how we mapped out our plan to save Earth.

Even now, during the Intragalactic Council Summit closing ceremony, as we stand on our dais as the united delegation of Planet Earth, I can't keep my thoughts on anything but Mira.

As our dais retracts to the side of the sphere for the final time, Wind Chimes's voice rings out, both in my mind and through the translator. "Earth delegation, may I have a word?"

The Youli soars across the sphere on a solo dais, coming to a hover in front of us. "Welcome to the Intragalactic Council. We are happy to put our years of conflict behind us and welcome your planet as peers."

Bai inclines her head. "We appreciate the Council's patience as we found our way."

"As I'm sure you know," Wind Chimes continues, "we owe a great deal to your young ones. Without them, this day would not be. Our people celebrate with song after the Summit. We'd like to bring your young ones back to our planet, just for the night, so that they may join our celebration."

My heart leaps in my chest. Will I see Mira there? "Of course we'll come!"

Ridders shoots me a nasty look. Guess I spoke a bit out of turn there, but I don't care. Ridders exchanges glances with Cole and Bai. When they both nod, he turns back to Wind Chimes. "Thank you. We accept your hospitality."

Later that day, Cole, Lucy, Marco, and I say farewell to the rest of the Earth delegation and cross the walkway to the Youli vessel. It's kind of eerie. Many of the docks are now empty since the Summit has ended and delegations are departing for their own planets. We board the Youli ship and activate the VR, transforming the orange wall into a replica of an Earth passenger craft. It's strange that Addy's not with us this time, but I got a vid message from her and my parents this morning. It was so great to see them all on-screen together, and Addy says her shoulder is already feeling much better.

The trip to the Youli home world passes quickly. When the Youli ship descends through the clouds to the tiered dock, I hold my breath. What if Mira isn't here? Luckily, I don't have to worry long, because as soon as we clear the clouds, I spot her.

I'm practically bursting by the time the ship's ramp is lowered. I leap off and race across the deck. Mira's off her feet, gliding toward me. We collide in a hug.

*I thought I'd never see you again,* I say, pulling her even tighter.

Mira fills my mind with sparkles.

"Don't let him take all the love, sweetie," Lucy says, breaking us apart and wrapping her arms around Mira.

When everyone has hugged hello, we stand in a circle, hand in hand, the five of us.

"We did it!" I say.

*You did it,* Mira says.

"Technically, *you* did it, Mira," Cole says. "If you hadn't trained us on the gloves, we never would have stopped the admiral."

"And don't forget the whole time-travel thing," Marco

says, nodding at Mira and me. "We really should say that *they* did it."

"Let's stick with *we* did it," Lucy says. "That has the best ring to it. Don't you think?"

*Definitely.* I float the words into our mental circle. *It's all about the pod.*

Thank goodness we can all communicate brain-to-brain. I'm barely holding it together. If I tried to use my vocal cords, I'm sure I would wind up bawling. I'm so overwhelmed that it's actually over, that my pod is safe and together again, that Mira's long fingers are securely resting in my palm.

*You're just in time for Union Song,* Mira tells us. She smiles and winks, and the next thing we know, we're bounding.

The song is in full swing when we arrive. Crystals twinkle and vines sway in time to the music as Mira leads us directly to the Travelers' chamber. She bows to the Youli standing guard, and they swing back the ornate golden doors.

The circular room is just as majestic as I remembered. The rich tapestries hold the music within the domed walls, and even the air seems to resonate with song.

*Welcome, young ones.* Wind Chimes's voice reaches us from across the room. *Find a seat.* After the words fill our minds, the Youli's voice rises in harmony.

I sink onto an empty jade cushion and close my eyes. My heartbeat slowly syncs with the tempo. Breathing in lavender and cinnamon, I add my voice to the song.

As I slip into the collective consciousness, I sense Mira. I feel her voice blending with mine. Our souls touch, and our melodies weave together as one.

The music goes on forever, but still it's over too soon. When the last note fades, I feel empty, lost, and utterly exhausted. I don't even want to know what comes next.

When I finally open my eyes, the small Youli who spoke to us the first time we entered this chamber is standing before me.

*Welcome back, Jasper Adams. There is much to celebrate. You have kept your promise and saved your planet. The preservation of one contributes to the diversity of all. And in diversity lies the true wealth of the universe. Tonight we honor you and your friends with our song.*

The gears in my mind shift as I force myself to focus. I've been here before, to the Travelers' chamber, and not just in the last days with my pod mates. This must be where Mira and I pled our case and begged for our planet. The Youli in this room gave us that chance.

*Thank you,* I say to all of them. *Thank you for believing in us.*

My mind fills with refracting light and echoes of the song we just shared. It must be the Youli's way of collectively acknowledging us. I bow my head.

A moment passes, and then the Travelers rise. One by one,

they exit the chamber until only Wind Chimes, Mira, and the rest of my pod mates are left.

*We've prepared a shuttle to take you to the pin sphere,* Wind Chimes tells us. *From there, you'll connect to your bounding base.*

"Do we have to go so soon?" Lucy asks.

"We've hardly had a chance to talk," Cole says. "I have so many questions."

*The Travelers have played their role. We must retire until we are needed again.*

A thick knot forms in my throat. Do I really have to say good-bye to Mira? Already? I grab her hand. *Before we go, can we have a few minutes alone?*

Something passes between Mira and Wind Chimes, then she reaches for my mind. *Yes, come.* She tugs my hand and pulls me toward the golden doors.

"Wait!" Cole says, tailing after us. "Can I just ask a few questions about time travel and the rift?"

Lucy grabs Cole by the shoulders and steers him back. "I'm sure our Youli friend would be happy to answer your questions."

"But—"

"Shut up, Wiki," Marco says, waving Mira and me out of the chamber.

When the doors close behind us, Mira turns to me and

smiles. With a twist of her mind, we bound, and the next thing I know we're in the VR pod room.

*Now I understand why you made this,* I say as we sit cross-legged on the green grass carpet. If I had to live on the Youli planet forever, I'd want to have a place that reminded me of home, too.

*Why* we *made it.* Mira sends me a memory of us together in this room, a memory we made in the abandoned timeline.

The knot in my throat tightens. *You know I don't remember that.*

She closes her eyes and fills the room with music and twinkling stars, just like she did in our real pod room at the end of our first tour of duty.

At least we share some memories that I actually remember.

I take a deep breath and try to freeze this moment in my mind. Make a new memory.

*Do I really have to go?* I ask.

She doesn't answer with words, but I can tell from the way her mind feels that the answer is yes.

"Why? I thought I was a time traveler, too. Doesn't that count for something?"

*You're technically not a time traveler. We intercepted you in the original timeline.*

"I can't really get my head around that."

Her mouth crooks into a sad smile. *I couldn't either at first, but I've had a long time to think about it.*

I lift her hands and lay her long fingers across my palms. Will I ever see these fingers stroke the keys of a piano again? I remember the first time I heard Mira play. That moment changed me. My impression of her had been so limited, and then it expanded beyond limits in the space of a second. For the first time, the assumptions I'd made about someone weren't just challenged, they were shattered.

"So are you really not going to age?"

She shrugs.

In my mind, we're in the future, and Mira hasn't aged a day. She looks like an angel, and I'm old and stooped like Gedney.

Our connection sparks with her silent giggles. *You'll never look like Gedney!*

*Hey! Stop reading my mind!*

She builds on the image I conjured, giving me gray hair and sprouty eyebrows.

I laugh out loud.

She throws her head back, shooting sparkles across my mind.

My heart is full. I wish we could stay like this forever, but I'm sure our time together is coming to an end. Any minute, Wind Chimes will show up and take me away.

**MONICA TESLER**

"Will I ever see you again?"

She pulls her hands back and curls her fingers. *I'm not sure. I'll try to bend the rules.*

That's not much, but it's enough for hope, and hope can sustain you through some pretty dark times. At some point, future Jasper—or maybe it was past Jasper? This time-travel stuff is impossible to keep straight—anyway, that other me knew this day would come. It was the only way to save Earth. One of us had to stay back, and one of us had to travel through time. We made a choice. I know in my heart it was the right one. But when I'm face-to-face with the fact that Mira has to live here as a Traveler, never getting to see her friends and family again, while I get to return to my life on Earth, it doesn't seem fair.

"Your sacrifice saved all of us."

She stares at me with her bottomless brown eyes. *It was your sacrifice, too, Jasper.*

I shake my head. *I don't know. Maybe I shouldn't have been the one to stay back.*

She grabs my knees. *You're the glue. It had to be you. It's always been you.*

Those were her words in the rift. They're seared into my memory, just like so many other moments with Mira. Our duet in the sensory gym. The night on the Gulagan Tundra. Her palm on the cell glass when we paid a visit to the alien prisoner. I raise my hand.

She presses her palm against mine and blinks a tear from her eye. *It's time to go.*

"Are you sure I can't stay?"

*No more talking.*

Okay, brain-talk. *Are you sure I can't stay?*

She looks at me with a shy smile. *No, really, stop talking.* Then she leans forward and presses her lips to mine.

My heart flutters like a kite bat in my chest. *Oh.*

She laughs, dousing me in sparkles. And for the next few minutes, I really believe that time stands still, and we're the only two people in the galaxy.

# Acknowledgments

A few years back, I had a story in my head struggling to take shape, a science-fiction adventure about a group of neuro-divergent kids who could bound through space and who saved the world. Little did I know that one day that story would become a five-book series. As I write this, I can hardly believe the Bounders series has come to an end. *Fractured Futures* felt like a long good-bye to these beloved characters who have lived in my head for so long. Even though I'm happy and hopeful about this final story and the resolution to the series, I definitely shed a few tears as I wrote the last chapters. It's been an amazing journey, and I feel incredibly thankful and blessed.

The Bounders series found its way into the world with a lot of assistance. I am extremely grateful to my editor, Sarah McCabe, who has helped me shape these stories over the last few years. I am also grateful to Mara Anastas and the entire team at Simon & Schuster/Aladdin for their support. In addition, I will always appreciate my original editor, Michael Strother, and my agent, David Dunton, who first saw the potential in the Bounders series.

I am blessed with a wide network of loving, supportive, and creative family and friends. I owe a million thanks to my children, Nathan and Gabriel, and my husband, Jamey Tesler. I'm also grateful for the support of my extended family, Lynne and Richard Swanson, Sarah Swanson, Alyson and Chris Anderson, and Cheryl and Michael Tesler. There are also countless friends who support and encourage me along the way, many of whom inspire me with their own creativity. They have my endless gratitude.

There are so many individuals who have helped me on my writing journey in big and small ways these last few years. I know I am missing some key people, so please forgive me and know you have my gratitude even if your name doesn't appear in these pages. In no particular order, huge thanks are owed to Lee Gjertsen Malone, Victoria Coe, Melissa Schorr, Jen Malone, Ronni Arno, Dee Romito, Bridget Hodder, Jennifer Maschari, Abby Cooper, Jenn Bishop, Janet Johnson, Laura Shovan, Elly Swartz, Erin Petti, MarcyKate Connolly, Katie Slivensky, Jarrett Lerner, Rob Vlock, Kim Harrington, Diane Magras, Jason Lewis, Jonathan Hickey, Shelley Sommer, Bill Grace, Gwendolyn Baltera, Totsie McGonagle, Kathy Detwiler, Lynn Mayo, Ethan Mayo, Will Teague, Owen Caulfield, Alexa Cohen, Maddie Chisolm, the Low Tide Band families, and all the readers who have reached out by e-mail or snail mail to let me know how much the Bounders stories mean to them.

Thank you to everyone who has read the Bounders books. A few years ago, the thought that even one person might read a book I wrote was mind-blowing. In many ways, it still is.

Finally, I'm fortunate to have five fabulous nephews. They think their cousins are lucky to have books dedicated to them. Now they do too. Connor, Lucas, Gavin, Nicholas, and Cameron, this book is for you.

**MONICA TESLER** lives south of Boston with her husband and their two boys. She earned her undergraduate and law degrees from the University of Michigan. She writes on the commuter boat, in coffee shops, and at her kitchen table. She tries to meditate every day but often ends up fantasizing about space, time travel, or strange lands, both real and imagined.